PENGUIN BOOKS
## FAULTY GROUND

Gabrielle Donnelly was born in Muswell Hill, London, one of a large Catholic family. She studied English Literature at London University, after which she became a magazine and newspaper journalist, contributing to *Options*, *Woman's Realm*, *Woman* and *The Times*. She now lives in California but continues to write for British magazines and newspapers. Gabrielle Donnelly is the author of *Holy Mother* (1987), also published by Penguin.

# FAULTY GROUND

*Gabrielle Donnelly*

PENGUIN BOOKS

PENGUIN BOOKS

Published by the Penguin Group
27 Wrights Lane, London W8 5TZ, England
Viking Penguin Inc., 40 West 23rd Street, New York, New York 10010, USA
Penguin Books Australia Ltd, Ringwood, Victoria, Australia
Penguin Books Canada Ltd, 2801 John Street, Markham, Ontario, Canada L3R 1B4
Penguin Books (NZ) Ltd, 182–190 Wairau Road, Auckland 10, New Zealand

Penguin Books Ltd, Registered Offices: Harmondsworth, Middlesex, England

First published by Victor Gollancz 1988
Published in Penguin Books 1990
1 3 5 7 9 10 8 6 4 2

Copyright © Gabrielle Donnelly 1988
All rights reserved

Made and printed in Great Britain by
Cox & Wyman Ltd, Reading, Berks.
Filmset in Bembo

*To my mother*
*Mary Donnelly*
*with love always*

It is a long way from London to Los Angeles. Susan Barnes recrossed her legs, long and thin in unfashionably faded jeans, tried and failed to find a position for her head which it had not already rejected as impossibly uncomfortable, and wondered yet again whether the large North Country woman sitting next to her found it necessary to breathe quite so hard.

The woman stared ahead, avoiding Susan's eye, as she had since her first, and only, attempt at conversation shortly after they had taken off.

'Going to Los Angeles, are you?' she had asked.

'Yes,' Susan had replied.

'Going for a holiday? To stay with friends?'

'Yes.'

'I'm going to Pasadena, me. To stay with my sister.'

Susan had refrained from reaction.

'Of course, she's lived there for forty years.'

Susan, who had been taught perfect manners, and could, when she chose, exhibit the most perfect rudeness, had turned on her a ferociously frozen smile.

'Of course,' she had agreed.

The woman had retreated into reproachful silence, and — having brought with her neither book to read nor whatever other activity women of that sort engaged upon, knitting, Susan supposed vaguely, or crochet — inaction. Susan herself had returned to her book, or rather, selection of books, none of which, as the flight took its course, seemed able to hold her attention — the serious literature being a little too demanding for her current state of mind, the light novels simply too

7

trivial. Throughout, the woman continued to breathe. It was extraordinary how profoundly you could come to dislike someone over an eleven hour flight.

Susan had, in the course of the brief conversation, lied twice. She was going, not for a holiday, but to work; to stay, not with friends, but with family. Not that she was not fond of her cousin Joanna; she was probably, in fact, more fond of her than of many she did regard as friends. But, they were, after all, cousins, Joanna being her mother's sister's daughter, and their pasts, presents and futures were thus inextricably entangled; let them love each other or not, neither would ever quite know the amicable satisfaction of having, with full consent, chosen and been chosen by the other. As to the work aspect of the trip, that, like the trip itself, was unforeseen. Just over a week ago, she had been sitting in her small, tidy flat off Haverstock Hill, surrounded by her books and what was beginning to be an interesting collection of paintings, planning her major task for London University's summer vacation — an introduction to a new edition of *Emma*. She had not, to be strictly accurate, been working, but rather, unusually for her (but then it was a sullen day with thunder in the air), daydreaming — recalling the lunch with the editor who had commissioned the work. 'For Christ's sake, Felix,' she heard herself say again, 'what can anyone write that's new about *Emma*?' 'That, my dear Susan,' he was replying, 'is precisely where your challenge lies,' as his languid manicured hand had reached to the cool green bottle to pour parchment yellow wine into sparkling thin glasses — when from nowhere came a volcanic crash, and the ceiling disintegrated, showering Susan, the books and the room with a lava of plaster flakes. The flat, the builders informed her next day with the glee peculiar to their kind, would be uninhabitable for at least six weeks.

It was on the second day, as she was preparing to move from a kindly neighbour's sofa to the most reasonably priced hotel she could find, that Joanna's letter arrived. As Joanna's letters

8

always did, it contained a glowing — Joanna had the gift of happiness — account of Southern Californian life; as always, it concluded with an enthusiastic, and, she knew, sincere, invitation to visit. Susan had for the first time considered the invitation seriously. She had not been to Los Angeles, nor had she ever intended to go. Were she to cross the Atlantic, she had always assumed, it would be by invitation to lecture at some reputable East Coast College, or possibly to explore Mayan ruins in Mexico; her plans, such as they were, had never reached to include a city she associated with sun-bleached surfers, movie stars and Disneyland. On the other hand, the plane ticket would cost little more than the hotel bill, and one should, she was aware, always take the opportunity to visit new places. Besides, it was six long years since Joanna, laughing through tears and clinging to the arm of her tall American husband, had left England, and her visits since had been too rare and too brief; it would be good to see her again. And the hotel was impossibly noisy, and the summer had, once again, been declared the worst for eighty years. Susan prided herself, once having made up her mind, on acting quickly. Hence, here she was, this late July afternoon, stuck for what felt like an eternity at an angle of exquisite unease, being breathed over by an offended North Country woman. She sighed, lit yet another cigarette, and yet again picked up her detective novel.

Since Susan was Joanna's cousin, they were driving Joanna's car to meet her. Mike had suggested his own car, which had the advantage of being larger, but Joanna had felt, obscurely, that it was her hostessly duty to be in the driver's seat when her guest arrived. Besides, Mike's car, which was not only large, but old, positively ate gas, and it was not as if they could afford to throw money away. She did not think Susan would be bringing much luggage: Europeans travelled so much lighter than Americans. Joanna had a theory that this was because

9

most American families contained, somewhere in the last four generations, at least one member who had been forced to flee his place of birth carrying only what he could take on his back. She had proposed the theory to Mike that very morning, and he had grinned the lazy grin that said he did not agree but was not about to argue, and ambled to the stove for more coffee, bending to kiss her as he passed. She looked at him now, slouched in the passenger seat, darkly handsome in that American way which is the product of mixed genes and excellent food, and wondered how he would take Susan's continued presence over the next few weeks.

Joanna felt protective of Susan, and always had, although she was just four weeks older, and a full three inches shorter. Partly, this was because the four weeks, stretching from August to September, had meant that Joanna was always a form ahead of her in the school they had both attended; but that was not the only reason. Susan was closed, cold, born, it seemed, with no instinct to make herself attractive to her fellow man or woman; and Joanna, to whom friendships were all important, worried about her. Many people found Susan difficult, if entertaining; Joanna saw her only, always, as sad.

Watching now with idle pleasure the sun striking the passing palm trees on Lincoln Boulevard, a part of her found herself back on the dark day of Susan's parents' funeral, saw the rain blackening the grey walls of the church, the shocked, wan February faces, and herself, separated for the first time from Mike, running to her cousin.

'Oh, Susan, I'm so sorry, so very, very sorry.'

'Yes.' Pale and plain in a severe black shirtwaist dress, Susan had looked at her with dry eyes. 'Yes. How was your flight?'

'Fine. Susan. . .'

'Good. Planes really are safer than cars, then, aren't they?'

Susan's parents had died together in a car crash. She had rarely spoken of them since, and Joanna's mother — with Joanna herself and her brother, Susan's last surviving relatives — said that afterwards, Susan had visited her neither more nor less often than before. Sad. Sad. Yet Susan was a good woman; and Joanna knew that Susan cared for Joanna.

How Mike and Susan would end up caring for each other, however, was another issue. He seemed happy enough at the prospect of having her for a summer houseguest. He was an American, and therefore naturally hospitable; having lived in London and married an Englishwoman, he fancied himself as something of an Anglophile; and on their brief encounters, Susan had usually made him laugh, and Mike always appreciated being made to laugh. But Susan over a couple of evenings during a London holiday, and Susan around the clock in Mike's home, were two different matters. And Susan and Joanna, for all their differences, shared so much that was so rich, that no one, not even Mike, could share. She hoped he would not feel excluded. She made up her mind to make an extra effort to be nice to him.

'How psychologically significant is it,' asked Mike, 'that in all the times we've come to this airport, you've always missed the turn-off?'

'I won't do it today,' she said.

'You just did,' he told her.

Sticky toothed and gummy eyed, Susan stalked off the plane. She had left London in the middle of the morning, and fourteen hours later, was arriving into the middle of the afternoon. She had eaten three main meals, seen two films, and conceived of a cordial hatred for her neighbour. At one point, she thought, but, speechless and unmoving, had been unable to test the theory, that she had got rather drunk. For some time, she had been unable to imagine that they would ever land. They had landed now, or so the stewardess's cool voice had told them, but only a part of her had disembarked. The rest would remain for ever, locked in the stale air of the vessel, winging through an eternity of plastic-wrapped food in the middle of the day.

Gingerly, accustoming herself to the new motion, she walked one step at a time — she who had crossed prairies in minutes and oceans in hours — down long grey corridors, past immigration officials and baggage claim carousels, and into the long dark hall of the arrivals lounge. A jumble of faces turned towards her, eager, of every conceivable shape and colour. She searched them fruitlessly, knowing for a moment with panic-stricken certainty that nobody would arrive to meet her, that the telephone number she would call would be out of order, the address she would go to be a hole in the road. Then she felt a hand on her shoulder, and turned around into Joanna and Mike.

'I'd forgotten how English you look,' said Joanna, as soon as speech became coherent. 'Oh, Susan, it's so good to see you again!'

She was right; Susan did look English, not with Joanna's own extravagance of blonde curls and plumply rosy skin, but in a more muted, brown on brown way, a way that Piers Plowman would have had no difficulty in recognising. Susan looked at her cousin with wary approval.

'You're not very brown,' she commented. She had expected her to look different, somehow, living so far away as she did; but she looked exactly the same.

'Joanna doesn't go brown,' said Mike. 'She likes her skin to coordinate with her accent.'

He was brown himself, not brown like a vain Englishman who had worked hard for a tan, but carelessly saturated with it, like someone who had always seen a lot of the sun. Joanna had once told her that, although his ancestry was predominantly Irish, he had had a great-great-grandmother who had been an Algonquin Indian. He took her suitcase, and Joanna hugged her again, pressing her arm as they made their way through the laughing, crying, kissing crowd. On the other side of the lounge, Susan saw the large North Country woman being greeted by her even larger sister, and what was presumably her enormous niece. She supposed they would all spend their evenings breathing over each other.

They left the airport and drove into a world where hot white light exploded around lacy palm trees and bounced off the tops of shiny cars and left oily dark shadows in the road in places where no shadows should be. They drove past parched grass and Spanish shop signs and supermarkets a block long, occasionally topping a hill to see miles of squat city spread out under a pinkish haze.

'How far is it?' asked Susan.

'Not far,' said Joanna. 'Five or six miles, perhaps.'

Susan did not understand miles. The life she lived, travelling by Tube during the day, taxis at night, and the occasional express train when she went away for the weekend, did not admit of such crude measures. It was faster for her to cross London to get to Tooting than to change Tube lines and get to Manor House, faster to go outside London to Leicester than to cross London for Kew. She leaned back and tried to react to the passing city. But the buildings were too large, set too far back, moved too fast past the car, and her eyes could not adjust to them. She did not even know whether she found them beautiful or ugly; they were simply like nothing she had ever seen.

'How's Ma?' asked Joanna.

'Blooming.' Here, at least, was something she understood and could respond to. 'A bit worried about the roses, as I expect she's told you.'

Joanna smiled. 'At length.'

'And she's sent you a fruitcake, which is why my suitcase nearly gave Mike a hernia.'

'Oh, smashing. Thanks.'

She had been wrong: Joanna had changed, or at any rate, her voice had. It was not that she had acquired an American accent, rather the opposite, that she was trying just a little too hard to preserve the Englishness of her vowels, and in doing so succeeded in sounding not quite English. And she had surely never said smashing when she had lived in London.

'Have you seen Tom?' Joanna asked.

'Yes, indeed. He's handsomer than ever, if possible, sends his love, and says he's not willing to commit himself yet, but he's almost made up his mind you're his favourite sister.'

'I'm flattered. Did you meet the girlfriend?'

'Briefly. She's even prettier than he is, which seems to confuse him a bit. But I think they're fond of each other.'

'Good. It's time he settled down.' She shot Susan a sidelong glance: Tom was four years younger than they. 'You can't stay footloose and fancy-free for ever.'

'Right,' agreed Mike, wound with hospitable discomfort into the narrow back seat of the car. 'But you could have a darned good time trying.'

'Ignore him,' said Joanna. 'He's in training for the seven year itch. I hope you don't mind, Susan. I've invited some people for dinner tonight.'

'Well, I didn't think you were going to abandon all human contact.'

'Yes, but your first night. It's just that it's a friend of ours' birthday, and I offered ages ago to give him a dinner party.'

'Offered, nothing,' said Mike. 'You got stuck. It isn't easy, Susan, being married to the softest touch in town.'

'I think you're very brave,' she said.

'Anyway,' said Joanna, 'it's not good to go to bed early with jet lag. You never get over it.'

'Plus,' said Mike, 'you get to meet all the gang at once. Think of it as one hour on the rack instead of Chinese water torture.'

'You know, I always thought Chinese water torture sounded rather relaxing.'

Joanna sighed. 'I can see it's going to be Laurel and Hardy all summer. Almost home now.'

They turned left around the corner that looked to Susan as indistinguishable from all the corners preceding it, and drove down a narrower road — although it was probably as wide as Haverstock Hill — lined with tumble-down gingerbread houses set in lawns that were lush and green under running sprinklers, or occasionally parched dry and dead of neglect. One house was covered with what appeared to be anti-nuclear slogans; in the porch of another, a swarthy elderly woman sat foursquare and inscrutable, while dark eyed children chased each other around a dusty cactus plant, shouting shrilly in a Spanish whose accent was recognisably not from Spain. The road led to the top of a hill.

'Oh,' said Susan.

Spread below them were more houses and a little main street; then a narrow strip of khaki; then, stretching far and melting into the sky, a shimmering, moving, silken expanse of blue.

'The Ocean,' said Joanna, unnecessarily. 'You never get used to it. It changes colour every day. Well, here we are.'

They had parked in front of a small, white clapboard house, immaculately clean, with a feathery jacaranda tree growing in the well-tended front lawn.

'Falling to pieces,' said Joanna apologetically as they climbed three wooden steps to the narrow front porch. Then, the irony of her words failing to mask the pleased pride of her tone, 'Home, sweet home.'

The living room, on to which the front door opened directly, looked like Joanna, warmly welcoming, with afternoon light streaming on to polished wood floors, well-thumbed books tumbling from shelves, and a faint smell of cut flowers in the air. Yet Susan remembered Joanna as being so English, and the Mexican rugs on the floors, the framed posters of little known movies on the walls, and the sturdy rocking chair in the corner, were not English at all.

'It's very American,' she said.

'Well,' said Joanna, 'I live in America. Come and see the rest, there isn't much.'

There was not. A large kitchen lined with cupboards of dark, honey coloured wood, a small bathroom, and a cool, simple bedroom, containing little but more books, a couple of chairs, and an old fashioned four-poster bed, covered with a comfortably fading quilt. On the white painted wall above the bed hung a plain dark crucifix. Susan raised her brows but said nothing. It had not been the custom among the family to discuss Aunt Betty's having married into the Catholic Church, or that curious, almost mediaeval business of her having been forced, in order for the wedding to take place, to sign a paper promising to bring up their children in that Church. Having made the promise, Aunt Betty had, creditably, kept it until her husband's death; although Susan could not help reflecting that, fond as she and all the family had been of Uncle Tony, it was not altogether unfortunate that that death had occurred before the education of either child was too far advanced. Not that Susan herself had anything in particular against Catholicism; she liked Evelyn Waugh, enjoyed the odd wily Jesuits who kept popping up in the strngest places in the history books, and had even been quite favourably impressed by the sheer drama of Joanna's own Nuptial Mass. In fact, now that she thought of it, she rather recollected having drunk slightly too much champagne and explained copiously to Mike's mother — one of those gingery, well-groomed American women, who had stood and sat and knelt through the complicated service with her eyes downcast, yet still crossing herself at all the appropriate places — precisely why it had been one of the finest pieces of theatre she had seen for some time. But Evelyn Waugh and a Nuptial Mass every quarter century or so were one thing. A crucifix in full public view, and over, of all places, the bed, was something else entirely. She would place bets that Aunt Betty did not know it was there.

'I'll show you your hidey-hole,' said Joanna. She led her through the kitchen and pocket handkerchief back garden to a small building off to a side. 'It used to be the garage, but we get more use from it as a guest room.'

'Oh, very nice,' said Susan.

It was exactly what she needed, cleanly spartan, with white

walls, a skylight, a narrow bed under a gaudily striped Indian rug, a desk, a typewriter, a telephone. There was a slight, and entirely agreeable, smell of paint.

'I use it as a studio, too,' said Joanna. She gestured towards some canvases stacked with their faces to the wall. 'I haven't been doing enough lately, though. Maybe you'll inspire me.'

'I'd like to see them,' said Susan. Joanna had painted since either could remember, producing works of a fierce, frightening power that were a surprise to everyone else and a constant, secret source of raging envy to Susan. 'I don't think I'm ready for them right now, though.'

'I shouldn't think you're ready for anything right now,' said Joanna. 'Look, why don't you have a nap? I'll wake you in a couple of hours, and you can shower and revive before people start to arrive.'

Naps, Susan had always believed, were for the elderly and the intellectually moribund. But then it was, she calculated, some twenty hours since she had been horizontal, and almost as long since she had been alone. Susan needed time alone. And the bed did look particularly inviting: nor did it have a crucifix above it.

'Would you think me a frightfully rude guest,' she asked, 'if I did just that?'

'This is Southern California,' Joanna told her. 'We all do precisely what we want.'


Susan woke to great gobs of golden early evening sunlight torrenting through the small window, and realised, lying in the pure clarity, that she had been wearing the same clothes for almost a full day and night. Joanna had mentioned a shower, which sounded an excellent idea. Feeling slightly drunk, which she supposed must be jet lag, she staggered to her suitcase and burrowed for her washbag, and a clean cotton print skirt and T-shirt, summer holiday clothes, barely worn in London, still folded for the journey. As she rummaged, she found a large Tupperware box. Aunt Betty's cake. She picked it up, and stumbled into the kitchen.

Joanna was preparing the meal, and Susan stood for a moment at the door, watching her. No cook herself, she was acutely aware of how others comported themselves in the kitchen. Joanna, clearly, was well in control of the room. She was not making messes, as her mother did, nor was she cheating with the tins and ready mixed sauces Susan had seen some use. She was simply, cleanly and efficiently, dealing with the food. On one scrubbed surface, a pan of fat fish lay ready for cooking; by the stove, a large jar of rice was placed conveniently next to a pan of water; Joanna herself stood, pristine clean and pausing occasionally to sip at a glass of white wine, by a tidy pile of well-nourished vegetables, absorbed in filling a massive yellow bowl with firm-fleshed avocados and crisply curling lettuce.

'Oh, you're up,' she said at last, noticing Susan. 'I was just going to call you. Have a glass of wine.'

'I think I'll shower first.' If she sat down now, drinking wine and watching Joanna cook, she would never reach the bathroom. 'Here's the cake. How many people are you feeding, an army?'

'She only cooks for armies.' Mike had appeared, and propped his height against the doorway. 'It's taken me till now to explain to her that for two people you only cook two boiled eggs.'

'Good Girl Guide camp training,' said Susan, and the cousins giggled like fourteen-year-olds, remembering one ridiculous summer, with a pompous patrol leader, and a girl who had insisted on wearing her Guide badge to bed.

'Poor Mike,' said Joanna. 'Now you're here, he'll have to start all over again teaching me to cook for three.'

'I'll leave you to your maths lesson,' said Susan, and went to wash off 6,000 miles of dirt.

When she came back, Mike and Joanna were laughing at a joke of their own, and Mike was picking at the salad.

'He's trying to get it down to regiment size,' said Joanna. 'Oh, you look much more comfortable now. The wine's in the refrigerator.'

Susan opened the refrigerator, oversized like the refrigerators she had seen in countless American movies and television shows, and noted with satisfaction that, although neither Joanna nor Mike was a hearty drinker, it contained several bottles. It also contained an ornate birthday cake, bearing the words *Happy Birthday Rick*.

'Who's Rick?' she asked.

'A friend of Joanna's,' said Mike. 'He's ten years old today.'

'He is not,' said Joanna. 'He's a friend of our friend Oliver's. And he's twenty-two today.'

'Twenty-two. Jesus. Susan, can you even remember being twenty-two?'

'Mike! She's younger than me!'

'Of course she is. You're the oldest woman I know.'

She swatted him with a spoon, and he ducked, laughing.

Susan tried to remember being twenty-two. It was not a memory that brought pleasure: on the whole, she usually rather pitied her students. There was a knock at the front door.

'It's open,' called Joanna.

A young woman walked in, of medium height, with brown hair and a wide mouth. She looked around, and grimaced comically. 'I don't believe it,' she said. 'I'm first to arrive again.'

'One thing about Kathy,' said Mike. 'She stays in character. Susan, this is Kathy. Kathy, Susan. Joanna's cousin.'

'Aoh, the brainy cousin.' Kathy's eyes, bright and dark, lit on Susan. 'From jolly old Lundun.' She caught herself. 'I'm sorry. It's just that I love the British accent.'

People really said that, then, registered Susan.

'Kathy's an actress,' said Joanna.

Kathy, transforming herself immediately into a 30's starlet, sidled to Mike, lips pouting, eyelids aflutter. 'Mr O'Connor's gonna make me a real big star.'

19

Mike made and directed films, small films, but, according to Joanna, highly thought of in the knowledgeable Hollywood community. Joanna had also said that he had more than once turned down quite a lot of money offered by the large studios to direct films that inspired him less than his own. Certainly their style of living, although far from poor, was clearly light years from that of the movie directors you read about in the gossip columns.

Mike put his arm around Kathy now, and puffed on an imaginary cigar. 'Stick by me, kid, and I'll see you right. Hey, anyone want some grass?'

'Help yourself to wine, Susan,' said Joanna as the sweet, summery smell filled the air. She was still on her first glass, and refused the joint as it passed her. She had finished the salad, and was mixing a dressing.

'Where's the birthday boy?' said Kathy. 'Listen, I can't stay late, I have an early class tomorrow.'

'I don't think anyone's staying late,' said Joanna. 'Rick and Oliver are leaving at 10.30 to meet some friends at some club.'

'Polite,' said Kathy. 'Real polite.' She began to sing, in a small, tuneful voice. 'It's my party, I'll eat-and-run if I want to, eat-and-run if I want to, eat-and-run if I want to . . . '

'Oh, I don't know,' said Joanna. 'I think it's pretty difficult being gay.'

'It's difficult being anything,' said Susan.

'Right.' Kathy looked at her, as if seeing her for the first time. 'Right.'

'Yes, but times like birthdays, you know? They both seem rather . . . rootless somehow.'

'I know,' said Mike. 'That's why I've signed them up for my next snuff movie.'

'Great security around here,' called a voice from the living room, and Mike laughed.

'It's an insurance scam,' he called back. 'We're hoping someone will steal the Picasso.'

The couple who walked in were different from the others, and after a moment, Susan identified the difference as money. It was not an obvious discrepancy: they were as casually dressed as anyone she had seen, and wandered into the kitchen with the ease of old and valued friends. But the man's battered jeans were just a bit better cut than Mike's, and the woman's chunkily exotic jewellery was of real gold.

'My accountant,' announced Mike with a flourish, indicating the man.

'My charity case,' the other countered. He looked at Susan, and smiled. 'Hi. I'm Bill. This is Nancy.'

'Are you Joanna's cousin?' said Nancy. 'You look so different.'

They did look different, everyone said so, Joanna being the image of her pretty mother, while Susan took after her father. It was not until you had been with them for a while that you noticed the similarity in their facial expressions, the trick both shared of emphasising one word in a sentence for irony or humour.

'Joanna's from the pretty side of the family,' said Susan, and Nancy exclaimed with pleasure.

'You're even more British than she is! God, I would kill for a British accent!'

Not so much people said it, then, as everybody said it: at any rate, two out of three had, and Bill's broad, good-natured face was nodding enthusiastic agreement. Susan began to feel slightly tired.

Nancy moved to the pan of fish, and inspected it with an expert eye. 'Looks good,' she said. 'You're such a great cook, Joanna. What's the herb, dill?'

'It's fennel, and you know it. Don't let her fool you, Susan, she's the best cook I know.'

'Hey, that reminds me. Barbecue on Sunday after softball, OK?'

'OK. Smashing.'

How could Susan have thought Joanna had not changed?

Joanna, whose image she instinctively placed over tea and Battenburg cake in her mother's chintz-hung sitting room, with the french windows giving on to the lawn and the famous roses, was actually at home here, at home and fully at her ease in this wood-cupboarded kitchen, among these suntanned people who smiled with bright teeth and talked of movies and barbecues and insurance scams. Joanna had changed a lot. Susan wondered whether she had changed so much herself: she rather thought not.

From the front of the house, a rusty doorbell sounded. Mike turned to Bill in delight.

'I don't believe you shut the door!'

'Believe it,' said Bill.

'Well, fuckin' go and open it.'

He did as he was bid, returning with a middle-aged man in a conservative grey suit, and a youth with tumbling black curls and a face just one step removed from a Botticelli. At the sight of them, the company burst into a ragged rendition of 'Happy Birthday To You' and the young man blushed.

'This is Oliver,' said Joanna, skilfully detaching the elder man from the mêlée of good wishes that surrounded his friend, and leading him to Susan. 'And this is my cousin, Susan.'

'How do you do,' said Susan.

He bowed in courtly fashion over her hand. 'Oh,' he said elaborately, 'but I love your accent.'

He caught her eye, and she felt for the first time that evening that here was someone with whom she just might become friends.

'Haven't you got one yourself?' she asked. 'An accent.'

'My goodness what a keen ear. Yes, I have. My family have lived in Virginia for what would not to one of your countrymen seem a long time, but what for us poor colonials . . .'

'Don't believe him.' The boy had materialised at Oliver's side. 'He's white trash from Tennessee. Hello. I'm Rick.'

'Susan. Happy birthday.'

'Thank you.'

'What presents did you get?' asked Nancy. 'Oh, *neat*.'

He exhibited a handsome watch, and smiled at Oliver, who smiled at him.

'It's not what I most wanted, though,' he said. 'What I most wanted was to be famous by now. You know, Mike's always using Kathy in his movies. Mike, why don't you use me?'

Mike, passing glasses of wine, paused to put a fatherly hand on his shoulder. 'Because,' he explained, 'you are a truly terrible actor.'

'You're not missing a treat,' said Kathy. 'He's like a bear with a sore nose when he's directing.' She positioned herself by Mike, a starlet again. 'Aintcha, Mr O'Connor?'

'Well,' said Rick, with a sly glance at her. 'At least he's not distracted by a pretty face.'

Kathy was neither pretty nor plain: she had an actress's face that could look at will elegant or coarse, seductive or sad. It looked now like one about to make a sharp retort, which, rather to Susan's disappointment, was not made, since Joanna at that moment ushered them all firmly to the living room table.

Susan should not have been hungry, but somehow found that she was. The fish was unfamiliar, but sweet and delicately flavoured. She remembered now that even at school, Joanna had done well at domestic science.

'Are you here on vacation?' asked Bill.

'Not exactly.' Terse lies, while convenient for silencing women on planes, would clearly not do for Joanna's friends. 'My ceiling fell in, London's full of tourists, and I have to deliver a 10,000 word introduction to *Emma* by September.' She thought of the drive from the airport, then of the streets of Highbury and Emma Woodhouse, who had never seen the sea. 'This should make for an interesting contrast.'

'More of a quantum leap,' said Oliver. 'I always carried a bit of a torch for Emma: she wore her snobbery so well.'

'*Emma*. That's Jane Austen, right?' said Kathy. 'I never got into her: she was always one of those people I felt I should read, and never did.'

'Well, you should,' said Susan, trying to conceal her surprise. She had never before met anyone — except for her department Head, a poet, and universally acknowledged as mad — who had openly admitted to not having read Jane Austen. Now, for the first time, it occurred to her that there might be others. She looked around the table. Joanna, she knew, had; very probably Mike; and obviously Oliver. But Rick was looking disturbingly blank, while Bill and Nancy both wore expressions of good-humoured interest that could have meant anything. With an increasing sense of her own foreignness, she wondered how many of them had learned Latin at school.

'I read a book once,' announced Bill.

'He did,' corroborated Mike. 'I was there. This guy and I go way back.'

'They were at film school together,' Joanna told Susan.

'Until,' said Mike, 'Bill knocked Nancy up and had to marry her.'

'Mike!' Nancy turned crimson. Bill only laughed.

'Had to marry her,' repeated Mike with relish. 'The wedding of the season. Bride waddling down the aisle, eight months pregnant in a white dress and veil . . . groom relaxed and smiling at the bride's father, who was pressing a shotgun to his head . . . bride's mother . . .'

'Mike, stop it! She'll believe you.'

'Nah. Susan doesn't believe a word I say, do you, Susan?'

'Not a word. Did you just say that story was a lie?'

Mike laughed appreciatively.

'He's such a tease,' said Nancy to Susan, her face returning to its normal colour. 'I don't know how Joanna puts up with it. You're a teacher, too, aren't you? Are you all teachers in your family?'

'Not all.' Susan was far too well bred to comment on having

24

her own professorship at London University thrown into the same category with Joanna's post of art teacher at what she referred to as a junior high school. 'Why, are you one?'

'God, no.' Nancy laughed. 'I'm not smart. I'm a potter.'

Susan had met a few potters in England, and Nancy could hardly have looked less like them. They had tended to the stocky of build, with square, strong hands, and clay embedded in the ridges around their fingernails. Nancy was tall and slender, and her long hands were scrupulously clean.

'That must be interesting,' she said politely.

'Oh, it is! I love the feeling of creation, you know?' The clean hands made interesting shapes in the air. 'The moulding, the making . . . I love making things. I make all sorts. I make jewellery, too.'

'Really?' Susan had never met anyone who claimed to be both potter and jeweller. But it appeared that Nancy, unlike the potters Susan knew, was not bound to her calling by the cumbersome chains of financial necessity.

'Yeah, really. I make good stuff, too.' She scanned Susan's face. 'Say. Why don't I make you some? You have great bones.'

Susan edged away in her chair. 'Thank you,' she said.

'I mean it. Come down to the house. Joanna, couldn't I design some great stuff for your cousin?'

Joanna, caught in another conversation, looked over and smiled with vague benevolence.

'Would you like some more salad?' asked Susan.

'No, thank you,' said Nancy. 'Listen, have Joanna bring you over one day, and we'll have a coffee *klatsch*.'

To Susan's horror, she appeared to mean it.

'Thank you,' she said firmly. 'But I am here to work, not to play.'

But the other was undeterred. 'Oh, you don't work all the time. Go on, it'll be fun. We can do girl talk.'

'Some time,' all but snapped Susan. 'If I'm free.'

'You'll find time,' Nancy assured her. 'It's a date, then. I'll call Joanna tomorrow, and we can fix a day soon.'

Suddenly, fatigue such as she had never known rushed in on Susan, and it seemed to her that she had landed in the very heart of an American nightmare, here in this circle of impregnably smiling faces, with a mercilessly well-meaning woman pressing upon her coffee *klatsches* and home-made jewellery, while across the table her own cousin was too busy talking to a man who had never read Jane Austen for Susan to ask her whether it were acceptable for her to smoke.

'If I'm free,' she said, trying, and hearing herself failing, to control the rising hysteria in her voice, 'I'll let you know.'

Her tone, at least, cut through to Joanna's ears. She broke off her conversation, and looked at her.

'Uh oh,' she said. 'Jet lag. Bad, huh?'

Feeling an absurdly childish sense of relief, Susan nodded.

'Well, you really shouldn't go to bed yet, you know. Do you think you can stay up till Rick's cut his cake?'

'I'll try.'

'If you truly try, my dear,' Joanna quoted their headmistress, 'you are doing all that anyone can ask. Here.' She reached behind her to a coffee table, and plopped an empty ashtray in front of her cousin. 'Have a duty free. And stop waiting to be offered things, because you're not a guest.'


When Susan tried, later, to remember the rest of the meal, it disintegrated into a kaleidoscope of noise. Loud comments were punctuated by louder laughs; the cake was brought in to a cacophony of cheering; the second singing of 'Happy Birthday' seemed to explode in her eardrums like the roar of a football crowd. At some point, she tried to refuse a slice of the cake, and Nancy exclaimed that, slim as she was, she surely did not need to diet. It was soon after this that Joanna, blessedly quiet, led her from the table and to the garage.

'I don't want to go and see Nancy,' said Susan, fully a child now, and a whining child at that. 'I don't want a coffee *klutz*, or whatever she called it, and I don't want any of her foul home-made potted jewellery. I don't.'

'You don't have to have them,' said Joanna.

Susan sat down hard on the narrow bed. 'You said I could do whatever I liked,' she muttered, but Joanna had already gone.


It was nearly a month since Susan had woken to a blue sky. She lay sybaritically with her arms folded under her head, revelling in the twin luxuries of fair weather and sheets cleaned by someone else, until there was a knock at the door, and there was Joanna with a cup of coffee.

'How are you feeling?' she asked, settling herself at the foot of the bed.

'Much better.' Susan gulped gratefully at the hot liquid. 'Oh, God. Was I very rude last night?'

'Not at all. That lot all know what it's like when you've just got off the plane. They liked you.'

'Good.' But then a memory swam back to her. 'But that woman. That Nancy. Wasn't I quite unpleasant to her?'

'She liked you the best of all. Said she loved your dry British wit.'

Yes, that sounded like the woman Susan remembered.

'Oh, God,' she repeated.

'Oh, Nancy's OK. Honestly. Once you get to know her. She's got a heart of gold.'

'And speaking of gold,' said Susan, feeling much more awake now, 'I bet she didn't make the jewellery she was wearing last night.'

'God,' Joanna sighed in exasperation. 'You and Mike. You're such clever dicks . . . '

'Doesn't Mike like her?' She had never thought of Joanna's easygoing husband in terms of liking or disliking anybody.

'Oh, he likes her. He just . . . I think he thinks she led Bill down the primrose path of materialism.'

'Well, she would. This is a materialistic society.'

'Says you after eighteen hours. How's Felix?'

'The same.' Susan shot a wary glance. Felix was not only her editor, but also her lover. Her married lover, who in five years had never pretended the faintest intention of leaving for her his wife and three teenaged children. Joanna made no secret of her disapproval of Felix.

'Still going on then?' she said now.

'Apparently.'

'Must be fun for his wife.'

Susan did not know, and had never asked, whether or not Felix's wife was aware of her existence.

'We can't,' she said, rather more defensively than she cared for, 'all be as happily married as you, you know.'

Joanna studied her feet, plump and bare in plastic flip-flops.

'You know, Susan, you don't just wake up one morning, and, abracadabra, you're happily married.'

'I'm sure you don't. But you are happy, aren't you?'

'Yes.' She thought, smiled, and took a companionable swig of Susan's coffee. 'Yes.' She handed the mug back. 'And are you? Happy?'

'Me?' The concept was not one she ordinarily entertained: life was life, and you got on with it. 'I suppose I am. Yes, of course I am. Should I get up?'

'When you're ready. You're not going to start work for a couple of days, are you? I thought we'd go to the beach.'

'Fine. We could even do some sightseeing at some stage.'

'Sightseeing! Aren't you European! You don't sightsee in LA, there aren't any sights.'

Susan was nettled. It had always been integral to their relationship that, while Joanna was the nicer of the two, Susan was the more sophisticated.

'What do you do, then?' she demanded.

'I don't know. Hang out. Go to the beach . . . Have coffee *klatsches* and do girl talk . . .'

Susan threw a pillow at her.

When Joanna returned to the kitchen, Mike was still sprawled there, drinking coffee, and making healthy inroads into the fruitcake.

'Your mother,' he told her, 'gives great cake.'

'And you,' she responded, 'are going to get an even greater stomach if you don't watch out. And why are you still here? Aren't you supposed to be off editing?'

'Ach, work.' He made a lazy gesture of dismissal, which fooled neither of them. Both knew that he would leave for the studio and his editing when he was ready and not one second before, and both knew that, once there, he would work full tilt. There were those who, on first meeting Mike, were deceived by his casual manner into thinking he did not take his work seriously; but that, Joanna knew with a pride so fierce it sometimes approached pain, was simply that, a deceit, a lack of the imagination to understand her husband. Mike was one of the hardest working people she knew.

'My father,' she said, for no reason remembering her childhood, 'used to take the 8.16 into the City every morning.'

'Jesus,' said Mike.

'And he'd come home on the 6.42 at night, and Ma would pour him a Scotch.'

'Jesus.'

Yet he had not been a dull man, her father: rather, as far as she recalled, the reverse. And there had been one summer's evening when he had arrived home, unexpectedly, a full hour early, and her mother had blushed like a bride. It was just that their lives had been so structured that both had known, beyond doubt or question, that from a certain hour they were to be apart, and from a certain hour, together.

It was not a structure which supported her own marriage, nor indeed, for that matter, presumably, Felix's. Joanna had never met Felix, but for an instant he was in the room, thin and silver grey, a Dickensian ghost, watching with wry detachment as Mike collected cake crumbs and licked them from his brown forefinger. Felix, she was sure, would not eat cake.

Through the open kitchen door, she looked towards the garage: there was no sign yet of Susan's appearance.

'She's still seeing him, you know,' she said.

'What?' Mike yawned, stretched, licked a stray crumb from his lips.

'Felix. Susan's still seeing Felix.'

'Felix?'

Joanna fought an urge to dump coffee grounds over his head. 'You know. That man. That awful married man. She's still seeing him.'

He frowned speculatively at the coffee pot on the stove. 'Maybe she likes him.'

'She can't possibly. He's married.'

He nodded to himself, rose, and poured another cup. 'I'm married. And people like me.'

'Don't be daft. He makes her miserable.'

'She seems OK to me.'

'She's miserable.'

He sat down again, shaking his head in resignation. 'And you're going to make her happy, right?'

'Well, I can try.'

'Softest touch in town,' he repeated.

She was a soft touch, she knew it, did not particularly approve of it, but could do nothing to change it. He teased her about it often, and she sometimes wondered whether, beneath the jokes, he found it irritating. Some people, she knew, did. But if he were seriously one of them, he had done a good job of hiding it over the years. She might have asked him about it, but at that moment, Susan appeared, wearing a tattered Greek caftan, and carrying her day's clothes over her arm.

'I'm going to shower,' she said firmly, as she marched past.

Joanna had forgotten how embarrassed Susan had always been about needing to use the lavatory.

It was just too far comfortably to walk to the beach, so they climbed into the car, Susan pallid and angular in shorts and a skimpy T-shirt, Joanna aglow in a dress of billowing cotton,

30

and drove down the hill to a half-filled parking lot giving directly on to the beach. Joanna looked around in disgust.

'Too many people,' she commented.

'Massed hordes. Look, there goes one of them now.'

'Well, you should come here one winter. It's completely deserted.'

'Hi.' A beautiful black girl, exuberant on a bicycle, rode past and around them. 'Great day.'

'Lovely,' called back Joanna.

'Luvly,' she mimicked amiably, riding off, and Joanna laughed.

'That's the marvellous thing about Americans,' said Susan. 'They're so friendly.'

'Oh, shut up. And bring your shirt, or else you'll fry.'

'Oh. Good idea.'

'I said, shut up.'

Barefoot, they walked across warm, crumbly sand, to firmer, moist sand, and finally to the Ocean itself, stretching around the globe until the West became the East, the left side of the map of the world became the right. They trudged along the very edge of the Occident, heads down, hands in pockets, salt water stinging their ankles, sand squelching under their heels and between their toes. It was, they both realised, although neither commented on the fact, the first time they had been fully alone together since before Joanna's wedding.

'Do you really like it here?' Susan asked abruptly.

Joanna laughed. 'Well, don't sound so surprised.'

'Well, do you?'

'*Yes*. Of course I do. Why wouldn't I?'

'I don't know, I've only been here eighteen hours.'

Childishly, Joanna stuck her tongue out at her. 'It's twenty-one by now, you're allowed an opinion.'

'Thank you.' But it was a while before she expressed one. 'It's just,' she said finally, 'so . . . different.'

'And is different so wrong?'

'No, no, no. It's just different. Do you really play — what is softball, anyway?'

'It's like baseball, but you play it with a soft ball, get it?'

She laughed; Susan groaned. 'Like baseball,' she repeated. 'With a soft ball. My God.'

'And to answer your question,' Joanna continued, 'yes, Mike and I do play, every Sunday, in a park near the house, and we're hoping you will, too.'

Barely perceptibly, Susan moved away from her. 'Is this the woman,' she inquired, 'once known throughout the Lower School as Tortoise Butterfingers?'

'Believe it or not,' said Joanna carefully, 'it's really rather fun.'

'Oh, I believe it,' said Susan. 'Myself, I can think of few experiences more exhilarating than . . .'

'It *is* different out here. And you shouldn't judge it until you understand it a bit better.'

She sounded hurt; Susan was contrite.

'I'm not judging it,' she said. 'The reason I asked the question is that it *is* so very different, and . . . you didn't exactly choose it yourself, did you?'

'I chose Mike.'

'But choosing a person isn't the same as choosing a country, is it?'

'In some ways, it's surprisingly the same.'

They walked for a while in silence through the lapping waves. Joanna looked ahead of them at the sand, soapy from the sea, its film of water reflecting seagulls, sandpipers, and the occasional child, digging into it with rapt lack of purpose, and back at their own feet, moving slowly in and out of the Ocean beneath their swaying bodies. Susan's feet, she noted abstractedly, were different from hers: longer and thinner, which she had always envied, but also pinched, their skin yellow, cold-climate feet that had been encased for months in nylon and leather. In a few days, they would relax, would breathe and turn brown. She herself avoided the sun, as Mike had remarked. But it was he as much as she who loved the pinkness of her flesh here in this bronzed city, loved how her rosy northern European limbs tangled with his own tough, tanned hide.

Thinking of Mike, Joanna's irritation was washed quite clean in a wave of pity. Locked as her cousin was in her own selfishness, what could she know of the joys of sharing a life? Of working in and around the faults, needs, and desires of another, of sacrificing a little to reach, in the end, so much greater a gain? And Susan was the loser by it; because her way of being had brought her only a portion of Felix, while Joanna's had brought — for all the better and all the worse, for all the sorrows and all the joys — the whole of Mike.

'If you tell anyone I said this,' she said, 'I will kill you. But softball is exactly — but exactly — like rounders.'

The Ocean's edge was divided by a line of rocks, and they turned and clambered up through the sand to the boardwalk, a cheerful *Bartholomew Fair* of street vendors, shysters, and strolling musicians. Stuck in the middle of the clairvoyants and cheap jewellery stands was a bookshop, and next to it a café, its seats spilling out on to the walk. An improbably handsome young man on roller skates showed them to a table, and took their orders for drinks.

'People are very beautiful here, aren't they?' said Susan, watching him glide off.

'It's the genes,' said Joanna. 'Beautiful people have been coming here since the movies began, and naturally they have beautiful children. And the sun doesn't hurt, of course.'

Susan raised her brows in the way Joanna knew indicated disapprobation. 'A master race, then,' she said.

'That's what I thought when I first came out here. And they're all so much taller than me, too. But you know, you get used to it, I hardly notice it now.' She heard the defensiveness in her own tone; and it occurred to her that Susan was not the only one who had grounds for criticism. 'Listen, what's going to happen about you and Felix?'

'Enjoy,' carolled the young man, setting down the drinks without breaking his roll.

'What do you mean?' Susan, on holiday until Monday, took her first sip of icy mid-morning wine.

'Well, what d'you think I mean?'

'Well, what's supposed to happen? He's got his life, and I've got mine. What's going to happen about you and your milkman?'

'We don't have milkmen here. And that's not an answer.'

Susan lit a cigarette. 'I'd forgotten,' she observed, 'quite how bossy you were. I suppose that's what comes of teaching children all day long.'

'Am I being bossy? Sorry.' But almost immediately, she started again. 'I just don't think half a love affair is enough for you, that's all.'

'Are you going to be like this all the time? Apparently, it is.'

'But . . . ' she paused, suddenly aware of how little she knew of her cousin's day-to-day life. 'Don't you get sad? Lonely? What do you do at Christmas? Or when you have a toothache?'

'What do I . . . my God, what a sad sack you think I am.' She tapped on her cigarette. 'Let's see. What do I do at Christmas? Last Christmas, I stayed at home, read Muriel Spark, and had a perfectly splendid time, as I told you over the phone. The Christmas before, I accepted the invitation your mother kindly extends every year, and then, too, had a perfectly splendid time, as I, then, too, told you over the phone. The Christmas before that, I was in Turkey, failed to reach you over the phone, but sent you a postcard which you never acknowledged . . . '

'Well, I never got it.'

'. . . describing to you the perfect splendour of my time there. When I have a toothache, I pour myself a large whisky, and moan softly. What do you do?'

'You know what I mean. I think you deserve more.'

'Well.' Susan was beginning to be annoyed. 'That's very sweet of you, and I'll quote you next time I apply for a job. But the question you're not asking is, do I want more? You don't seem to believe that I honestly haven't the slightest desire for any more involvement than I've already got, and that, strange as it may sound to you, I actually quite like my life the way it is now.'

She was right. Joanna did not believe it, could never fully believe it, so far outside did the concept lie of her own frame of reference. Yet Susan did not usually lie to her, nor did she look as if she were lying now.

'And if you want to know,' she continued, 'as extraordinary as you think my life is, I think it's even more extraordinary that you should have been willing to uproot yourself completely, to leave your home, your friends, your job, your family, and travel halfway across the world, simply for one person.'

'You see,' said Joanna. 'You do disapprove.'

'No, I don't.' Susan stopped, watched the carnival going past, the limber black youths on roller skates, the derelicts who under the dirt could have been any colour, the near naked, perfect bodied girls, the street comics, pickpockets, policemen, drug addicts. She had travelled far in her life, had visited countries in the old world where she could not read the alphabet, much less speak the language; but nowhere had she felt so profound a sense of alienation as in the twenty-four hours she had here. 'I really don't . . . It's just such a long way to come, that's all.'

In the small cluttered studio, Mike, hunched over reels of picture and sound, absent-mindedly reached into the tiny refrigerator for a Cola. He drank, barely aware of the ice-cold can in his hand, the bending back of its metal ring, the taste of the fizzy liquid, sticky against his teeth and throat; but when the sugar and caffeine hit his system, he felt it inside him, exploding into energy. A deceptive energy, because when the let-down came, it would come hard; but he would deal with that when it happened.

He was working on his latest film, doing, since his budget was too low to admit of even the most menial post-production crew, the synching on his own dailies. There was no creativity in synching, but he did not mind. He had had creativity enough in the shooting, the three bickering, exhilarated, overworked weeks when he, a cameraman, a kid from UCLA film school, and four actors had crammed into a cabin in the Mojave to film his story of love and betrayal under the blistering desert sun. He would have creativity later, when he had synchronised, when thousands of feet of disjointed action, scenes shot from all angles, lay jumbled together with no regard to story or sense, waiting to be selected and smoothed and spliced into a movie. Into his movie. That would be creation.

For the time being, though, he was simply a machine, synching, matching the reel of sound to the reel of picture, the most boring job in the world, and yet a job in which it was essential to keep fully alert: one second's inattention, one tiny frame too early or too late, would murder a whole illusion, would show the clumsy framework holding together the whole delicate fantasy, and by doing so, destroy it completely. Mike, as he worked, could feel himself ageing, growing dull with drudgery, could feel his mouth drying, his eyes losing their shine, sinking dimmed into dark-pouched sockets.

As he grew more established, he supposed, as he became able to command more money without compromising his artistic control, he would acquire assistants to do the donkey-work for him, a sound crew, even an editor. It would be expected, and offered, and would leave him free to devote his energy purely to directing, and he knew he would never refuse it; but he knew that when it came, he would miss these tedious days. To be simply the director would be like having an affair with a woman you only saw when she was bathed, scented, and smiling winningly: it would be sweet, but there would never be the comradeship of two who had been dreary and dirty together. Besides, he loved the cutting room, its rickety work bench, its scattered cans of reel, the one, blankly accusing eye of the moviola. Their very unloveliness touched him, moved him, seemed to mark him indelibly as one with the moustachioed men who had come from the East all those decades before, and sent their tramps and cops and big-eyed girls on to the steep streets of sleepy Hollywood to fashion fantasies that would fuel the world's imagination.

A conversation floated in from the corridor, two other small directors talking shop. It hung in the airwaves and passed over his head. He was on another plane, far from this time or this place, existing only in the two lengths of sprocketed reel, the all-consuming necessity of marrying the two with compatibility perfect beyond perfection.

It was neither his eyes nor ears, but his nose, that picked up Kathy. She had slipped in silently, as sometimes she did, and had stood leaning against the refrigerator for he did not know how long, sipping occasionally at his can of Cola, watching her own invisible image being matched to the silent track of her voice.

'Hi,' she said. 'How're you doing?'

He blinked at her, adjusting the focus of his mind. 'You been here long?'

'A bit. Have a break, you look like you could use one.'

'Yeah.' He blinked again, shrugged his shoulders, and perched on a precarious high chair. He took the Cola from her hand and drank, then leaned over and kissed her, lingeringly, on the lips. They had been lovers, on and off, for three years.

She nodded at the film in the synchroniser. 'So how's *Marina*?' she asked.

'Synching up. Why aren't you at class?'

'Class is over, it's past noon. You wouldn't notice an earthquake, would you? Thanks for last night.'

'Yeah.' Gradually, he felt himself returning to the real world. 'Yeah, it was a good evening.'

'Good evening, good food, good company.' She paused. 'Pity Rick had to be there.'

He wondered, in slight irritation, why she found it so

necessary so often to make sharp comments about others. Joanna did not do it. He decided to ignore it.

'What d'you think of my cousin-in-law?'

She met his eye, laughed at the change of subject, but answered him. 'I liked her.' She drew her upper lip into a straight line. 'Teddibly British. But I liked her. Don't know what she thought of us, though.'

'She said she really liked you all.'

'Oh, the British. They're so polite.'

'Not all.' He stiffened his own upper lip : although she was the actress, his British accent was better than hers. 'Some are just — teddibly — rude.'

'Joanna isn't.'

'No, Joanna'd need a correspondence course to get a little bit fresh. She's a good kid, Joanna.'

'Yeah. Some women make you want to be sick.'

But that was said not sharply, but with real, even wistful, affection, and he kissed her again.

'How are the House of Horrors?' she asked. 'How's your buddy Mac?'

*Marina* was financed by a consortium of dentists; successful, professional men looking to save some spare dollars from the taxman by investing them in a project that combined the ring of glamour with an at best marginal chance of any return on their investment. Most of the consortium had been satisfactorily content to sign over their money and forget it. The exception was Neal MacDonald, who fancied himself to be a movie buff and Mike to be his friend.

Mike now grimaced. 'Jesus, he's persistent,' he said. 'Has to have lunch with me next week. I can't shake him off. Polo Lounge again.'

'Oh, poor baby.' She mimicked compassion.

'Listen, if you want to go instead, you're welcome.'

'No, I won't deprive you of your chance to gussy up.' Mike's dislike for formal wear was famous. 'What'll it be this time, the sports jacket?'

'No, that was last time. It's the suit's turn.'

'I always think you look cute in that suit.'

'Well, I'm glad it gives someone somewhere some pleasure. I'll think of you when I put it on.'

She looked down, traced a pattern with her finger on the refrigerator. 'I think you look cute out of it, too.'

He frowned: she should know that, when at work, he was off limits. She herself, preparing for a scene, was positively unapproachable.

'Can you lock this door?' she asked.

'It's not soundproofed.'

'Who's to know? Anyone hears, they'll just think you're making a porn.'

He thought, then shrugged: after all, he had achieved a lot that morning. 'OK,' he said.

They had sat so long, gossiping and getting to know each other again, that it was lunchtime. They ordered salads, vast bowls bursting, brimming, and overflowing with outrageously fresh vegetables, cheeses, cuts of meat. Wine came yellow in a cold carafe, drops of water condensing and trickling down the outside. The Ocean was in the air, and neither they nor anyone in sight had pressing business to attend to. Susan felt herself thaw into the sunshine and the nourishment.

'This is very nice,' she said. 'I really feel as if I'm on holiday.'

'I still do,' agreed Joanna. 'Always. Of course, at the moment, I really am.'

'Well.' Even among her own kind, Susan leaped to the instinctive academician's defence of the summer vacation. 'You mean you're not actually teaching.'

'Oh, Susan!' She shook her head, laughing. 'Thanks for the vote of confidence, but honestly, I'm not doing anything.'

'You're recuperating. Refreshing yourself.' She thought of the canvases stacked in the garage, and felt again the familiar envy twisting in her entrails. 'Presumably painting.'

39

'Oh yes, the painting.' She looked down at her wine glass, cheeks pinkening. 'I did tell you yesterday that I'd gotten awfully lazy. And there's really no excuse, you know. I mean, *look* at all this.' She waved a hand at the blue sky, the crayon-yellow sun, the brown sand, the multi-coloured people. 'And I keep thinking I should *do* something with it, but . . . I don't.'

'That's odd,' said Susan. 'This seems to be such a creative place. I mean, most people last night seemed to be — as you put it — *doing* something.'

'Oh . . . people around here talk a lot, you know. Nancy — well, as you picked up, she doesn't quite know what she does, but whatever it is, she loves doing it. Kathy and Rick both claim to be actors — and actually, Kathy's very good, when she gets the chance — but she earns most of her living as a temporary secretary, and Rick does a bit of modelling and lives on Oliver. Oliver claims to be a journalist, but he writes one article a year and lives on some vast sum of money his grandmother left him . . .'

'Rick told me he was white trash.'

'Did he? Well, somebody left him, anyway; he's a bit of a mystery, is Oliver. But anyway, the only person of that lot who really does what he says he does is Bill, and everyone's terribly rude about him.'

'And Mike. He does what he says he does, doesn't he?'

'Mike? Oh, yes.' She smiled in sudden, shy pride. 'Yes, he does.'

Susan, digesting this information, missed her smile.

'That,' she said finally, 'would drive me quite mad.'

'Actually, I find it rather refreshing. In England, everything's such a hassle, even to get started. I like it that here you can just say you're a painter, and, bingo, you're a painter.'

'Except that you say you're not painting.'

'Well, that's true, Susan. Thanks for reminding me.'

'Well, you did say it.' All the same, and envy apart, she was looking forward to seeing the effects of this place on her cousin's work. 'I'd like to see what you have done, anyway. When we get back.'

'Oh, sure. Sure.' She studied her wine glass again. 'You might not like it, you know. I've changed quite a lot.'

'I wouldn't have expected you not to.'

'Well, I have. Come on, drink up and let's go.'

When they arrived home, the afternoon sun lay heavily on the grass and around the white painted walls; but inside was shuttered and deliciously cool.

'Cup of tea?' offered Joanna.

'Paintings first.'

They went into the garage. Joanna turned the canvases around, and propped them against the walls, the bed, the desk. Susan looked at them.

'You have changed,' she said.

'I told you I had.'

'They're not as angry.'

'They're not as good.'

She was right. The paintings Susan remembered, full of the nightmarish, not quite distortions, the suggestions of shadows about to leap out of cupboards and from under beds, had disappeared. What was in their place, beach scenes, a portrait of Mike, one of the Mexican woman they had passed the previous evening, was pleasant enough to look at, competent; even, in the portrait of the Mexican woman, inspired. But the anger had indeed left her work, and as it had gone, so had what it was about it that had set it apart from the ordinary.

'What happened?' said Susan.

'I don't know. You say they're not angry, and I suppose *I'm* not angry any more. I never really felt I was, but I suppose I must have been, mustn't I? Or unhappy or something. Because look at the way I used to paint in London. And now I'm happier than I've ever been, and my painting's just gone . . . like that.'

Susan knew with a crashing, trumpeting, fiery-sworded sense of loss that she would never again envy Joanna her gift.

For that, and for a moment, she wished her all the ill in the world.

'So long as you're happy,' she said. 'I suppose that's the main thing.'

'You don't suppose for one second,' said Joanna. She glanced through the garage door, and her face changed. 'Oh — Eileen.'

A late middle-aged woman had climbed out of a shiny car, and was striding jauntily across the garden towards them. After a minute, Susan recognised Mike's mother.

'What a lovely surprise!' Joanna's cry of welcome, and the warmth of her kiss, were genuine enough: there was, at least on her part, no apparent in-law problem here.

Eileen advanced towards Susan. 'I came to welcome our cousin to Los Angeles. Welcome, my dear, it's so good to see you.'

Susan did not like to be appropriated, without consultation, into the family of a comparative stranger, even if she were Joanna's mother-in-law. But she politely took the freckled, manicured hand that was held out to her.

'Thank you,' she said. 'How do you do?'

'How do you do! Isn't she British!' laughed Joanna. 'Stay for some tea, Eileen.'

'Tea. Don't you young people drink anything but tea? Isn't there a real drink about the place?'

Susan, conscious of having taken the majority of lunch's carafe of wine, looked at her with new interest as they crossed the yard to the house. She must be in at least her late fifties, but was as erect as a woman twenty years younger, and carried herself with the unmistakable assurance of one leading a life that was both demanding and fulfilling. Susan thought of Joanna's own mother, gently silvering over her tea service and Townswomen's Guild. It was like imagining a being from another planet.

'How is dear Betty?' asked Eileen, seeming to read her thoughts as they settled into the living room. 'That woman has the most gorgeous skin, I hate her.'

'Eileen, of course, is a prune.' Joanna, who had hurried into the kitchen, reappeared with a glass full of ice and a bottle of Irish whiskey, and affectionately patted her mother-in-law's cheek. 'There you are. My mother-in-law the lush.'

'My own father-in-law,' said Eileen, 'was never without a whiskey by his side.'

'And he,' finished Joanna, evidently recounting a tale often told, 'died on his way home from Stations on Good Friday, aged ninety with all his teeth and a full head of hair.'

'Well, he did that, Miss, and you should show some respect for your elders and betters.' She turned to Susan. 'Are you not drinking, dear?'

'Sorry, Susan,' said Joanna. 'The kettle's on for tea, but would you rather have a whiskey? You really will have to stop being so polite, you know.'

As they both looked at her, warm and kind, Susan felt the mellowness of the lunch wear off, and herself grow prim, and sallow, and stiff. 'A whiskey would be very nice, please,' she said.

'That's my girl! And a smoker, too.' Eileen raised a glass to her. 'I can see you and I are going to be friends.'

Susan smiled thinly. A shared taste for whiskey and cigarettes did not, in her view, a friendship make. 'Do you live nearby?' she asked. She had had the impression that Mike had come from Chicago.

'Twenty minutes' drive. But I'm always over here: these poor kids can't get rid of me.'

'I wish. Susan, you don't know what a rare treat this is. Eileen does something terribly complicated with computers at the hospital, and they don't usually let her out of the building.'

'Honey, I don't usually let myself out of the building, but I just had to greet our guest. And to see how the party went.'

'Oh, fine. Didn't it, Susan? Although it would've been nicer if you'd been there, but if you will lead such a packed social life . . . But we all enjoyed ourselves. Well, Rick did, which was the main thing.'

Eileen frowned. 'That boy is no good,' she said.

'Poor Rick,' said Joanna. 'You say he's no good, Mike says he can't act, Kathy hasn't a kind word to say for him . . . You know, I feel rather sorry for him, everyone disapproves of him so much.'

'They're right to,' snapped Eileen. 'And the one I feel sorry for is Oliver. These men who keep boys, well, it's the way they are, but they're asking for nothing but trouble. And that Rick's a parasite, and Oliver's a nice man.' She looked directly at Susan. 'Isn't he a nice man?'

'I liked him,' agreed Susan, wondering what, if any, were Aunt Betty's views on homosexual couples.

'Well, there you are, you see. Your cousin would feel sorry for Adolf Hitler if they gave her the opportunity.'

'I know.' The brief spark of sympathy that had kindled was effectively doused. Susan did not feel the need to have Joanna explained to her by a woman who had known her for just half a dozen years.

'Well.' She drained her glass. 'I should be on my way. But the other thing I wanted was to invite you over to dinner on Sunday.' She winked at Susan. 'Those two can sip their wine, and you and I'll have real drinks and get to know each other.'

'Oh, dear,' said Joanna. 'That would have been lovely. But we said we'd go to Nancy's for a barbecue. What a shame: I don't suppose we could make it Saturday?'

'Oh.' Eileen frowned again; but it was a different frown, one that smacked less of disapproval, and more of personal affront. She did not, evidently, relish having either her invitations refused or her plans subjected to change. 'No, Saturday's no good. I'm busy myself.'

'With Dr Weintraub?' Joanna asked, smiling slyly.

Eileen's pale cheeks flushed, and she smiled herself, almost giggled. 'You mind your own affairs, Miss,' she retorted. Then her smile faded. 'Oh, darn. Well, then, I don't know when . . . ' She snapped her fingers. 'What about tonight?'

Tonight, Susan knew immediately, was out of the question. She caught Joanna's eye, and signalled a 'no' that was as unmistakable to her cousin as it was unrecognisable to anyone else.

'Oh, dear,' said Joanna again. 'Can we take a raincheck, please? I have a couple of things to do, and God knows, this one will be here for ever.'

'What things?' demanded Eileen.

'Oh, you know,' said Joanna. 'Laundry. Letters. *Things.*'

'Well, do them this afternoon,' said her mother-in-law. 'And then come over.'

Susan shifted in her chair. She was by no means sure whether she liked this Eileen, whether she would grow to like her over the course of her visit, whether she would ever grow to like her, but of one thing she was certain: she would not dine with her tonight. She stared at the older woman, hoping to make her look back, knowing that when she did, the expression in her eyes would speak more than Joanna's politely feeble excuses. But Eileen continued to look at Joanna, her own greeny-blue eyes — wherever, it occurred to Susan, Mike's Algonquin ancestor fitted in, it was clearly not on the maternal side — registering annoyance, accusation, determination.

'Well, I'm not sure,' floundered Joanna, 'that I can.' She shot a questioning glance at Susan, and caught the force of Susan's gaze. 'And anyway, Mike . . .'

'Oh, who needs Mike?' interrupted Eileen. 'If he comes home in time, bring him, and if not, why, we'll have a hen evening.'

This, Susan decided, was simply too much. The woman was even more persistent than Nancy. Well, she, for one, was not to be bullied into good fellowship. She leaned forward into the conversation.

'What Joanna is trying to say,' she said firmly, 'or rather, trying not to have to say, is that she's tired and I'm jet-lagged, and thank you very much for the invitation, but we'd really rather take it up another evening. If it's all the same to you.'

45

The two women's eyes met at last, and sparked just for a second into mutual hostility.

Then Eileen smiled, an attractive, American smile, wide mouth crumpling soft cheeks, showing strong, slightly protruding teeth. 'Honey, I'm sorry,' she said. 'Of course you must take your time to get used to the place. Joanna, call me next week.' She rose to go. 'And give my love to that no good husband of yours.'

'Which husband's that?' A male voice joined theirs, Mike loomed at the door, and Eileen's face turned silly with love.

'That was a short day,' said Susan.

'What day? I'm just starting. Came home for a sandwich. Did you guys eat yet?'

'He often does that,' said Joanna. 'He says the drive clears his head.'

She spoke about him as if he were not there; and he himself, after politely kissing his mother, threw her the most perfunctory of nods before disappearing into the kitchen.

'Just like his father,' said Eileen, watching through the open door as he pulled bread, mustard, and ham from the cupboard and refrigerator. 'He's not with us at all. Thinking, all the time he's thinking. Mike, don't you use a plate?'

'Sorry, Mom.'

'You don't have to say sorry to me, it's not my kitchen.'

'Sorry, Joanna. Sorry, Susan. Sorry, everyone who ever lived or died or had hay fever, or swept the floor, or went to the desert.'

'Ah, there's no talking to him. Just like his father. Joanna, you have the patience of a saint.'

'Well,' said Joanna. 'You should know, Mrs O'Connor.'

'Indeed I should,' said Eileen, 'Mrs O'Connor.'

'They gang up on me,' said Mike vaguely to Susan, wiping a mustard-stained hand on his jeans as he trailed out from the kitchen.

'So I see,' said Susan. She was thin, cold of spirit, and older than all of them.

'See you later,' said Mike.

'Walk me to my car, Mike,' said Eileen, and he transferred his sandwich and held out his free arm to her.

On her son's arm, she looked up at Susan. 'So good to have seen you, my dear. And I hope before you go, we get to know each other real well.'

'I'm sure we shall,' said Susan.


'You have great hands, Susan,' said Bill, handing her a paper plate groaning with moist chicken and substantial potato salad.

'Thank you,' said Susan: she assumed it was a compliment.

She had been in Los Angeles now for five days. She had been up the rocky coast road to quiet Malibu, and down wide, car-crammed, palm tree lined avenues to the skyscrapers and office blocks of downtown LA. She had eaten burritos, doughnuts, and sushi, had watched a game show on television, and had so far resisted being taken to one of the large movie houses for a film. She had sent a postcard to Aunt Betty, to her neighbour at the flats, and to Felix. She had got over her jet lag, and thought she was accustoming herself to the constant bright light, the scale of the roads and buildings, even to the idea that, far and wide as the city reached, from desert, to mountains, to the Ocean, it still contained no real centre, no theatre district, no historical museum.

What was more difficult to adjust to was the unremitting pleasantness of its inhabitants. True, Joanna herself was pleasant to most people most of the time; but she had always been so, and Susan had long grown blind to it, as one stops noticing the birthmark that mars the face of a loved one. A nation of Joannas, however, was rather more than she had bargained for. Everyone, it seemed, was on terms of the warmest cordiality with everyone else. Waitresses introduced themselves by first names; shop assistants chuckled as they packed goods, discussing the weather, the prices, the latest

47

show business scandal; everyone loved her accent. Once, on a street corner downtown, she had heard two voices raised in what sounded like altercation, and had turned eagerly, hoping for some sign that all was not sweetness here; only to see two young black men, grinning widely and slapping palms, an exchange of insults clearly basic to their friendship.

The softball game, predictably (exactly like rounders, as Susan had sturdily not repeated Joanna's description), had been a veritable orgy of good feeling. She had been cheered by her own team when she had picked up the bat, cheered again when she had made contact with the ball, and apologised to by Bill on the opposing team when he had run her out on second base. She had been deluged with offers of the loan of a glove when her team went to field, and cheered tumultuously when — although uninterested in games, she was wiry and naturally well coordinated — she had caught Kathy out. Halfway through the game, some children crossing the park — baseball-capped, black, oriental, and freckle-faced white, like extras from a sentimental Hollywood movie — had stopped to join them, and had demanded cheerfully to know why she and the other lady talked funny. You could not fault sporting spirit or racial harmony; yet Susan, after less than a week, was beginning occasionally to experience a frantic feeling of drowning in a sea of treacle. She was (somewhat to her surprise, because she did not usually) missing Felix.

The food, at any rate, here at Nancy and Bill's comfortably sprawling house, was good — insofar as one could judge barbecue food — and plentiful, and Nancy, on her own native heath, was proving herself to be an efficient, and unexpectedly unobtrusive, hostess. Nor, to Susan's unspeakable relief, had she resurrected the idea of the jewellery session. A boy who looked like Nancy, and a girl who looked like Bill, were mingling among the adult company with a self-assurance no British child knew, and both Bill and Mike were keeping her plastic cup well filled with wine. A drift of smoke from the barbecue caught a cooling evening breeze, and, far from disagreeably, stung her eyes. She looked down, and realised that she was starting to turn brown.

'Do you play sports in England?' Kathy was standing beside her, attacking a hot dog with enthusiasm. 'You're very good.'

'Thank you,' said Susan. She faintly, she thought, remembered a time and a place when she was able to begin a conversation with other phrases. 'No, I haven't played since I was at school.'

'Don't you play cricket?'

'Good God, no.' Nor did she know anyone who did. Felix followed it, but that was yet another side of his life they did not discuss.

'I always thought it sounded so elegant.' Kathy tossed her head, and spoke in aristocratic tones. 'A game of cricket, old chap? . . . How do you play, anyway? Is it like baseball?'

'It's complicated.' Susan was most certainly not prepared for a dissertation on the rules of cricket. 'Have you been to England?'

'No, I'd love to. Mike's always talking about it, he had such a great time when he was there. You know, he talks about it more than Joanna does.'

'Actually, you should go if you're an actress. The London stage is really very good. The. . . ' She broke off abruptly, a memory from the dinner party asserting itself. But an actress must surely be familiar with at least Shakespeare?

'Miss Barnes, the authority on Miss Woodhouse.'

Oliver had arrived. Unlike Rick, he had not joined the game, and looked cool in a lightweight suit and Italian leather shoes.

'You didn't play,' said Susan.

'I did not,' he agreed. 'I don't. A wise countryman of ours once warned us to distrust all enterprises that required new clothes, and since I have not, and have no intention of acquiring, a pair of sneakers . . . How is Miss Woodhouse, anyway? I suppose that when her sister married she did graduate from being Miss Emma?'

'I'm sure she did.' She could relax with Oliver, who not only had read, and apparently understood, *Emma*, but also reminded her very slightly of Felix. 'Actually, she's still sitting unopened on my desk. I start work on her tomorrow.' And how refreshing it would be to walk again in a world where amicability, although pleasing, was of so incidental an importance. 'I didn't know there was an element of free will attached to softball.'

'Well, Rick and I have an agreement.' He raised his head, scanning the green lawn, dotted with people, that ran down to the swimming pool. 'I don't take him to films with subtitles. And he doesn't take me to events which involve round flying objects. Where is Rick, anyway?'

'Somewhere. Over there.'

On the other side of the garden, Rick was deep in conversation with the son of the house. They were almost by the side of the pool, but even from the distance, his cheeks were visibly flushed and his eyes shining from the afternoon's play.

'He's found his intellectual level,' said Kathy, and Oliver laughed.

Susan had forgotten the exchange between Kathy and Rick in the kitchen. She remembered it now, and noticed how readily Oliver enjoyed her joke.

'He's very beautiful,' she said.

'Thank you,' said Mike, passing with a full wine bottle and a glass for Oliver.

'But he's so-o-o-o dumb.' Kathy smiled teasingly up at Mike as she held out her own plastic cup for a refill. 'Mike, how come Oliver gets a glass glass, and the rest of us get these?'

'Take it up with the management. I just do what Nancy tells me. Susan, finish that before I pour. This is Oliver's wine, and it's class stuff.'

'If you knew Susie,' sang Kathy, 'like I know Susie: Oh, oh, oh what a gal.'

'I made the mistake,' Oliver told Susan, 'at one point during my misspent youth, of studying wine. I gained a palate, and ruined my bank balance for ever.'

'She's none too choosy is our young Susie . . . but I guess if you're drinking Oliver's wine, you must be choosy after all.'

Susan drank. It was very good. 'It's very good,' she said.

'Veddy good,' said Mike.

'Teddibly good,' agreed Kathy.

'A frightfully amusing little wine.'

'After a while,' said Joanna, joining them, 'you get so used to people being terribly witty about you, that you stop noticing it. Oh, is that Oliver's wine?' She sipped from Susan's glass. 'Nice.'

'This is pathetic,' said Mike. 'One bottle of good wine, and a bunch of adults goes crazy. You'd think we lived on methylated spirits.'

'My grandfather used to tell me,' said Susan, 'that you can get drunk from toothpaste. Unfortunately, he died before I was old enough to ask him how.'

'Family can be selfish,' noted Oliver.

'Who's selfish?' Rick had left his other conversation, and joined them, edging his way between Kathy and Oliver. 'Hi, Oliver. You made it, then.'

'Apparently,' said Oliver, turning away. It became apparent to Susan that here, at least, were two people who were not, for the moment, in perfect harmony.

'Apparently,' Rick mimicked, and laughed. 'So go on. Who's selfish?'

'All sorts of people,' said Oliver.

'Ancient relics of over forty,' said Mike.

Rick laughed again. 'Did you bring that wine, Oliver? Oh, you guys are drinking it. It's good wine. Isn't it good? You have to admit Oliver has good taste. If nothing else.'

Oliver, staring ahead, said nothing. It also became apparent that Rick's glow was due to more than exercise.

'If you like it so much,' said Kathy, 'I'm surprised you're

not drinking it.' She stared at the beer can in his hand. His hands, Susan noticed, in contrast to his features, were surprisingly coarse.

'I don't need to.' He slid her a glance under heavy eyelashes. 'I get plenty at home.'

'I like your T-shirt, Kathy,' said Joanna, quickly.

'You've seen it before, it's from that festival thing I was in. I have another at home you can have.' She eyed Joanna's curves: she herself was sparely endowed. 'If you can get it over those gorgeous great tits.'

'Oh, it's so rough to have to be slim and elegant.'

'Oliver likes me to wear T-shirts,' announced Rick. 'Don't you, Oliver? I was wearing one when we met. Wasn't I?'

'What festival thing was that?' Oliver asked Kathy.

'Oh, an Inge thinge,' said Kathy. 'Just, when, round about the time you guys were being cultured together.'

'Oliver and I met,' explained Joanna to Susan, 'at a class we both took. Art history.'

'I thought you already knew about art history.'

'American art history, you clot.'

'Clot?' Kathy's ears pricked up at the new word. 'What's a clot?'

'A dumbbell,' Mike explained. 'You'll have to excuse Joanna, she's spent the week reverting to racial type.'

'Oliver's British,' said Rick to Susan. 'I always say that's where he gets his uptightness from.'

'Very possibly,' said Susan. To her shame, she found she was rather enjoying Rick.

'I mean.' His gaze swept the circle, and rested, briefly, on Kathy. 'I mean, some people are uptight, and you can see why they're uptight. And some people, like Mike here, aren't uptight at all. Are you, Mike? But old Oliver, he's just uptight for no reason. Just like the British.'

'Joanna, how rude of me,' said Oliver. 'I haven't yet thanked you for a truly outstanding meal the other night. Wasn't it outstanding, Rick?'

'What?' Rick turned, focused on him. 'Oh, yeah. Outstanding.'

'He's already thanked me,' said Joanna. 'Thank you all for thanking me. Isn't it funny how we get one British person in our midst, and suddenly, everyone becomes terribly polite?'

'You see what I mean?' Rick demanded of no one in particular. 'Uptight. I'd already thanked her.'

'I'm quite sure,' said Oliver, gallantly, 'that no one's ever *not* polite to you, Joanna.'

'I'd already thanked her,' repeated Rick. 'And I'd told her what a great time I'd had, and . . . and I'd asked her to dinner with us, next Thursday. Hadn't I, Joanna?'

'Rick.' Joanna leaned over, and took his hand. 'Shall we go and get some coffee? You look like you could use it.'

He glared at her, his glow deepening to scarlet. 'Hadn't I asked you to dinner? This coming Thursday? I'm going to cook chicken.'

'Rick,' she said, 'I think some coffee . . .'

'Hadn't I?'

'Well, actually, Ricky, it's very sweet of you, but since you mention it, no.'

'Well, then.' He was unabashed. 'I'm asking you now. All of you. Come to dinner on Thursday. I'm cooking chicken.'

His glare widened to include the whole group. Joanna looked at Mike, who shrugged. Oliver stared, stonefaced, over Joanna's left shoulder. 'How nice,' said Joanna, at the second before the silence grew painful. 'That's very sweet of you, we'd all love to come, and Kathy too, right? Come and get some coffee.'

'Chicken,' he stressed. 'I'm a very good cook.'

'I know you are. Look, let's leave these kitchen illiterates, shall we, and go and talk recipes indoors? Come on.'

'Kitchen illiterates.' He nodded. 'Right. Yes, let's go talk.' He began to move with her, and then stopped. 'You're a good cook, too, Joanna.'

'Thank you.'

53

She led him, stumbling slightly, towards the house. At the door, he paused, and turned. 'Kitchen illiterates!' he shouted.

Oliver smiled once, and detached himself from the group without a word. Mike and Kathy exchanged rueful glances.

'Thursday's going to be fun,' said Kathy.

Susan said nothing. Inexcusably, she was really quite looking forward to it.


Joanna lounged under the jacaranda tree, a glass of iced tea and a magazine to hand, watching the shadows on the lawn, still, not shifting like English shadows, and rejoiced in the felicity of being, for the first time in nearly a week, alone. Mike had just left, growling and pulling uncomfortably at his suit and tie, for his appointment at the Polo Lounge; and earlier that morning, Susan had carried into her garage a sandwich, an electric kettle, a jar of instant coffee, and the largest ashtray she could find, declaring it her intention not to emerge before late afternoon. She was, Joanna knew, for those few hours as completely gone as was Mike; more so. Mike had simply driven a few miles up the road; while Susan had gone over continents and through centuries to a rainsoaked Surrey village, and Boney, magnificently unmentioned, marching through Europe across the sea.

She was, she thought, now giving herself a chance to assess Susan's visit, definitely pleased with the way it was so far going. Her cousin, while all too obviously never a natural Southern Californian, was nevertheless as obviously doing her best to understand, if not to enjoy, the place; their friends, while slightly puzzled by her, appeared on the whole to like her; and Mike, bless him, had accepted her as intrinsically a part of the environment as if she had come with the house. It was, she decided with a mixture of self-congratulation and relief, all going remarkably well.

It was tiring, however, being a hostess, even to someone as close as Susan. She had had no real time to herself all week, and Joanna needed time to herself, treasured it, even craved it. She sometimes would visit Nancy, and, watching while the other interrupted herself constantly to answer questions, slap hands, and apply kisses and bandages to cut knees, would ask in a tone that she could hear to be midway between admiration and horror, how she could bear to be *on* all the time? To which Nancy would reply, with a blank look, that it was not something you bore or did not bear, but simply did. Maybe, she would add, Joanna would do it herself one day. Maybe she would; almost certainly she would; but not yet. Not yet.

A day's joyous solitude stretched, long and lush, before her, as it had for all of July, and would for all of August. It was the first year that they had been able to afford for her not to take a temporary job during the summer vacation, and she was enjoying her idleness, she sometimes guiltily thought, almost more than was decent.

She had not, of course, intended to be idle. She had intended to be productive, to take Spanish conversation classes, to exercise ten pounds from her hips, to paint. But somehow, day slipping into long day, she had done none of those things, but only sat under the jacaranda tree, looking up into the leaves. Soon it would be too late even to start: for the Spanish classes, it already was. Perhaps she would go to the health club later today. Perhaps — probably not — she would paint.

She had not, in fact, painted for some time: the end results, these days, were so boring that they scarcely seemed worth the effort. She recognised this, but did not, unlike Susan, mourn it; her talent, she knew, was not dead but sleeping, lulled to slumber by a life of perfect harmony with a husband she loved, friends who loved her, and a sun that shone, although not usually too hard, on most days of the year. Whether it would continue to sleep was an open question. It might, one day, wake itself, refreshed and renewed; she might, God forbid, for some reason too painful to foresee, be forced to kick it to wakefulness. Or it might just continue to sleep. She did not know, and could not, right now, find the energy to speculate.

She sipped at her drink, and lay luxuriously back into the

battered plastic sunlounger. A hummingbird flew out of the sun into the tree above her, and remained, sipping on a last, blue, bugle-shaped flower, left over from the spring, its small sleek body motionless, tiny wings battering at a sinister speed. Probably the health club would wait until tomorrow. She stared up at the bird in the tree, and tried to pretend she did not hear the car draw up, the car door open and shut, the footsteps walk towards her up the path. Something filled with savage hatred for whoever was coming to her was conceived, brought to term, and expelled from her as she turned her head with a smile of welcome towards her visitor. She had been so looking forward to the day.

It was Rick.

'Rick!' she said. 'How lovely to see you.'

'Hi, Joanna.' He bent to kiss her, unshaven, his breath smelling of sour morning, and coffee, and breath freshener. 'How you doing?'

'Fine. How are you?'

'Not good.' He perched on the end of the sunlounger, almost overtoppling it. He did not look well. 'Oliver sent me. To apologise.' He sighed. 'He says I was drunk yesterday.'

Joanna tried, and failed, to repress a laugh. 'Well, Ricky, you weren't exactly sober, were you? Come in and have some iced tea.'

He followed her in, and dropped heavily into a chair by the large kitchen table. Joanna, who had intended to take the tea outside, glanced briefly through the door at the shadows on the grass. Then she looked properly at him. He was pale, and his hair was lank; he looked, almost, ordinary.

'You don't look well at all,' she said.

'I keep telling you. I'm not.'

'Well, do you want something to eat? Eggs? Or look.' She checked the Tupperware box: miraculously, there was a small chunk of the cake left. 'Have some of this. My mother made it, it's guaranteed to cure all known ills.'

'Looks good. Thanks.'

He took a slice, and ate for a while in silence. Joanna watched him, reflecting on how different from hers were American eating habits. It would not have occurred to her to eat cake at 12.30 in the afternoon.

'Hey,' he said at last. 'I meant it about Thursday evening, you know.'

'Too right you meant it, or we'd have been battering on your door.' But he did not laugh. She tried another cheering tack. 'I've told Susan about your chicken.'

A small smile appeared, then. 'Did you?'

'Oh, yes. Are you going to do it that new way?'

The smile grew: his latest recipe was his most successful yet. 'Maybe,' he said.

'And do you think,' she pursued, 'that if I were very nice indeed to you, you might even give me the recipe?'

The smile erupted into a grin as he finished his cake. 'I doubt it.'

'Well, I think you're jolly mean. And just to show you how nice I am anyway, do you want the very last piece of cake?'

'Yes, please.'

'I thought you might.' Ruffling his hair affectionately as she passed, she went to the shelf for the almost empty Tupperware box.

When she returned to the table, his smile had gone. 'You are nice, Joanna,' he said.

Sitting, she sketched a curtsey. 'Well, thank you, kind sir.'

'Really. You are.' He reached over and helped himself to more tea. 'This isn't just hangover, you know.'

'Isn't it?' She had thought it was not. 'What is it, then?'

'Oh.' He sighed, his mouth drooping at the corners. 'Oliver. You know.'

'What about Oliver?'

'Oh, you know. Everyone says he's so kind and so smart and I'm such a bum . . .'

'Oh, Ricky!' But she could not deny it: it was true.

'Yes, they do.' He picked unhappily at his cake. 'And he *is* kind and smart, and I *am* a bum, probably, but it isn't as simple as that.'

It probably was not: it rarely was. It was true that none of their group had approved of Rick, not since he had appeared in Oliver's life, quite suddenly it seemed, soon after Christmas, coming from no one quite knew where, with little but his looks apparently to recommend him. But then again, neither did anyone quite know where Oliver came from: talking often about the South of his origins, he never mentioned actual mother or father, school friend or childhood pet. Joanna had known him for over a year, but had no idea of when his birthday was. As for Rick, he could not help not being a genius; and the look on Oliver's face when the other spoke was not always kind. The question of how Oliver put up with Rick was often asked; looking at Rick now, she wondered for the first time just what it was that had driven or drawn an able-bodied twenty-two-year-old into being kept by a man more than twice his age.

'What do you mean?' she asked.

'Oh.' He sighed again. 'He's very demanding, you know. And he's . . .' He paused, searching for the word. 'He's so . . . *middle aged.*'

'Well.' Oliver did, after all, provide his food, and for all she knew, his clothes, too. 'He can't help that.'

'Well, I can't help being young, either.'

Something then in his voice reminded her of her brother Tom; not Tom as he was now, the overworked young doctor running from surgery to housecalls, with barely time to fall in love with his senior partner's daughter, but Tom as a part of him would always be in her mind, the sulky schoolboy late with his homework. She rather missed Tom. She cast a last look at the sun and shade outside, and settled down for the afternoon.

'What exactly do you mean by demanding?' she said.

\*

All the valet parkers at the Beverly Hills Hotel knew Mike. Rather, they knew his car, a battle-scarred Oldsmobile, dingy grey, which stood out among the gleaming Mercedes and Jaguars like one dead tooth in an otherwise expensively cared for mouth. It had occasionally been put to Mike that he might invest in a more cosmetically impressive vehicle, a suggestion which he dismissed as beneath contempt. Mike loved his car. He thought of it in the most secret depths of his heart as the Mikemobile; it had been with him since before Joanna, almost, it sometimes felt, since before Mike. Presumably, it would not last for ever, but he did not dwell on the thought. He only knew that to abandon it now, purely because it was no longer beautiful, would be worse than pointless, would be perfidy, would be unpardonable. Besides, should the occasion arise where he needed to cut a dash, he could always borrow Bill's Mercedes.

Striding across the hotel lobby, heavy with the scent of flowers and expensive perfume, he caught his own eye in a flatteringly lit mirror, and exchanged with himself a brief glance of disgust. Kathy had said he looked cute in his suit. He did not feel cute, he felt uncomfortable: constricted and faintly foolish. His Algonquin ancestors had not worn suits; nor, except for Sunday Mass, had his Irish. His father, the hotshot Chicago lawyer, had had a wardrobe filled with suits, a different one of which he had worn every weekday of his life, and had succeeded, in all of them, in looking like nothing so much as a one-eighth Indian, one-quarter Creole, black Irish peasant wearing a suit. Which, as his father had been well aware, had of course been a potent part of his professional charm.

Although he was on time, or as near as made little difference, MacDonald was already sitting at the table, waving to him eagerly across the pastel coloured room. No matter how early Mike arrived, Mac was there before him: no matter how late, he was delighted to see him. Mike shifted his shoulders in his suit as he crossed to the table: the man's naked excitement at being involved in the movie business made him feel subtly ashamed, dirty, dirtied, as if he had been caught peeping through a bedroom keyhole. But it was Mac who was the investor, Mac who held the purse strings. Without Mac and his colleagues, there would be no independence for Mike, no making of his own movies; he would be lost in one of the major studios somewhere, churning out expensive froth to suit the fads of that year's public or the whim of that year's studio head. So it was that Mac was able to issue unrefusable, unnecessary lunch invitations. Mac was in the position of power, after all.

'How're you doing?' he said, reaching across the table to shake Mac's scrubbed dentist's hand.

'Hello, Mike. Time to "do lunch" again, right?' He giggled, as he invariably did at the joke, and Mike looked away. 'I'd like you to meet my colleague, Celia Fletcher.'

Mike for the first time became aware of the woman sitting on Mac's right. Interesting looking, he noted, with glossy black hair and strong bones hinting at an Indian ancestry like his own, but set off by a poise that could be East Coast or could be European. The hand she extended was both strong and shapely, and she wore her own well cut linen suit with an ease he himself would never attain.

'I hope you don't mind,' she told him. 'I couldn't resist the opportunity to meet a real movie director.'

'An award-winning director,' noted Mac.

'It was only a film school award.' Mike sat down with a frown. To tap dance in private was humiliation enough; to be exhibited in public was beyond the pale.

'Well.' Quickly reading the situation, she allied herself with him. 'Mac can't talk about awards, he has a whole wall full of them in his surgery.' He had: Mac was highly respected in his profession. 'Let's order soon. I'm hungry.'

'Celia wants to talk to you,' said Mac. 'About financing a movie.'

'Mac, please.' She caught Mike's eye in complicity. 'Give him a chance to sit down.'

'Let's order,' said Mike.

'I know what I'm having,' said Mac. 'The low calorie plate.' He patted his stomach. 'Got to watch the waistline.' He was lean to the point of gauntness, but liked to affect a Hollywood paunch. In the early days of their association, he had tried quite hard to persuade Mike to play tennis with him on Saturdays.

'So how's it coming?' he asked after they had ordered. 'When do I see a rough cut?'

'Soon,' said Mike. It shocked him to realise how little he wanted Mac to see his dailies, to let his avaricious eyes swarm over the intimate inception of his movie. Mike's movie. 'Real soon,' he repeated. 'It's going OK.'

'Soon. OK.' Mac raised his eyes, and turned to the woman. 'The guy's making my movie, and he won't even talk to me about it.'

'That's a pity,' she murmured. She was looking at Mike, Mike now realised, with frank admiration.

'Won't even talk to me,' he repeated. 'Never happened to Louis B Mayer.'

'What I can't get Mac to understand,' said Mike, 'is that talking about making movies is very probably the second most boring thing in the world.'

'How disappointing,' she said. 'And the first?'

'Making movies.'

'Well.' She raised her shoulders in an elegantly philosophical shrug. 'There goes another illusion. So much for my glamour investment.'

'Oh, listen, lady.' He began to relax: the lunch looked as if it might be more enjoyable than he had anticipated. 'You've got money to invest . . .'

'She's got money,' put in Mac. He rubbed his fingers together and stared significantly at Mike. 'Serious money.'

'Then take my advice. Find something exciting to put it into. Like Formica.'

'Really? I was thinking maybe pig iron.'

'Well, there you are. Great conversation among pig iron people.'

'And I have high standards. Did you ever hear a roomful of dentists talking?'

A small noise emitted from Mac's breast pocket.

'I don't believe it,' he said. 'They're bleeping me.'

'You don't get an argument from me,' said Mike.

'They're bleeping me,' he repeated. 'I told them I was coming here, and if they wanted me, they were to page me. And they're bleeping me. In the Polo Lounge. Excuse me.' He sprang to his feet, and strode angrily from the room.

They waited until he was decently away before they laughed.

'Heads will roll,' said Mike.

'He's really an excellent dentist,' she said. 'And he's told me a great deal about you.'

'Curious. He hasn't told me anything at all about you.'

'Well, I only really met him a couple of weeks ago. At a dinner. And I happened to mention some friends and I were looking to lose some money somewhere, and . . .'

'And at 3.00 in the morning, he still had you pinned to the wall, feeding you misinformation about camera angles.'

'Something like that, yes.'

'Well.' She apparently had more money at her disposal than had Mac's group, and who knew what other misinformation Mac had been feeding her? 'I should make it clear right now that as far as film making goes, I'm strictly small fry.'

'I know,' she said. 'I've seen your stuff.'

He raised his eyebrows. Well respected as he was among the film community, he was little known outside it. 'You have?'

'I saw *Hollyweird* at Filmex. And Mac showed me *The Foxes* and *Ring o' Roses* on his video.'

'And you liked?'

'As far as I could tell.'

Unusual it was in this town where everyone fancied him or herself to be an expert, to find a non-film maker who resisted giving him her opinions of his film. Mike, who often barely restrained himself from a detailed criticism of Mac's teeth, raised a silent glass to her.

'So,' she continued, 'might you be interested?'

'I might,' he said. 'When I've finished *Marina*, of course. Might you?'

'I might well,' she said and smiled at him.

'Good.' He had his own code of honour: now was the time to mention Joanna. 'Listen, don't think I'm crazy here, but are you Ms Fletcher or Doctor Fletcher? My wife's British, and I get confused as hell about titles.'

She continued to smile; her teeth, he noticed, were excellent. 'I'm Celia,' she said.

'Goddamn woman.' Mac was back, muttering irritably. 'Goddamn bleeping me for a goddamn false alarm. She's got to go. Ah, food. Did you know Jack Nicholson's in the next room?'

The waitress served them, and left. Celia looked over her broiled fish with professional appreciation at Mike, demolishing his steak at speed. 'You have great teeth, Mike,' she said.

Mike realised that her knee, bare under the linen skirt, was nudging his. At the same moment, he had a brief, vivid picture of her wearing her white dentist's coat. Well, he had told her about Joanna; and she was, besides, a potential investor.

'Wanna get into pictures, kid?' he asked with a leer.


Susan's concentration sputtered, faltered, died. She recognised the symptoms: a woolliness in the head, the handwriting, always small, dwindling to little more than one straight line, and knew that it was time to call it a day. She did this slowly, unwillingly, sitting still at the desk, flicking with blind affection through the well thumbed pages of her Penguin edition, then through the notes she had taken, assessing their volume, waiting for Emma's world fully to recede so that she could resume her place in her own world, a world of cigarette-rasped throat, aching eyes, and coffee-jangled nerves. She sat for some minutes, not here, not there, not anywhere, before reality reasserted itself, this new reality of fierce sunshine on the bed's striped rug, and the Mexican children's voices lilting raucously in from the street. It was a quarter to six.

She had worked well, surprisingly so, considering how rudely she had been uprooted. But then she had been exposed lately to so much that was foreign and strange, and *Emma* was so well ordered, so familiar. Were she a sentimental person, she could almost have felt sentimental about it. As it was, she had worked energetically, arranging and rearranging thoughts and ideas, imposing, finally, a workable structure on which to build her 10,000 carefully chosen words. Tomorrow she would begin the actual writing. Felix would be pleased.

She smiled to herself, picturing Felix as he doubtless was at this moment, sitting thin and erect in his hopelessly cluttered office high over an alley in Covent Garden, a cigarette drooping from his lips, pouring a glass of white wine to celebrate the end of the day. In a few minutes, Malcolm from the next office would insert his ferret-like head around the door, and the two would sit drinking wine and swapping gossip as the evening sun warmed and yellowed on the age-old stones of the alley, and . . . no, foolish woman that she was, in England the sun had set hours ago, and Felix was at home.

She tidied her papers, picked up her overflowing ashtray and drained coffee mug, and left the garage. The sun was full on the garden, and she stood for a moment to bask. She heard Joanna's voice coming from the kitchen, and another voice, young, male, light, which after a moment she identified as Rick's. She frowned — she had not been expecting company, but then people, she remembered, did tend to drop in on Joanna — but went inside anyway.

'Hello,' she said, emptying the ashtray, and depositing the mug in the sink.

They were sitting over a pot of tea, Rick looking rather flushed, and Joanna rather tired.

'Susan!' Joanna's joy at seeing her was transparent: Susan wondered what had been happening that afternoon. 'Would you like the last cup of tea?'

'I'd rather have some wine, thanks.' She went to the refrigerator and poured herself a glass, Rick watching with eager interest as she did so. But she caught Joanna's eye, and did not offer him any.

'How was your day?' asked Joanna.

'OK.' She sat down, and sipped at her glass. 'Rather good, actually.'

'Well.' For a split second, Joanna stared at her harder than was necessary. 'Did you get a chance to think which movie you wanted to see?'

'Movie?' She had made her views on American cinema well known. But she had caught and understood her cousin's look. 'No, I thought I'd leave it to you. Since I'm still a backward European who calls them films.'

'Oh, shut up.' She turned to Rick. 'Listen, Ricky, I'm afraid I'm going to have to throw you out.'

'Why?' He perked up. 'Are you guys going to the movies tonight?'

'If we can find something to suit my clever cousin, yes. So . . .' She stood up.

But he remained seated. 'Well, I go to the movies a lot. Actors do, you know. Maybe we could all go together.'

'Oh, listen, you don't know this woman's tastes.' She stood over Susan, pointing down at her, and mouthing ostentatiously. 'She thinks Kurosawa's a lightweight.'

'Kurosawa?' He looked at Susan challengingly. 'I saw a movie of his once. I thought it was boring.'

Susan lit a cigarette. 'I imagine you did,' she responded.

He continued to look at her for a moment, then broke into his broad, childlike smile. 'That's the sort of thing Oliver says. But I'm a great cook. You'll see on Thursday, won't she, Joanna?' His smile vanished. 'I guess I have to go back to Oliver now.'

Joanna grimaced in sympathy. 'I think you'd better. But tell him I said he was to be nice to you.'

'Tell him . . . ' He smiled again. 'Yeah. I'll tell him that. 'Bye, Joanna. You're terrific.' He kissed her. 'She's terrific,' he told Susan.

Susan found herself smiling back. 'I know,' she said.

The two cousins waited until they heard the car door slam, and the engine purr off down the street. Then Joanna sat down with a dramatic groan, laying her head on her arm, and thumping on the blond wood table with her small fist.

'I take it,' said Susan, 'you were getting to know him rather well?'

'I thought he'd never go,' said Joanna. 'I thought he'd never go. He arrived before lunch — before lunch, Susan! And he's told me all about him and Oliver, and Oliver and him, and him and his mother, and him and his father, and him and his sisters, and he's got three, can you believe it? And we went through them one by one, and then . . . '

'I'm beginning to grasp the general theme of the conversation.'

'Oh, dear.' Joanna raised her head. 'Poor Ricky. I'm sure Oliver *isn't* easy to live with, and he does so want to be an actor, and Mike says he can't act for toffee. Poor Ricky. It's just . . . oh dear, oh dear.'

Susan finished her wine and her cigarette in silence. She had long run out of sympathy with her cousin's squandering of precious compassion on those who marginally if at all deserved it. She went to the refrigerator and refilled her glass.

'Would you like some wine?' she said.

'No, thanks. Mike's late, I wonder what he's doing.'

Susan grunted, and took her wine into the garden. She sat on the sunlounger, now in the mellow sun's full light, and turned her face to the sky, letting the kind heat wash over and around her, soak through and through her, warming her, browning her, sweetening her. She surrendered herself to it, knowing she had earned it, slowly letting the last cold traces of the day's scholarship melt from her mind.

Two large hands clasped her narrow waist, and she exclaimed. It was Mike.

'Jesus, you're thin. We'll have to fatten you up some.' He sat beside her on the lounger, and nodded at her wine glass. 'Enjoying an attitude adjustment hour?'

'My God, is that what they call it?'

'Aoh, mai Gawd, these colonials. What will they think of next?'

He playfully nudged her bare leg with his own, and she realised he was not wearing jeans.

'You're wearing a suit,' she said.

'Yeah. Like it? Think it looks cool?'

'Actually, it looks rather hot to me. Have you really been at lunch all this time?'

'Yeah, well, it went on a bit. Where's my wife?'

'Indoors, recovering. She's had a hard afternoon.'

'What happened?' He cocked his eye towards the kitchen. 'Long line at the market?'

'I'll tell her you said that. Actually, Rick was here, and decided, apparently, to pour out his soul.'

'Rick? Didn't know he had one.'

He was uncharacteristically sharp about Rick: she wondered if he were jealous. Rick was, after all, even in this town of beautiful people, so extraordinarily beautiful.

'Well, he's got a full afternoon's worth, anyway, and poor old Joanna's seen it from all angles. Shall we go in and cheer her up?'

'Yeah, OK.' But he did not rise. 'How was the garage? You manage to work OK?'

'Fine, thanks. Yes, I got quite a bit done. How's your work going?'

He shrugged. 'OK.'

He rarely, it occurred to her, talked about his work; remarkable, surely, in a city where, as she had seen, the movies formed a staple of many conversations? For the first time, she wondered just how he worked, just what he did.

'You don't talk about it very much,' she said.

'Don't I? I guess I think it's boring.'

'But people are always talking about cinema here.'

'Sure.' He smiled, flatly. 'Everyone's an expert.'

'Yes, I suppose that must be fun for you.'

'Oh, it is.'

'Well, you don't have to worry about me,' she said. 'I can't remember the last time I saw an American film.'

'Don't blame you. Bunch of crap they're making nowadays.' He smiled. 'Except for mine, of course.'

'Have you read *Emma*?' she asked suddenly.

'Yeah.' He looked at her in surprise. 'In school. Why?'

'I just wondered.' She squeezed her eyes into the evening air. 'You'll have to excuse me, I'm not quite yet back in the real world.'

He nodded, understanding.

'Takes a while sometimes, doesn't it?'

'Doesn't it.' With a flash of fellow feeling, she remembered the glaze over his eyes the day he had come home for the sandwich.

'Doesn't it. I've been there.' His voice trailed off into an almighty yawn as he leaned back on his hands to watch the sun through the tree. 'Been there . . . seen the movie . . . bought the sweatshirt.'

They sat together in friendly quiet until the slow sun worked its way past the tree.

'Come on,' he said then. 'Let's go bug Joanna.'


'And in the end,' said Joanna, 'I had to pretend Susan and I were going to a movie, and throw him out almost bodily. Otherwise, I swear he'd still be there now.'

Nancy laughed over her mug of coffee. Morning sunshine flooded her wide, white-walled living room, and through the open screen door came the splashings and shrieks of children in the swimming pool. 'Poor Joanna,' she said.

'Poor Rick, you mean,' said Joanna. 'He doesn't know whether he's on his head or his heels. I mean, he's never been the brightest of boys anyway.' She paused, turning over in her head the new picture she had, of Oliver seen through Rick's eyes. 'But I think they're fond of each other, actually. I really do. I didn't before, but I do now.'

'Well, that's nice.' Nancy was the only one of their group who was never unkind about Rick. But then, Nancy was never unkind about anyone. Joanna smiled at her, feeling a surge of affection for her. Had she not married Mike, it would never have occurred to her to become friends with anyone like Nancy.

'How's Susan?' said Nancy.

'Fine. She's working hard this week. She does work hard, you know.'

Nancy smiled; she was well capable of self-mockery. 'She won't be coming over to make jewellery, then?'

Disloyally, Joanna raised her head, and pinched her lips. 'If I'm *free*,' she imitated irritably, 'I shall let you *know*. I shall be receiving in the withdrawing room . . . Poor old Susan,' she added, not because she pitied her, but because they were poking mild fun at her.

An anguished scream came from the swimming pool, and Nancy turned her head sharply. Then she relaxed. 'False alarm,' she said. 'I don't care about my two, but there're other people's kids out there. Susan should have kids, she'd know you're never free. She seeing anyone?'

'Yes.' Joanna stopped: Susan very possibly would not want her affairs discussed throughout their group. 'Well, no.' But this, after all, was Nancy. 'I mean, I'm not sure she'd like me talking about this, but she's seeing a married man.'

'Oh.'

'Yes. He sounds a pig, but . . . Wouldn't it be lovely if she'd meet someone out here and fall in love?' It was said frivolously, but then, on the other hand, wouldn't it? 'Really. Someone nice, and kind, and not married. Do you know anyone?'

'Me?' said Nancy. 'I don't know any intellectuals.'

'Yes, I suppose he'd have to be, wouldn't he?' Mates for Susan, of course, would never come two for a penny. But how good it would be to have the worry attached to her removed, to have her settled, committed body and heart to one man; or at least, to free her from Felix.

'Honestly,' she said. 'These women who think married men are so glamorous. If they could see them the way we do.'

'I tell you,' said Nancy. 'I looked at Bill the other night, and he was sitting with his gut out, staring at the TV, 'cause he couldn't be bothered to turn it off, and he'd taken his lenses out so he was wearing those goddamned John Lennon granny specs, 'cause he hasn't bought glasses since 1969, and he was picking his toenails. And I looked at him, and I thought, this is the guy that fifteen years ago, I had mad, passionate fantasies about?'

Joanna laughed. 'It's a passion killer, isn't it? Listen, do you want to go to the gym?'

'Can't. I have to take Barbara to her ballet lesson.' She looked at her watch. 'In about five minutes.' She rose, and went to the windows. 'Barbara!'

Apart from meeting Susan at the airport, it was weeks since Joanna had had to be anywhere. Probably, she would put off the gym until after lunch. She watched as Nancy's ten-year-old, plump and dripping, padded wetly through the tiled room, her mother dealing a friendly slap to her bottom as she passed.

'She needs these lessons,' she said, as her daughter disappeared up the wide staircase. 'Alex is OK, but this one has to watch out. If she's not careful, she's going to be fat.'

'Oh, so what,' said Joanna. 'I was a fat teenager. I'm still fat, and it's not the end of the world. Some people are.'

'Not my daughter,' said Nancy. 'Anyway,' she added hastily, 'you're not fat. You're curvy. Like Marilyn Monroe.'

'Will you marry me?'

'I told you, I'm busy today. Hey, what are you guys doing on Thursday? Bill's bringing some clients in, and I'm cooking.'

'Thursday?' She thought. 'Oh, drat, we can't. Remember I told you, it's Rick's famous dinner party?'

'Oh, right. Well, have a terrific time.'

Joanna rolled her eyes. 'I'm sure we shall.'


Oliver's apartment was in a squat block in the no man's land west of West Hollywood, three floors up on the small elevator, and a long walk down a gloomy corridor thick with deep pile brown carpet. The apartment itself, however, once reached, was welcoming enough, in a masculine way, with solid Spanish furniture built for large people to sprawl in, and good Oriental prints on the light, plain walls. Curled barefoot in one corner of the wood-framed sofa was Kathy.

'I did it again,' she said, raising a glass of Oliver's excellent wine in salutation as they entered. 'Arrived first.'

Mike, dropping into the hefty armchair next to her, shook his head in reproof. 'You'll never make it in this town,' he chided, 'if you can't make an entrance.'

'Yeah, well, the temp agency isn't big on entrances, you know? Hi, Susan. You're brown.'

She was: it was surprising what one hour in the morning and another in the evening could accomplish. 'Hello,' she said. She possessed herself of the opposite armchair, leaving Joanna to flop on to the other end of the sofa.

'I do like this apartment,' the latter announced, squinting smilingly around the room. 'Look, Susan, Oliver goes all over the place looking for those prints. That's my favourite there, the lady and the bird. It's quite rare, and he bought it for a song.'

'It's very nice,' said Susan. She had been brought up to believe that it was rude to comment on people's homes in their presence, and even ruder to mention money. But then again, so had Joanna.

Certainly, it did not seem to occur to Oliver, busily pouring wine, to take offence. 'Not quite a song,' he corrected, handing Joanna a glass. 'Unless maybe a rather intense aria. But yes, she's right, it cost me less than it should have, and I'm ashamed to admit I was capitalist enough to be proud of it.'

'Proud? He preened for weeks.' Rick appeared from the kitchen, a smudge on his face, a bowl of nuts in his hand.

'Nuts, anybody?' said Oliver. 'I'd advise you all not to hang back, because when the maestro's in the kitchen, he tends to forget such tedious matters as the time.'

The two exchanged glances. Whatever differences they had had had evidently been resolved in the intervening days.

'I have to get back to my chicken,' said Rick.

'Do you want some help?' asked Joanna.

'No, stay where you are. This is my evening.'

'Leave him,' said Oliver as he left. 'He's perfectly capable of asking for help if he needs it. Susan, you're looking alarmingly well, I hope these beach bums here haven't turned you into a California girl.'

'We're grooming her for stardom,' said Mike. 'The lobotomy's scheduled for next week.'

'Can I get one, too?' said Kathy. She was hunched over her drink, looking rather small. Mike kicked her gently.

'They didn't call back?'

'Nope. I mean, it wasn't a part I'd have killed for, or anything.'

'But it still depressed you.'

'Right. And that makes it almost worse, you know? Because you can see getting depressed about not landing Blanche Dubois for Polanski, but when you get depressed because you didn't get The Girl for a cop show . . . That's what she was called. The Girl.'

Mike laughed sympathetically. 'Not even The Pretty Girl?'

'Not even that.'

'I think you're amazing,' said Joanna. 'I don't know how you keep going, I'd have killed myself ages ago.'

'Jumped off the Hollywood sign? It's been done already. No, I shouldn't complain. There was that thing in January, and then *Marina* . . . I've had a good year compared to some.'

'Some what?' said Susan. 'People or years?'

'Both.' She grimaced. 'But that's enough about that. Life's a bitch, and then you die, right?' She held out her glass to Oliver, affecting a bar room slur to her speech. 'Fill 'er up, Jack.'

He did so, patting her shoulder as he leaned over her.

'This business,' said Mike. 'We must all be nuts to put ourselves through it. Hey, Susan, think we're nuts?'

Susan smiled politely, and sipped her drink. Her own work was important to her, more important than many things in her life, she could not imagine a world without it, or a Susan who was not a scholar. But then scholarship — even should she, unthinkably, somehow become unemployed — would always be available to her, there would always be books, libraries, pens, and paper. How much greater must be Kathy's dedication, than her own, even than Mike's, holding fast as she did to a professional ideal when so much of the time she was denied even a profession to practise. Perhaps, after all, everything in this place did not arrive quite as easily as ripe fruit plucked from the tree.

'She's not saying anything,' said Kathy. 'She does think we're nuts.'

'Did you say you want more nuts?' Rick was standing at the door, a bag in his hand.

'Useful things, nuts,' said Mike with a wink at Kathy. 'Wouldn't be without them, myself.'

'Mike, do shut up,' said Joanna. 'Actually, we could use a refill here, Rick, yes, They're lovely, where did you get them?'

'A place I know.' He filled the outstretched bowl carefully. 'Don't eat too many, though, dinner's nearly ready.'

'I don't know what you said to him the other day,' said Oliver to Joanna, as Rick returned to the kitchen. 'But whatever it was, I want to thank you. He's been much easier ever since.'

'I think he's just been depressed,' said Joanna. 'People often get depressed around their birthdays: I know I do. And he so wants to be an actor, and it's just not happening at all, is it?'

'Oh, God,' said Kathy.

'I don't care, Kathy, he does. And he wants it for different reasons from you, and of course he'd be a different sort of actor, but the thing is, he wants it, and he's not getting it. And you of all people should know how rough that is.'

'Well, thank you, anyway,' said Oliver. 'I don't know what to say to him when he gets like that. I'm not easy to live with, you know.'

'Well, is he?' asked Kathy.

Oliver smiled. 'I am not, my dear Kathryn, quite so besotted as to claim that he is. But he has the excuse of being young.'

'Not so young.'

'Younger than this fading roué, then. Oh, dear.' He sighed humorously. 'Look at me, the ageing queen, trying to recapture his youth through the pretty boy. What it is to be a walking cliché. More wine, Susan?'

'You're simply not artistically credible,' said Susan, accepting. 'I've known people like that. Well, Joanna's mother, for one.'

'Ma?' said Joanna.

'Yes, your ma. She is such a sweet English lady that if you read about her in a book, you wouldn't believe her for a single paragraph.'

'*Ma*?'

'Hadn't you noticed?' said Mike. 'She's Celia Johnson. I keep wanting to pull on my flying goggles, and go off to fight Jerry.'

'Do you?'

'The woman preserves her own rhubarb. And darns socks. On a, what d'you call it, Susan?'

'Mushroom,' nodded Susan.

'Mushroom. Not something I've noticed her daughter doing.'

'Well, I might if you ever wore socks.'

Rick was again at the doorway. 'It's ready,' he said.

They followed him into the dining area, and arranged themselves on the carved chairs around the dark wood table. Lamps flickered on a bowl of oranges like a detail from a Siglo de Oro court portrait; but no long-jawed descendant of Isabel and Fernando would have recognised the kitchen just visible around the corner, with its blenders and grinders, its automatic washers and waste disposal units.

Rick served the meal: salad, rice, and chicken in a faintly spicy sauce.

'Rick,' said Joanna. 'If you don't tell me how to make this chicken, I shall never speak to you again. It is delicious.'

'It's good,' said Mike. 'Real good.'

'I think,' said Oliver, 'I'll let him stay. For the time being.'

Susan ate in silence. The food was good, but not excellent; but it clearly did not do to say so. She wondered whether the omission of salt from the table was deliberate, and decided, regretfully, that it was.

'Where d'you learn to cook, Rick?' asked Kathy.

'I've always cooked,' he said. 'My sisters taught me. My Dad used to hate it.'

'Yeah? I never cooked, and my Dad hated *that*.'

'Fun daughter you were,' grunted Mike.

'Really. Didn't cook, didn't play with dolls, wouldn't wear dresses.'

'Your poor mother,' said Joanna.

'Oh, Mom was OK about it, really. She's a neat lady. But poor old Dad.' Kathy laughed, the cloud that had sat over her shifting slightly. 'I was like his worst nightmare.'

'My Dad hated me,' said Rick. 'I had a terrible childhood.'

'Oh, mine liked me well enough. I was just . . . I used to *see* him, you know?' She dropped her fork, and peered comically around the table. 'Watching other little girls, who were proper little girls, and pretending he wasn't, and thinking, "Why me, God, why me?"'

She made a gesture of despair, and her fork clattered to the floor. Amid the laughter, Rick stood up and handed her a replacement.

'Here's another,' he said. 'Your chicken's going cold.'

'Thanks.' But she let it lie beside her plate; she had barely touched her food. 'Poor guy, he comes to see me now, and he walks through the door of the apartment — you've met him, Mike, you know how he stands there — and he just looks around, and it's like . . . ' the expression on her face became her father's, affectionate, puzzled, sad. 'Now, if I'd been a son, he'd have been fine. Hey, Rick, perhaps we should have traded families.'

Rick looked her full in the face. 'I don't think so,' he said.

She returned his gaze, and her own eyes turned to stone. 'Fine by me,' she replied, and returned to her chicken.

Through an atmosphere grown several degrees chillier, Susan heard Mike draw in his breath.

'What's that supposed to mean?' he asked.

From where Joanna was sitting, opposite, came an unmistakable marital kick under the table.

Rick fixed Mike with clear eyes.

'What?' he asked.

'What you just said,' said Mike.

'What, about . . . Oh, I just meant I wouldn't wish my family on anyone. Would I, Oliver? Sorry, did it sound rude?'

'Great chicken,' said Kathy.

'Thank you,' said Rick.

Joanna began, firmly, to talk about movies.

Susan pushed her food around her plate; she was tired, no longer hungry, and abominably alone. Rick had been rude to

Kathy, appallingly so; not rude as a European might be, with the rapier of malice dancing in the delicate hand of good manners, but bluntly, openly, as with one coarsely skilful shot from a six gun. And, Kathy, for all her quick wit, had not responded as a European might, deflecting the blade, turning it back upon its owner; she had simply absorbed the shot, registered the pain, and continued on her path. And Mike had seen, and Mike had commented, and Joanna had kicked Mike under the table for commenting. And now, not sixty seconds later, they were all of them talking comedies and car chases, yes, even Mike, who had told her he did not like to talk films with lay people, with as full an appearance of cordiality as if nothing had happened. Mike made a joke, and Rick laughed; Rick made a joke and Kathy laughed, not as hard, but then, it was not as good a joke. It was as if what had been, had not been. Were she to stay here for ever, she thought despairingly, she would not understand these people.

She took a mouthful of food, and tasted sugar. There was Marsala in the spicy chicken sauce, honey in the dressing drenching the crisp lettuce, raisins were buried in the plump white rice. She gulped at the smoky wine, but sweetness lurked there, too; it lashed out at her, washing over the sugared tastes already in her mouth, filling it full and overflowing with syrup. Who was it, she tried to recall, cold in the knowledge that she was the only one at the table who might know the answer, who had drowned in a butt of Malmsey?

At the thought, her loneliness turned to a yearning so sharp it was almost physical, for Felix. She and he, of course, were never invited to social occasions as a couple, but quite often would arrive separately at the same lunch, or even dinner, he leaving early to catch the late train to Oxford, and would spend the time carefully ignoring each other, and as carefully watching the company, taking notes for future comparison and dissection; and, once, somewhere during the course of the few hours, he would catch her eye, and would raise the very end of his left eyebrow, while she would twitch the right corner of her mouth, and that would be their bond.

She looked at Joanna, and wondered what it would be like to have someone always and acknowledgedly there, someone to kick secretly, someone whose anecdotes to interrupt and correct, as her cousin was doing now, laughing, stretching a rounded, Indian gauze clad arm across the table to touch Mike's bare wrist, while he, laughing back and shaking his head, held to his own version of the story. She wondered whether she ought to envy Joanna. Joanna seemed to think, and society seemed to agree with her, that she had, on the whole, a better deal than Susan. But Susan had never cared much for the opinion of society; and Joanna had kicked Mike under the table.

'More chicken, Susan?' said Rick.

'No, thank you,' she said, realising for the first time that she had finished the whole plateful. She handed him her plate, and cast an unobtrusive glance down the table.

'My cousin,' announced Joanna, 'is wondering whether it would be rude to ask to smoke. Shall we let her?'

'Only if I can have one, too,' said Kathy.

Susan pulled gratefully at the cigarette, feeling the harsh tobacco smoke flood her lungs with ill health. That, at least, was not sweet.


It was Saturday morning; they had no duty but their pleasure; they lay content in the garden, finishing mugs of cooling coffee, their stomachs luxuriously laden with eggs, potatoes, and buttered whole-wheat toast.

'I suppose,' murmured Joanna, fingering her newly washed hair in the shade of the jacaranda tree, 'that since you're a visitor, we should show you something. I must get my hair cut soon.'

Susan rearranged her long limbs in the full sun's light. 'You said,' she reminded her, 'there was nothing to see.'

'What nothing,' said Mike. 'Plenty of stuff. Disneyland. Universal Studios. Hey, let's take her on the tour of the stars' homes.'

'It's what I've always dreamed of,' said Susan. She had worked hard that week, and, leaving Emma to her own life, was perfectly happy to spend these two days of rest in soaking up the sun. Besides, there was that stretch of blue that all week had lain just out of reach, but so tantalisingly in view, at the bottom of the hill. 'Actually, I thought I might go for a walk on the beach.'

'Ooh.' Joanna pursed her lips in warning. 'It's crowded at the weekends. I've got an idea. Why don't we all go and hang around Bill and Nancy's pool?'

'I want to go to the beach.' Susan had had enough for the time being of returning pleasantnesses to pleasant Californians. She could even, it struck her, use a short break from Joanna and Mike; as she was quite certain could they from her. A memory swam from early childhood, of clotted cream teas in her grandmother's salt tanged, riotously flowered Devonshire cottage garden. 'The blood of Bart Hawkins still runs deep, you see.'

'Granny Forrest,' Joanna told Mike, 'used to swear we had an ancestor who was hanged for piracy.'

'I know,' said Mike. 'I was wondering when you'd get around to mentioning it. Tom told me seven years ago.'

'Tom would.' Joanna snorted in sisterly disgust. 'At one stage he talked of little else.'

'And you didn't talk at all. You see what happens, Susan, when you think you're marrying into a respectable British family?'

'They're her family, too, Mike.'

'Wash your mouth out. I was left by the gypsies.' Susan sat up on her hands, and blinked into the hot blue sky.

'I'll drive you to the beach,' offered Mike.

'Thanks.' Unable to drive herself, in London she would have considered this an impossible imposition; but she was, she noted with mild interest, apparently beginning to be used not to being in London now. 'When you're ready.'

'I'm ready when you are.'

'OK.' How easy it would be to fritter away the day sitting in the sun, making plans that had no hope of being carried out. She stood up. 'I'm ready now. I'll get my things.'

As Mike's car roared into jubilant life and buffeted down the hill towards the Ocean, Joanna sat back, leaning her damp hair against the rough bark of the tree, and faintly jealous of the other two, so rich in their enjoyment of the weekend. Idleness was very well, but to be fully appreciated, it had to be earned. Well, she obviously did not want that appreciation badly enough to earn it. She would be back at work soon enough. Back at work, and Susan back in England, and everything as it had been. She sighed, thinking about it: she would miss Susan.

If only, she thought again, lazily, remembering her conversation with Nancy, Susan would indeed meet someone here, meet and fall in love, and — what ties, after all, did she have in England? — marry and move to Los Angeles. Contented, and more than contented, as she was in this new life, Joanna sometimes found it in her to envy Mike, so casual about his mother twenty minutes up the road, his sister an hour's plane ride away in San Francisco, both of them available to see and to speak to in a way she knew she could never again speak to her own mother or to Tom. How sweet it would be to have one of her own family close by to have time to fritter away with, to recommend hairdressers and secondhand bookshops, to pass on jokes not worth remembering, to trudge with in bored silence to the bank or the launderette. Sitting there, she allowed herself to drift off into an outrageously self-indulgent fantasy of a married Susan, living close by and visiting often, of long evenings at one or the other's house, with Mike and the husband (someone tall, she thought, and unpretentious, not unlike Mike himself) glued to beer and the game on television, while the two women sat in the kitchen and drank wine, and talked about their men in a way they now could not, not with Joanna's feelings about Felix. Felix: she frowned. What a wicked man he must be, to step outside his own, naturally paired state, and by doing so, to block Susan's chances of joining a pair at all.

As she sat, the familiar engine sound began, grew louder, and stopped, the large door creaked open and slammed shut, and Mike dropped beside her, fitting his familiar body to hers.

'You've got to learn to relax, kid,' he said. He squeezed her. 'Alone at last, huh?'

'Mm.' She leaned against him, comfortably. Dearly as she loved Susan, it was good to be alone with him, not just in the bedroom, but here in the open garden. 'D'you drop Susan all right?'

'Uh huh. She went a bit white when she saw the crowds, but then she stiffened her lip, straightened her back, and strode off into the blue yonder.'

Joanna laughed. 'Poor old Susan,' she said, as she had said at Nancy's the other day.

'Lucky old Susan, you mean. Having two terrific cousins like us to come and stay with.'

But Susan was not the lucky one, as Joanna knew. She was not precisely unlucky, but she was not lucky either, as Rick was not, nor Oliver, nor Kathy. Joanna was lucky, was superlatively lucky; and she must never forget to be grateful for her good fortune.

'Had I really not told you about Bart Hawkins?' she said.

'Not a word. You can be quite secretive, can't you?'

'How strange. We used to talk about it a lot when we were kids.' Strange that she had not thought to share that part of her childhood with him. But stranger to think that a man whose blood ran in her veins had once swaggered through the Spanish Main, capturing galleons laden with mother-of-pearl and pieces of eight. Stranger still to know that at that time, and half the world away, a man of her husband's blood had squatted in a teepee, with paint on his face, and feathers in his hair. While very possibly, in a Paris whose streets would soon run red with the blood of its aristocracy, forebears of her French great-grandmother, and his Creole great-grand-father, had passed each other in the street with not a look or a word. 'Aren't we all civilised these days?'

'Ask the men in Washington,' he said.

'I don't mean we're nicer.' She paused, weighing a sloop bristling with cutlasses against a bomb; beggars ignored on the streets against starving continents ignored on the television. 'But we're civilised. I wonder whether Susan's missing Felix?'

He grunted, somewhere between a laugh and a groan of irritation. 'Why don't you ask her?'

'Oh, I couldn't. She doesn't talk about him much, does she?'

'Secretive, you see. Runs in the family.'

She stuck out her tongue at him, but absentmindedly.

'You know what I'd really like?' she asked eventually.

He sighed. 'I can't possibly imagine.'

'To have her meet some really nice man — some really nice unmarried man — out here, and fall madly in love, and come and live here. Wouldn't that be lovely? Do you know anyone?'

He thought, laughed.

'There's Mac.'

'Oh, shut up. Really, though, wouldn't it be lovely? Nancy and I were talking about it the other day.'

'Bet Nancy had some great ideas.'

'Oh, go and boil your head. Eileen said she might come by today, I'll ask her if she knows anyone. I don't know how you got such a nice mother, I really don't.'

He yawned. 'I have great taste.'

They sat for a while, and watched as the hummingbird flew into the tree, perched on a branch, poured from its frail throat its harsh, confident song, and flew off, wings awhirr.

'Seriously, Mike,' she said. 'No, seriously. Don't you know anyone for her? Anyone at all?'

'No,' he said. 'No, I don't.' He paused. 'I don't think,' he said finally, 'she's the kind of person you can do that kind of thing with.'

'Why not?'

'Well.' He frowned, his face wearing the expression of earnest bafflement of a man trying to imagine how it feels to be a woman. 'She's just not,' he said.

She laughed, and threw a jacaranda blossom at him. 'Want to bet?' she said.


Joanna was right, the beach was crowded. Oxford Street crowded, rush hour crowded, Christmas shopping crowded. But it was a crowd different from London crowds: on the throng of faces, Susan could count on the fingers of one hand those she saw that were tense or frowning. It was a crowd with nothing but happiness in its heart. She should not, she knew, equate happiness with stupidity. But she could not, for instance, picture Felix here; and she certainly could not imagine what Emma, magically transported from fiction to reality, from her time and place to this, would make of it.

She picked her way among the roller skaters and skate boarders, the children and the cheerful derelicts, the jugglers, the mimes, the musicians and street vendors. Just ahead of her, a youth hailed a pretty Mexican girl.

'Hey!' he called. 'Hey, Maria!'

'Yeah?' The girl stopped, turned to him.

He moved towards her, smiling ingratiatingly. 'Don't you remember me, Maria?'

'I never met you before,' she said.

'Sure you did, how would I know you're called Maria?'

'Everyone's called Maria.'

She stood, slender in white dress and proud head held high,

torn between amusement and impatience, wondering how far she would let him advance.

Skilfully around them skated a man in a white turban, a guitar in his hands which he occasionally plucked, on his face the beatific smile of the stoned.

A man in a frock coat played ragtime on the piano.

A young black comedian perched on top of a telephone booth, holding forth to an appreciative audience. 'I *love* the President,' he was insisting. 'I tell ya, I *love* that guy. Why? 'Cause he's gonna bring back *slavery*.' An impeccably timed pause. 'And when *that* happens, I'll be *workin'* . . .' The crowd burst into uproarious laughter.

Above it all, the seagulls swooped and soared in the still blue sky.

Susan left the crowd on the boardwalk, and went down the beach, passing large family groups, gleaming bodied muscle builders, and mumbling solitaries who might have been actors running lines, or might have been lunatics. She reached the water's edge, and walked through the waterline, feeling it wash at her feet and lap at her legs, as she had in Scotland and Italy, Turkey and Northern Africa. But the sea, too, was different; pure, virginal, untouched by history. Neither explorers nor merchants had crossed that blue water, no hawk-faced Spaniards, no Greeks bearing gifts, no bushy Bart Hawkins. It was a sea not for function but for pleasure, not for the past but for the present, for the bleach-haired surfers, the squirming children, the bronzed lifeguards watching for misbehaviour, the pretty girls watching the lifeguards.

She walked for maybe a mile, or maybe two, and turned back, edging her way around the roller disco to the bookshop next to the restaurant where she and Joanna had been that first day. It was a model bookshop, cool inside and welcoming, the books helpfully sorted, low stools dotted around for the comfort of browsers. She gazed for a long time, both sitting and standing among good books that were well tended, and finally picked out a crisp new novel by an author with whose name she was unfamiliar.

'Great choice,' commented the woman who took her money. She had frizzy hair, wore no make-up, and her face was alive with intelligence. 'I keep telling people to read this guy. Did you read his last one?'

Susan shook her head. She felt a sudden, sword sharp pain of longing for the surly illiterate who had last served her in Foyles.

'Well, I guarantee that after this, you will want to.' She dropped the book into a bag, added a paper bookmark, and handed it over with a flourish. 'Enjoy.'

'Thank you,' said Susan, taking the package.

She left the shop, and on an impulse walked away from the beach, down a shaded alley, and up a narrow lane lined with shabby wooden houses. Further along, she knew, was a Main Street. Not a proper street with butchers and greengrocers, but a pretty, pretend place of shops selling luxury items, soaps, paper novelties, expensive clothes. Here, however, was residential. Tropical plants rioted through gardens; a cat which had fallen asleep in the sun awoke in the shade, and shook itself indignantly; on the porch of one of the houses, a no longer young prostitute peacefully told Tarot cards as she waited for custom.

Then, everything changed.

'Motherfucker!'

The shrill tone screeched through the street, poisoning the air. Susan looked up. A television switched on too loudly? A tropical bird protesting captivity? But no, the voice came again, and it was human, and it was real.

'Motherfucker, motherfucker!'

Susan looked around. Just behind her, a woman was leaning out of a car, yellow hair showing black at the roots, screaming vitriol at a man who stood over her. 'You owe me money, motherfucker. They're your fuckin' children, too.'

The man leaned down placatingly, hatred taut in every line of his body. 'I gave you money,' he said.

'Not enough.' She leaned further out of the car, and her sharp-fingered hand clawed viciously at his trousers. 'You didn't give me enough. What d'you think we eat, one meal a year? One fuckin' meal, think that, motherfucker?'

'I gave you enough money,' he said.

Susan watched intently. The scene was of rage, of boiling, blood-red anger, and she drank it in as one parched takes gulps of icy water.

'Enough money!' shouted the woman. 'What the fuck enough money! The only one you give enough money to is her, right? Your whore. Your baby!'

She got out of the car and stood, taller than he in short shorts and teetering high heels, jabbing him in the chest with a finger.

'You don't see her asking for money, right? 'Cause you fuckin' give it to her. And our children go hungry. Our fuckin' children, motherfucker.'

'How do I know,' he asked, 'they're my children?'

'How . . .' Her red face turned redder, and she grabbed tauntingly at his crotch. ''Cause they are, motherfucker! Couple of fuckin' times you got it up, I got fuckin' pregnant! Couple of times, motherfucker!'

He drew a gun, and shot her through the heart.

She looked surprised, and slid with strange grace to the ground, crimson spreading and clashing with the shocking pink of her cheap T-shirt. The prostitute screamed; the cat jumped and ran up a tree; Susan stood silent and rooted to the spot.

In no time, a crowd had gathered; in little more time, the police were on the scene, grim in heavy uniforms and bulging holsters. They took the man, who still stood, gun in hand, over the lifeless body, and led him to the car. The key witness, the prostitute, followed them, eyes aglitter, her day transformed.

Susan stayed on the edge of the crowd that stood, as crowds will at disasters all over the world, watching with nothing to watch, talking with nothing to say, desperate, delighted to be safe and not alone. Soon, she became aware of something thick and mud coloured trickling down the sloping gutter towards the Ocean. It was blood. She had never seen shed blood before, and wondered who would clean it, and when, and how long it would take.

She left the alley, and walked back down the boardwalk, seeing the people there for the first time through undazzled eyes. For the first time she realised how, among the perfect bodies were so many crippled, golden girls with legs plastered from sporting accidents, derelicts with limbs that simply ended in a sleeve or trouser leg sewn up, like a Bonfire Night Guy. For the first time she noticed, here and there among the beautiful people, the not merely plain, but ugly, the monstrous women, fatly licking ice-creams, eyes peering like malicious buttons over bulging, quivering cheeks, the men with whole chunks of their faces eaten away by who knew what disease. The guitar player in the white turban skated past again, and his eyes above the smile were staring like those of a dead fish.

There was, then, a dark side to the place. It was not all sweetness, not simply a confection spun of sugar melted in the sun, but held passion, too, a violent passion indeed, such as she with her civilised, Northern European breeding, had never thought to witness. But the people here, after all, were different: they came, she now reminded herself, not from Hampstead or the Home Counties, but from countries torn by war, famine, persecution; they had herded into ships and fled across the murderous seas, they had crammed into frail wagons and hacked their way across the mountains to this place; this place which was not so secure after all, since the Ocean flooded the streets, brush fire burned in the mountains, the earth moved along the San Andreas Fault, and men carried guns and would use them.

She found her turning place, and walked through another quiet alley into the make believe Main Street. It was mid afternoon, and she had seen enough, and plenty, of the beach to keep her thoughts well occupied. She had arranged to telephone the house from one of the public telephones frequently placed, and invariably in working order, along the street, to have someone pick her up; but looking up at the steep hill, high and unshaded in the glare of the afternoon sun, she decided instead to walk.

It was a long walk, and the hill was even steeper than it had looked. Susan, climbing the baked asphalt, felt herself becoming too hot, felt her cheeks redden, and the moisture collect under her armpits and run down her back. A large truck passed her, belching black smoke over her, and as he passed, the driver leaned out to shout something lewd. The city was beginning, just beginning, to take on a definite shape.

By the time she reached the house, the sun was starting to lose its edge, to ripen slowly from afternoon cruel to evening kind. She heard laughter from the back, and went around the side, to find Joanna and Kathy sitting at the worn, friendly kitchen table, sharing a jug of iced tea and a plate of oatmeal cookies.

'Hello,' she said, trailing her sweat and her grime into the gratefully cool indoors.

'I thought you were going to call,' said Joanna. 'I'd have come and picked you up.'

'I had a revolutionary new idea. I thought I'd walk.'

'Oh, she's so witty, my cousin. Tea?'

'Wine.' She went to the refrigerator, and took out a full-bellied carafe, not of good wine like Oliver's, to be sipped and discussed from fine glasses, but of cheap stuff, plonk for sloshing into thick tumblers and knocking back, icy cold on a hot, hot day.

'Did you enjoy the beach?' said Joanna.

'Yes.' She thought about it. 'Yes, if you like that sort of thing.'

'Many people?'

'A good few.' There was no point in not telling them. 'I saw a shooting.'

'*What?*'

'Shooting. You know. A man shot his wife, they were having a row. There was blood everywhere. Or maybe she wasn't his wife, I don't know.'

'Oh, Susan!' White-faced, Joanna stared at her. 'Susan, I'm sorry. Are you all right?'

'Yes, of course I'm all right. *I* wasn't shot.' She lit a cigarette and inspected her own feelings. So busy had she been in rearranging her ideas of Los Angeles, that she had scarcely had time to register the impact of the violence on herself. 'I'm fine,' she concluded.

Which was more, it seemed, than could be said for her cousin.

'This bloody country.' Still pale, Joanna stood up, reaching across the table to pour an unsteady stream of tea into Kathy's glass. 'This bloody country. There's violence everywhere, it happens all the time. That won't even be in the papers, you know. And the policemen with their great big guns, it's a disgrace.'

'Most policemen have guns,' said Kathy. 'I can't imagine them without.'

'Well, that's a disgrace, too,' said Joanna. 'And look what it leads to. A man and his wife quarrel, and someone gets shot. *That* should be the sort of thing you can't imagine.' She stopped herself, and grimaced apologetically. 'Sorry. *You* can't *not* imagine it, can you?'

'*I* wasn't married to Mike,' said Kathy.

'Kathy's husband shot her,' Joanna explained to Susan.

'I'm sorry?' said Susan.

'My husband,' repeated Kathy. 'He shot me. Look.' She lifted her T-shirt. On the right side of her narrow midriff was a purple, puckered scar.

'Good God,' said Susan.

Kathy shrugged. 'It was for the best,' she said. 'Made me leave him. Even I can't find an excuse for a bullet.'

Susan poured more wine in silence. The violence was for everyone, then, not just for women with bleached hair and plastic shoes, but for the middle classes, too, for people she herself had dined with.

There was a knock at the door.

'It's open,' called Joanna, leaping up nevertheless. 'Oh — Eileen. I'd just about given you up.'

'Another crisis at the hospital.' Her mother-in-law strode into the kitchen, workday practical in green trouser suit among the casual Saturday clothes of the rest of them. She dropped into a chair. 'Boy, could I use a drink.' She looked around, smiling, quite unaware of the change she brought to the atmosphere. 'Don't you all look comfortable. Hi, Kathy, did you get your hair cut? It's pretty. Hi, Susan. Where's Mike?'

'Getting his car smog-tested.' Joanna handed her a glass of whiskey. 'He should be back soon. Assuming he can find a garage willing to take him.'

'That car. You'd think he'd have some pride in his possessions.' Eileen shook her head, her pride in her own possession flooding her face, and turned to Susan. 'Well, Susan, how does LA stack up to London?'

'I'm just beginning to realise how very different it is,' said Susan. Eileen, she thought, coming from Chicago, and indeed, the Chicago of thirty years before, might well have some interesting views on guns and violence. But before she had finished even her brief comment, the large eyes had slid from her to Joanna.

'Now, look here, Missy.' Eileen rapped sternly on her daughter-in-law's arm. 'I will not take a no this time. You and our cousin and that deadbeat husband are coming to supper tomorrow, is that clear?'

'I wouldn't dream of arguing,' said Joanna. 'That'll be lovely, won't it, Susan?'

'Very nice,' agreed Susan.

The telephone rang, shrill and urgent. Joanna reached to the side table, and picked up the receiver. 'Hello?' she said. 'Oh, hello, Rick.' She looked at the others. 'It's Rick,' she mouthed.

'How are you? . . . Are you? . . . Oh, dear, *are* you?' She looked to the others again, rolled her eyes, and slumped her shoulders. 'But I thought you were getting on so much better . . . Oh, did he?' Rick and Oliver were, evidently, no longer getting on better. 'Me? No, I'm not busy. It's just that I'm in the kitchen, and there are about a million people here, that's all. Hold on, and I'll take you into the living room. Hang on.' She picked up the telephone on its long cord, and took it next door, waving a despondent farewell to the cheerful kitchen company as she did so. The door shut behind her.

The three looked at each other, and as one, shook their heads.

'That girl,' said Eileen, 'is a marshmallow.'

'She is so sweet,' agreed Kathy. 'I don't know how she manages to stay so nice all the time.'

'Well, she's married to my son,' said Eileen. 'And they say suffering purifies the spirit.'

The two laughed and simultaneously sipped their drinks, women in sympathy.

'You ever been married, Susan?' asked Kathy.

'No.' A bald enough answer, but what more was there to say? 'I didn't know you had.'

'I didn't know you hadn't.'

'You kids.' Eileen clucked her tongue. 'The way you get divorced these days. You should try to stick to your marriages, you really should.'

'You sound like my Mom,' said Kathy. 'Before she divorced my Dad.'

'Your Mom was right the first time,' said Eileen. 'Marriage isn't a bed of roses, and it was never meant to be. But it was meant to last. What God hath put together, let no man put asunder.'

There was a frown between her brows, and beneath carefully applied lipstick, her thin Irish mouth was drawn into a line of disapproval. Presumably, thought Susan, Eileen's husband had never shot her.

'That's all very well,' said Kathy. 'But what would you say if Mike and Joanna got divorced?'

'The same.'

Kathy raised her eyebrows.

'The same. Mike's my son, and I'll always love him, and Joanna's a dear girl, and I hope I'll always love her, too. But if they did something like that, I promise you, I wouldn't pretend to approve.'

'Oh, Eileen! You sound like Bing Crosby.'

'Oh, you kids think it's all a joke.' But Eileen was not laughing. 'You'll find out, all of you. You think you can have everything, but you can't. You have to have rules, or everything collapses. You'll see. It wasn't meant to be easy. We were meant to pick up our cross — our daily cross — and carry it.'

She was wearing a cross herself, a small gold one, winking on a fine chain around her neck. Susan had not realised quite how ardent a Roman Catholic she was. But then, the crucifix above Mike and Joanna's bed had to have come from somewhere; it certainly had not come from Aunt Betty. Eileen noticed her gaze, and turned to her, her mouth relaxing into a smile.

'Honey, you're brown,' she said. 'I can see you don't take after Joanna's family, that one's as sickly white as I am. And slim, look at her, Kathy, don't you just hate her?'

'She probably has no personality,' said Kathy.

'Oh, you.' She swatted Kathy with a hand, and turned back to Susan. 'Did you spend much time at the beach, dear, or what?'

Susan began to wonder whether this woman had ever heard a word she had said.

'As a matter of fact,' she replied, 'I've been working quite hard. On *Emma*.'

'Honey, I'm sorry, I keep forgetting. I get so used to Joanna's visitors being on holiday.' Having, apparently, accorded Susan enough attention, she turned back to Kathy.

'Did you ever meet Tom? He went down to the beach every morning, and came back every evening with a different girl.'

'Well, don't confuse Susan with Tom, or she'll kill you, and I can't say I'd blame her.' Joanna came into the room, plummeted into a chair, and reached for a cookie. 'I've got to do something about Rick, he's suddenly decided I'm his mother.' She tossed an envelope to Susan. 'This arrived for you.'

The envelope was flimsy, airmail, and addressed in old fashioned, italic handwriting. Susan's heart skipped like a foolish girl's. Felix's handwriting.

'It's from my editor,' she said. Not the politest thing in the world to open it now, but who knew when these people would leave? 'It might just be urgent. Excuse me a moment.'

She went into the garden, and sat out of view of the kitchen on the sunlounger. She opened the letter, read it, and then read the third paragraph again to make sure she had read it right:

'So since I shall be in New York anyway, and the blasted man — who or what *is* UCLA, by the way? — is so unshakeably keen to meet me, I can see no alternative but to fly out to Los Angeles for a few days. I'll be arriving on Wednesday week, by which time you may or may not have received this missive. You, by then, I trust will be enough of a native to let me know with some authority whether there is indeed, any "there" there.'

Felix was coming, he would be there in four days' time. Susan sat turning the information in her mind, as a miner, spotting a nugget of gold among the dirt, turns and returns it until he is sure that what he is seeing is more than merely the sun's reflection on broken glass. Felix was coming.

'How was the beach?' A heavy, masculine weight dropped to the sunlounger beside her. Mike, although probably no taller than Felix, was much broader.

'It was there,' she told him. 'How's your car?'

'Perfect.' He circled thumb and forefinger. 'Heavy duty perfect. The ultimate car.' A peal of different laughters came from the kitchen. 'Who's that?'

'Your mother and Kathy.'

'Jesus. Three of them.' He saw the envelope, and took it from her hands. 'Now, there's a sight. An English stamp. Is it first class or second class?'

'It's from my editor. He'll be in town next week.' A dull thought struck her: "in town" here could mean up to eighty miles away with no public transport. She retrieved the envelope, and consulted the letter. 'In Westwood, near UCLA. Is that far?'

'Just down the street, near where my Mom lives. So. You'll have someone to talk British with, right?'

'Apparently.' His eyes were still on the envelope, white in her brown fingers, and the look in them was almost envy. 'You must get a lot of letters yourselves, though.'

'You. And Betty. One or two others. People I know don't write letters too much. Pity, because I like them, they're so . . . civilised.'

There was something about the late afternoon sun, and the other, familiar voices floating from the house, that was conducive to confidences. 'You liked England, didn't you?'

'Man.' He shook his head, and hunched forward on the seat, tipping it slightly. 'I had the best time there. The best.' He looked up at her; he was, for once, perfectly serious, and she was surprised to find herself flattered. 'I mean, I sometimes thought I shouldn't have, being Irish and all, but . . . You know what I really liked? People there mean what they say. Here, you can say any damn thing, and anyone will believe you, hell, you'll believe yourself. Over there, you have to mean it.'

She fingered her envelope. 'Have you ever thought of living there?'

'Nah, I couldn't. Two years was my limit. It's all so structured there, you know? You know who you are, and where you are, and that's great if you're Betty, or Tom, or

94

your pal Emma, and you know how to work inside that, but here . . . ' He sat back, and stretched his arms into the high sky. 'Here, anything can happen.'

Anything, she thought, could indeed happen.

'I saw a shooting today. A man killed his wife.'

'Jesus.' Sobered, he brought his arms down, and laid a large brown hand on her knee. 'Hey, I'm sorry. You OK?'

'Yes. Yes, actually I am.' Somehow, she found herself saying to him that which she would never have dared to say to Joanna. 'In fact, it was quite interesting. I mean, it was awful that it happened, obviously. But seeing it helped put a lot of things here into perspective.'

'Yeah.' He nodded, understanding as Joanna never would. 'Hey, you know what? One day, if you're not too busy, I'd like you to come see my movie.'

Flattery upon flattery. 'I'd like that,' she said.

'Mike.' Eileen was standing at the front door, her smile failing quite to mask a frown. 'I thought I heard your voice. Why didn't you come in and say hello?'

'It was Susan.' Mike put an arm around her shoulders. 'She wouldn't stop talking.'

'Well, you might say a proper hello to your mother, now you noticed her.'

'Sorry. Hi, Mom, it's great to see you, you're looking great, how are you?'

As he got up to kiss her, his leg, bare in tattered shorts, brushed Susan's. It was brown, springy-haired, and felt warm. Felix's legs were always white, and the hairs on them were long and lank.

'I don't know what to do with you.' She looked up at him, and shook her head. 'Just like your father. Susan, how is he as a host?'

'Very efficient, thank you,' said Susan.

'Well.' Once again, she ignored the answer to her own question. 'I'll see you kids tomorrow, I can't stand here gossiping.' Interesting, reflected Susan, the difference between pleasantness and politeness: she would think about it when she returned to *Emma*. 'Mike, walk me to my car.'

As the two slowly walked towards her car, standing shiny new a little way down the street, Susan wondered with a twinge of guilt whether it might be arranged that Felix and Eileen should meet. Then she went indoors to where Joanna and Kathy were laughingly dividing the last cookie.


Susan caught the ball, ran, made contact, and Nancy was out.

'All right!' shouted Bill.

'Jolly good show,' called Bill's brother, Ted.

Kathy put two fingers in her mouth, and emitted a piercing whistle.

Susan smiled graciously, and made a modest bow of acknowledgement.

Joanna, sitting under the slender shade of the park's fence and waiting her turn to bat, watched in satisfaction. There was no question about it: Susan, despite her terrible experience of the previous day, was noticeably more relaxed than she had been last week. Which was especially convenient for today, because she wanted Susan to make a good impression on James this evening.

What a stroke of good fortune had been Susan's going into the garden soon after Eileen had arrived. And how quick Eileen had been on the uptake, a moment's thought producing a doctor to the hospital, new to town, and, she knew, unattached, to whom, indeed, Eileen had recently promised a dinner in exchange for some work on her car. The doctor, she was assured, was tall, responsible, and witty. 'They won't know what's hit 'em,' Eileen had predicted with a wink. What a satisfactory mother-in-law she was. Joanna wondered what James' mother was like.

Listen to her, marrying Susan off to a man neither had even clapped eyes on. But the fact was that Susan should be half of a pair, it was the natural order, the way things were. Susan

herself, if asked, would doubtless reply snappishly that Felix
was as much of another half as she wanted or needed. But
Joanna, wise in her married state, knew that Felix was the
other half not to her but to his wife. What sort of a mate was it
whom it evidently did not even occur to you to call when you
had witnessed something so terrible and distressing as an
uxoricide?

Granted, it was easy enough for her to pontificate, being
happy in her own partnership. But hers was not the only
happy union she knew. Look at Bill and Nancy, for instance,
or Ted and his girlfriend Lauren. And Kathy was alone, and
patently unhappy in that state.

And Rick and Oliver, she thought; how happy were they?
Rick, it was becoming apparent to her, was not a happy
person. Not sophisticated enough even to realise that he
lacked the sophistication of Oliver and his friends, he was
blundering through his days, unsatisfied, knowing it, and not
knowing why; while even his ambition to be an actor, sincere
as Kathy's, was based on so little talent that it brought him,
not sympathy, but laughter. And it had not, now that she
thought of it, been kind to Oliver to take him from whatever
milieu had been his, to thrust him into so new a one, and to
turn away when he sank rather than swam. Perhaps it was not
so very desirable to be beautiful, after all.

'You look serious.' Rick was standing over her, watching
her.

'Do I?' Caught, she felt herself blushing. 'I was having a
deep think. Quite painful, if you're as stupid as I am.'

'Don't say that,' he said. 'You're not stupid.'

'No? Well, that's nice to hear. How are you, Rick?'

'Oh.' He sat down beside her, gripping the edge of the
wooden bench. 'I'm feeling better since yesterday. But I
always do feel better after I talk to you.'

Poor Rick, she thought, suddenly reminded of the sort of
stray animal that attaches itself to anyone who will pet it. On
the other hand, it would do no one any good if he were to

97

become so attached to her: and the look in his eyes was ominously hopeful of confidences. Happily, at that moment, salvation lumbered up in the form of Mike. She rose quickly, and took an icy draught from the cold beer can he held in his hand.

'Thank you,' she said. 'I needed that.'

'Is it nearly over?' Nancy joined them, trim in pink cotton shorts and running shoes to match.

'Not till the fat lady sings,' said Mike. 'Sing, Joanna.'

'Oh, he's lovely to live with,' said Joanna. 'Such a subtle sense of humour. Nancy, how come you never sweat?'

'She never moves fast enough.' Bill was leading his team off the field. 'Move it, you guys. It's our inning, or hadn't you noticed?' He picked up a bat lying on the grass by the bench, and swung it experimentally. It landed dangerously close to Rick's face.

'Hey,' said Rick.

'Sorry,' said Bill. 'Didn't see you sitting down.'

'Well, I was here,' said Rick. 'I've been here all along.'

'Whew.' Mike whistled, and shook his head. 'Hate to think of the law suit if you'd broken his nose.'

'Don't listen to him, Rick,' said Joanna. 'He's jealous of both of us. Mike, are we going to play, or are you going to stand around being funny all afternoon?'


There was something about Eileen's pleasant apartment that made Susan distinctly uncomfortable. It was not the place itself, large and light, nor the cheerfully battered old furniture; nor had their welcome been anything short of enthusiastic. But there was that in the place that made Susan, perched on the end of a capacious sofa, a stiff whiskey and an ashtray to hand, even less at her ease than she had been since her arrival in Los Angeles.

Joanna and Mike, in contrast, sitting opposite, sharing a bowl of nuts, their account of the day's game each interrupting and tumbling over the other's, seemed almost more at home than they were in their own home.

'I still say,' said Joanna, 'that it was jolly mean of you to get me run out like that. You wouldn't have done it to Susan. And you've taken the last cashew.'

'Course I wouldn't have done it to Susan,' said Mike. 'She can run faster than one mile an hour. Hey, if you really wanted that cashew, I can spit it out.'

'God, you're disgusting.'

'Did you enjoy the game, dear?' Eileen bent her laughing gaze on Susan.

'Yes,' said Susan. 'Thank you.'

'She's jolly good,' put in Joanna loyally. 'Isn't she, Mike?'

'Susan's fine. Pity about the rest of her family.'

'Oh, shut up.'

But still, Susan's spirit had intruded into the conversation, like a broken spring, which, once discovered in a mattress, cannot be ignored.

'How about you?' She turned to Eileen. Unable to be jovial, she could at least reach for politeness. 'How was your day?'

'Honey, it was terrific, I did nothing. Got up late, read the papers . . .and went to Mass.'

She looked pointedly at Mike, who, bent over the nuts, appeared not to have heard. 'What's for dinner, Mom?' he asked.

Her eyes softened. 'Pot roast. He loves my pot roast,' she told Susan. 'This one only cooks him chicken and fish.'

'Red meat's bad for you,' said Joanna. 'If he wants to clog up his arteries, he can do it without my help. I would have thought Dr Weintraub would have taught you a bit more about nutrition.'

Eileen chuckled. 'You leave Dr Weintraub out of this, Miss. Mike's Grandfather O'Connor had steak for dinner every night of his life but Fridays.'

'Tell me, Mom,' said Mike. 'How old was he when he died?'

'Oh, you. Ah.'

She showed no sign of surprise at the doorbell, and Susan, glancing at the dining space, noticed that the table was set for five. Perhaps it was the mysterious Dr Weintraub.

But the man who stood at the door was surely a couple of decades younger than Eileen; nor was her manner towards him, although instinctively flirtatious, that of a woman greeting a beau.

'Come in, James, come in and meet the gang. Mike, Joanna, this is Dr James Biggin from the hospital, my son and daughter-in-law. And this,' purposefully, she led him towards the sofa, 'is Joanna's cousin from England, Susan.'

Susan tensed in horror. There could be no mistake of Eileen's intention. She was being introduced. Matched. Mated like some village girl, she, Professor Susan Barnes of London University. The effrontery of it quite took her breath away. She sat up straight, and, an unusually sympathetic memory of Miss Murdstone entering her mind, proffered the very tips of her fingers.

'How do you do,' she heard herself murmur, icily languid, as if she grudged the very effort of lungs and tongue to form the phrase.

Dr Biggin, however, appeared to notice nothing strange about either her or her greeting but with an amiable grunt dropped, large, male, and bearded, next to her on to the sofa, and grinned at Joanna, while Eileen fussed with whiskey and fresh nuts.

'So you're the British daughter-in-law we hear so much about.'

'Do you?' Joanna smiled and blushed faintly. 'Nice things, I hope.'

'Oh, nothing but nice things. Whereabouts in Britain are you from?'

Susan, after ten days, was beginning to feel that if she were asked that question one more time she would scream. But Joanna, after so many years, gave every appearance of hearing it for the first time.

'The South,' she said. 'Just outside London. Have you ever been to England?'

'Once. It was beautiful.'

They had all been once, and were all irresistibly impelled to tell you about their visit. And Dr Biggin, it transpired, had even a great-grandfather from Dorset whose village he had tracked down, churchyard and all. Joanna listened carefully, only occasionally darting sidelong glances at Susan, as if waiting for an opportunity to draw her into the conversation. Well, she could wait. Susan fully intended to give Dr James Biggin from Dorset via Pittsburgh, Ohio, or wherever he came from, neither a jot nor a tittle of her rather valuable time and attention.

Instead, she turned to Mike. 'I really would like to come and see your movie,' she said. '*Miranda*, isn't it?'

'*Marina*.' The eyes that met hers were laughing, but his voice was grave enough. 'Sure. Wait till I'm synched up, and we'll fix a date.'

'Now, now.' Eileen had bustled out of the kitchen to join them. 'I don't want any huddles, we'll have general conversation, if you please. And, Mike, I don't want to hear any shop talk about your old movie.'

'Sorry, Mom.' He cowered exaggeratedly in his chair, and looked across at James. 'Bullies the hell out of me,' he observed.

The other man nodded. 'Mine, too.'

'Of course she does.' Eileen flourished her glass. 'And how would you two great tall guys have grown up if your Moms hadn't made you eat your spinach?'

'How's your car?' said James.

'Oh, doing nicely, thank you. This man is so smart, he's a brilliant mechanic. But can you believe this one?' she pointed at Susan. 'This Londoner here? She can't even drive.'

Susan stared ahead. She did not recall having discussed her driving abilities with Eileen; and she refused to have thrust upon her the undignified role of damsel in potential distress.

Yet politeness, and her position as Joanna's guest, demanded that she make some response.

'In London,' she said, again barely moving her mouth, barely exercising her throat, 'you can always find a cab.'

And she turned to meet any indulgence in his eyes with her own flinty stare.

But he looked at her only just as long and as warmly as was polite before turning back to her cousin. 'But your British roads,' he said. 'They're so narrow and winding. I think they'd be quite dangerous.'

It came to Susan in a burst of outrage that he was ignoring her fully as much as she him; and worse, that he was being rather more graceful about it than she was. Then, catching Mike's eye, she saw that he saw that, too, and that his enjoyment of what he saw was intense.

'I think,' he said, leaning forward and into the conversation, 'that Susan was just saying she'd like to learn to drive. If she could find someone car-minded enough to teach her. Weren't you, Susan?'

Susan smiled, and reflected on the inconvenience of the fact that you could only acceptably kick under the table those to whom you were married.

'By the way,' Joanna put in hastily. 'You'll never guess who I saw the other day. Frank Sinatra. Coming out of a restaurant. You know, people always say Los Angeles is such a sprawl, but I'm always amazed at the number of famous people you see just walking around.'

'Sinatra.' Eileen frowned. 'That guy's face is a picture of debauchery. He should go back to his wife.'

Joanna laughed. 'Which particular wife, Eileen?'

'His wife,' Eileen repeated. 'His wife in the eyes of God and the Church, and the mother of his children.'

It was then that Susan realised what in the apartment was causing her discomfort. The place was festooned with religious artefacts. Walls were hung with crucifixes; shelves dotted with plaster figures of the Virgin or of the saints; the dining area dominated by a polychrome Jesus rending his garment to reveal a redly bleeding heart. It was quite barbaric, and extraordinary that she had not noticed it before.

'Can we eat, Mom?' said Mike. 'I'm starving.'

They clustered around the dining table, Eileen sitting at its head, and passed plates of comforting childhood food, thick meat, mashed potato, and vegetables glistening in gravy. There was even salt on the table.

'Great pot roast, Mom,' mumbled Mike through a mouthful. 'Wish I could get Joanna to cook like this.'

'In my day,' said Eileen, 'we believed in feeding our men. But I will say that if you like the rabbit food you kids go in for, Joanna cooks it very well. Do you cook, dear?'

She had addressed Susan, and was actually waiting for a response.

'No,' said Susan. She could, sitting at other tables, be entertaining about her lack of culinary skills; but here, the short syllable was all that she could muster.

'No! Then all I can say is, you must have a lot of young men take you out to dinner.'

It was the moment to mention Felix, to discomfit Eileen, to discourage, should discouragement be necessary, James. On the other hand, why should she pay the situation that compliment? She would not mention him; but she would tell him, in just a few days, and with what relish would she tell him, all about it.

'Usually,' she said, 'I take myself out.'

Joanna's elbow nudged hers. There was, it occurred to Susan, an interesting treatise to be written on what went on under dinner tables.

But Eileen only laughed. 'That's my girl! I'm all for liberation. And what about you, James? Are you a liberated man, or do you live out of cans, like most bachelors?'

'The latter, I'm afraid.' He, like Mike, was attacking his food with gusto. 'When my wife left, she took all the pots and pans. I sure do miss home cooking.'

Susan caught a glance, of alarm and amusement respectively, between Joanna and Mike.

But Eileen appeared conveniently not to have heard the middle portion of his statement. 'Well, I declare, the pair of you are as bad as each other. And look at you both, skinny as rails. Joanna, you should invite James over, fatten them both up.' She nodded at James. 'Go over there one evening. You'll have a swell time: she's a good cook.'

Enough was enough, Susan felt. She turned to Eileen, sitting freckled and sallow under the wild-rose cheeked, ripe-corn haired, bleeding Jesus. 'I don't know,' she said brightly, 'that it's ever been proved that good food necessarily ensured a good time. This is delicious pot roast, by the way.'

Just for a second, Eileen's face crumpled, became old. Then she recovered. 'Do help yourself to more wine, dear,' she said. 'Don't stand on ceremony around here.'

Looking across the table, and avoiding Joanna's eyes, Susan found herself staring straight into the suddenly interested gaze of Dr James Biggin.

'What part of London did you say you came from?' he asked.

The atmosphere, driving home in Mike's comfortable old car, was anything but cordial.

'You didn't have,' said Joanna, 'to be quite so rude.'

'Rude!' echoed Susan, driven by guilt to defence of her position. 'You did see, didn't you, what she was trying to do to me and that James man?'

'Yes, Joanna.' Mike, at any rate, appeared to be deriving pleasure from the evening. 'You did see that, didn't you?'

'Throwing us at each other like two retarded teenagers.'

'Well, he was a perfectly nice man.'

'That's not the point, and you know it. I don't care if he was Albert Schweitzer. The woman . . .' A knee in her back through the back of the seat stopped her. 'Sorry, Mike. I'm quite sure Eileen meant well, and it was probably very kind of her. But I'm afraid I just do find that sort of thing the most awful intrusion.'

'I'm not surprised,' said Mike. 'I would myself.'

'Well,' said Joanna. 'If, God forbid, it or anything like it ever happens again while I'm around, d'you think you could bear to be just a bit less embarrassing about it?'

'Point taken. Sorry, Joanna.'

'And you, Mike, it didn't exactly help to have you sitting there all evening grinning like an idiot.'

'Sorry, my love.'

In the front of the car, Mike and Susan exchanged a furtive glance of the camaraderie of the disapproved of.


'Don't you have work to do?' said Bill.

'Sure,' said Mike. 'Don't you?'

'Nah. I got employees to do that stuff.'

Mike was all but finished with his synching. When it was over, he would force himself to take a few days off to clear his brain: then he could start on the real work, the editing. Partly in celebration, partly to put off the hour, he had decided to visit Bill's office on the way to the studio. Mike took a half shameful pleasure in visiting Bill at work. It pleased him to amble in jeans and grubby T-shirt past the razor-efficient secretary in reception to flaunt his freedom in the deep piled office where his friend sat locked in a suit behind his gleaming desk. He enjoyed dropping his sneakered feet on the magazine laden coffee table, and letting film terms, synchroniser, code numbers, master shot, fall casually from his lips while Bill's eyes flickered with the envy of a man hearing news of a once beloved, deserted mistress. Bill had once loved the movies: then he had met Nancy and left them. Mike's father, the lawyer, the rich man, would have considered Bill, not Mike, to be the success in life. But then, Mike's father was dead.

'Saw your wife,' he said. 'She came to see Joanna. On her way to pottery class.'

'Jewellery class.'

'Some kind of class. She likes those classes, doesn't she?'

'Seems to.'

While Joanna, it struck him, who had, or who had had, genuine creative talent, appeared content to idle away her summer in telephone calls and cups of iced tea. He thought of the Joanna he had once known, the Joanna of London, who at weekends and school holidays would take herself up to her light filled attic with an expression of purpose he never saw in her now. He wondered whether he missed that Joanna.

'That Susan,' he said. 'She works, boy. Takes her breakfast, sits in the sun till 9.45 — never 9.40, never 9.50, just 9.45 — and then she's in there. In that garage. Working.'

'How's Kathy?' said Bill.

'OK, I think,' said Mike. He took a swig of coffee, watching Bill over the rim of the cup. He sometimes wondered how much Bill, who had, after all, known him longer, and in some ways even better, than Joanna, suspected about him and Kathy. 'Why?'

'Just wondering. Any sign of work?'

'Don't think so.' Although if the deal with Celia and her colleagues were to come off, there might well be a part in it for her. But he had not mentioned Celia to anyone yet: and she had not, as far as he knew, even contacted his agent. 'Jesus, I wouldn't be an actor.'

'Alex is talking about it,' said Bill. 'Acting. Can't say I like it.'

'He's eleven years old.'

'Twelve. But I'll tell you one thing, I'm glad he knows people like Kathy. I mean, he sees his school friends' dads, and he sees some of my clients, and it all seems rich and glamorous. I'm glad he sees the other side of the movies, too, people like Kathy, and . . .' He stopped himself. 'And even Rick,' he finished.

'And me,' Mike supplied.

'Yes,' said Bill. 'And you. You know what I mean.'

Mike knew what he meant. He knew, too, that if Alex did eventually decide to pursue acting, the most expensive of classes would be available to him, the finest of coaches for his voice, of photographers for his publicity shots, of everything down to the most impressive of clothes for his auditions. It was more, far more, in the material sense than he himself could ever hope to offer his own son. But it was more than had been offered, for instance, to Bill; and look how Bill had turned out.

A buzzer sounded on Bill's desk.

'My client,' he said. He jerked a thumb. 'Out.'

Mike swung his feet from the table, finished his coffee, and started towards the door.

'Not that way,' said Bill. He pointed towards the back door, leading not to the mirrored elevator, but to the service stairs. 'That way.'

Mike raised his brows and whistled. 'Important client, huh? OK, buddy, I won't show you up.'

And, too generous to point out the difference between his friend's morning and his own, he padded down the narrow back stairs into the joy of making his movie.


'You poor thing,' said Nancy.

'Don't!' said Joanna. 'We had Susan hissing vitriol at Eileen, and Eileen, well, you know how Eileen can get, and in the middle of it all, there was Mike, deciding it was the funniest thing he'd seen all year. As for James, God knows what he thought.'

Although she could have sworn that he had liked Susan, had even liked her more as the evening had progressed. Curious, because she herself, were she meeting Susan for the first time, would not have liked her at all. But who could predict who would find what sort of behaviour attractive? At any rate, James had seemed a nice man. She had half a mischievous mind to take up Eileen's suggestion and invite him for dinner.

'It's such a pity,' she said. 'He was such a nice man. And she wouldn't even give him a chance.'

'When's this Felix arriving?' said Nancy.

'Soon, Today. And that's another thing, you know. Here he is, almost on her doorstep, and there she is, just working away calmly, as if it were just any old day. I mean, I'd be a basket case, wouldn't you?'

'I guess so,' said Nancy.

'Guess! Imagine if you weren't married to Bill, and you hadn't even seen him for two weeks.'

'Heaven.'

'Oh, well.' Joanna laughed. But at the same time, she was struck, sharply as with a period pain, by an annoyance with Susan. She should be able to talk like this to Susan, too. 'It's all wrong,' she said. 'She's a daft idiot, really . . . My God, she was furious with Eileen. And for what? For introducing her to a nice man. Daft ha'p'orth.'

'She know it was your idea?'

'Ssh! No. My God, no, she'd go mad. She . . . Oh.'

The telephone rang. She reached over and picked up the receiver. A rushing sound came from the earpiece, telling her the call was long distance.

'May I speak to Susan Barnes, please?' said a man's well-educated British voice.

'Oh, yes.' Joanna's stomach swirled excitement for her cousin, censure for herself. 'Who is it speaking?'

'Felix Grahame,' said the voice.

Joanna laid the receiver on the side table, crossed the garden, and knocked on the garage door. There was no answer, so she opened it and peered around. Susan was sitting at the desk, bolt upright, staring at a piece of paper in the typewriter, her lower lip caught between her teeth, her right hand scrawling blind boxes, crosses and grids on a scrap of paper beside her.

'Susan?' she said.

Susan turned around, saw her, and frowned. Joanna saw Uncle Peter, in the days when she and Tom, too young to know better, had crept into his study to disturb him at work. Uncle Peter had worn glasses: but from the look of the furrows around Susan's eyes and brow, it would not be long before she needed them, too.

'Yes?' said Susan. 'What do you want?'

'Telephone call,' said Joanna. 'It's Felix. You can take it in here if you want.'

'Oh. Oh, thank you. Yes, I will.' She nodded, a polite nod of dismissal. 'Thanks.'

Reluctantly closing the door, Joanna heard the click of the receiver being picked up, and her cousin's cool voice speaking into it. She returned to the kitchen and quickly, before she overheard anything she should not, replaced her own receiver.

'It's all wrong,' she said to Nancy.

'Leave 'em to it,' said Nancy. She stood to go. 'Come by later for lunch. If you can stand the kids.'

'I have a mass of shopping to do. I promised Mike I'd make curry. He says if I give him one more salad, he'll start having nightmares about Elmer Fudd.' The telephone rattled as the receiver was replaced next door. 'And Susan might need a lift somewhere.' Susan, poor Susan, who had no idea of what it was like to live with a man all the time, to cater to his voracious appetite, to find his socks under the bed, to displace her own well ordered life to accommodate someone who was large, and untidy, and always hungry. 'It's all wrong,' she repeated.

The last inch of sound was married to the last picture frame, and the synchronisation was finished at last. Mike rolled his head between his sore shoulder blades, crumpled his empty Cola can, and let out a groan of sheer relief. The slog was over. The next time he worked, he would be enjoying himself, editing, making his movie. His movie. His *Marina*. He smiled, rubbed aching palms into aching arms, and smiled again around the dingy cutting room. He was even early; he would be able to go home and watch Joanna cooking the curry.

He was not sure, but he rather thought he might be growing tired of Joanna's open laziness. It was true that he himself had urged her — not that she had needed much urging — to take the summer off; but he had had, in doing so, no clear picture of what it would be like. Inflamed with the excitement of being able to afford a few weeks' leisure for his wife, he had simply presented it to her, assuming that she would find something to do with it that was, if not necessarily so puritan as to be productive, at least worthwhile. What he had not bargained for would be that she would take his precious gift and waste it, wantonly, hour after hour; that he would leave her, idle, morning after morning to go off to work, and return, evening after evening, to find her idle still.

She suffered, of course, by contrast with Susan. Accustomed as Mike was to having guests who simply sat in the sun all day —extraordinary how long the British could sit in the sun — he was finding it a distinctly refreshing change to have someone around who was working as hard as he was. It was really rather nice.

Really rather nice. How British he was becoming, the effect, no doubt of that same Susan, whose unassimilated voice had for some days now been echoing in his head, shaping his thoughts to her own dry turn of phrase. Presumably, it would get worse when this Felix was here; when he was gone, Mike would hardly be able to think a thought in good American any more. Well, he could live with it.

He whistled a few bars of 'Rule, Britannia', as he locked the studio door, and set off down the grubby, ill-lit corridor.

'You're happy.' Celia Fletcher was standing in front of him, dark hair, creamy skin, a lily blooming in a junkyard.

'What are you doing here?' he said.

'I was passing, and I remembered you were working here, and I just wondered if you were still at it.' She paused. 'I live nearby, remember?'

He met her eyes and remembered her when she was less cool, no lily, but a rambling, lascivious rose.

'I remember,' he said.

'Well?' she said.

'I haven't heard from my agent.'

'I haven't spoken to him yet.' She looked down the dim corridor: her nose was slightly too long. 'Is this really where you work?'

'Told you it wasn't a glamour investment.'

'Well, we're not looking to cut corners, you know. Wouldn't you even like an assistant?'

'Depends on the assistant.'

He could go home, shower, roll a joint, and talk to Joanna. But she was there in front of him, and her fresh linen jacket fell so beautifully over her brown and white dress, and Joanna would not expect him yet.

'Come on,' he said, and as she smiled and turned to lead the way out, he put a hand on her slim hip.

It was at that moment that Kathy rounded the corner.

'Oh,' she said.

Oh, shit, thought Mike. 'Kathy!' he said aloud, too loud. 'Great to see you. I don't know if you've met Celia Fletcher, who I'm hoping to interest in financing my next movie? Celia, this is Kathy Schneider.'

The two shook hands, murmured polite greetings. Mike had seen Kathy in red silk and high heels looking desirable; he had seen her in old jeans and a sweatshirt looking irresistible. She never looked less attractive than she did in her office clothes. Standing beside Celia, she was reduced to an awkward kid sister, one who would try forever, and never achieve, what to the other came as naturally as drawing breath.

'Kathy's an actress,' he said, 'A darned good one. You might have seen her. I use her whenever she'll let me. I like to think of her as Robert de Niro to my Martin Scorsese.'

'Thanks very much!' said Kathy, and the two women laughed rather harder than was necessary.

'Well.' Better, he decided, to leave it at that. 'Listen, Kathy, we have to go talk business; but why don't you come by the house later? I won't be late, and Joanna's fixing curry.'

'No.' She waved a casual hand. 'I just stopped by. I have a date later on.' She smiled, seductive, suggestive, under aching eyes. 'More fun than business.'

'You bet,' said Mike.

They walked out together, and he kissed her affectionately before they parted.

'She's a good kid, Kathy,' he said, watching her little yellow Volkswagen breeze gallantly down the road towards Santa Monica and home.

'She seemed a real good kid,' agreed Celia.


It was fortunate how little power the outside world had to distract Susan from her work. Los Angeles could not. Not the first bland, blond land of sunshine, nor the new Los Angeles where men drew guns and shot their wives; nor, apparently, could the news that Felix was on his way, flying swiftly and fantastically high over ancient forests and cities that in Emma's day had not even been there. She worked as hard as she had planned on Jane Austen's small canvas, until she reached the point she had anticipated. Then she shut her books, leaving Emma, and Jane Fairfax, and silly Miss Bates in deep-laned Highbury; she showered; she wanted to call a cab to the hotel where Felix would be staying, but Joanna, requesting her not to be so daft, bundled her into the car and drove her over, leaving her with instructions to call when she wanted to be driven home.

'If, of course,' she added, looking carefully out of the window at the early evening traffic, 'you are coming home, I mean.'

Susan, inspecting the front of the hotel from her own window, did not reply. She had rarely spent the full night with Felix, and the few occasions on which she had, she had not enjoyed. She did not like him in the mornings, a scratchycheeked intruder in her small, neat kitchen, who sat at the table with his bald patch showing, slopped his coffee, and read her paper before her, so that by the time she got to it, it was second-hand, its virginity taken. But that was in her flat, all those miles away across the world. Perhaps he would be different in a hotel.

No perhaps about it, she told herself, sitting waiting for him in the peach-lit, piano-tinkling cocktail bar. Of course he would be different, they both would be; foreigners in a strange land, acid-tongued, civilised Britons, who alone spoke each other's language. Two weeks since she had been in Britain; three since she had seen Felix. She felt as if she had not seen him for years and years.

And there he was, tall and beak-nosed, striding across the room towards her, and of course it was not years, but only days, only twenty-one days.

'My dear Susan.' He bent over and kissed her cheek. There was no one, in the hotel, in the whole sprawling city, who might know his wife; but so used were they to behaving unlike lovers in public that they did so now, even here, without a thought.

'Felix.' She drank him in, his narrowness, his nicotine-stained teeth, his pallor, here in this town where everybody was beautiful and strong. 'You made it.'

'Barely.' He sat down, and crossed his legs; many people, on first meeting Felix, assumed that he was homosexual. 'I was seated next to a woman with a repulsively wholesome brat who kept asking searching questions about the working of the aeroplane. I always thought intelligence in children was highly overrated.'

She laughed. How long it had been since anyone but herself had made her laugh.

'And when I arrived, the desk clurk — as he persisted in referring to himself — greeted me as if we'd been suckled at the same breast. "How are you today?" he said. "No different from yesterday," I told him, which threw the unhappy youth into a state of complete confusion. You, incidentally, if I may comment, are looking rather delicious today.'

She had thought she looked well before she left the house, a cream silk shirt deepening her tan, her eyes bright with pleasure. She caught sight of their two reflections in a mirror on the wall: next to him, she looked positively Californian.

'Can I get you something, madam, sir?'

Yet another Adonis, honey-haired, golden brown, was standing over them, and Susan's reflection shrank to its customary North European dreariness.

'I imagine you can,' said Felix. 'Certainly, you may. I should like a very large, very dry Martini, straight up, with an olive, and . . .'

'And the same for me, please.' Wine was fine, but it was long, too, since she had shared a serious drink with anyone but Eileen.

'The burning question,' he said as the waiter moved off, 'is, do the Los Angeles martinis stand up to New York's?'

'I wouldn't know. I haven't been to New York, and this will be my first Martini here.'

'Your first? My poor angel, what have they been doing to you? Cigarette?'

'Thanks.' How different was her life from Emma's, flying 6,000 miles for a summer visit, sitting in trousers in a strange hotel, accepting a cigarette from her married lover. Jane Austen had put on the spinster's cap when she was thirty, and Susan was already thirty-two. '*Emma*'s going well,' she added.

'Excellent. Your brain isn't quite fried in the sun, then?'

'Only lightly scrambled. Oh, Joanna sends you her best wishes, and if you're not too busy tomorrow evening, would you like to come to dinner?'

'Ah.' He smiled, a yellow smile. 'The famous Joanna, the *cousine sans peur et sans reproche*. How is it going with her, badly I hope?'

He had always teased her about Joanna, and in London she found it amusing. Here, somehow, she did not. 'It's going very well,' she replied. 'They're both being very nice to me indeed.'

'But of course they're being nice, Americans are nice.' He puffed dismissively at his cigarette. 'All that hospitality. But how's it *going*?'

Susan did not reply.

'I mean,' he continued, 'do they surf to their analysts and force feed you recycled bean sprout juice?'

He was mocking himself as much as he was mocking California, and two weeks ago, Susan would have laughed along with him; half an hour ago, she would have thought she could laugh still. But, surprisingly she found that she could not.

'As a matter of fact,' she said, 'they're perfectly intelligent, sophisticated people. And Joanna's English, anyway.'

'But what a disappointment.' He was unruffled. 'I was hoping at the very least for astrologically matched jogging shoes.'

This was wrong. Susan had been in his company for barely ten minutes, and here she was, snapping at him. He had, after all, just got off the plane: and it was so much more fun when they were laughing together.

'Well,' she said slowly. No, she would not throw Joanna or Mike to his satirical wolves; but they were not the only people she had met out here. 'Joanna and Mike are pretty well British, anyway. But there's this other couple they're best friends with . . .'

'Enjoy.' Adonis returned, and set their drinks in front of them. Susan tasted. It was very good, and quite soon she forgot the uncomfortable feeling at the edge of either her stomach or her soul as she started to tell Felix everything about Nancy and Bill.


Joanna shifted the receiver against her ear: Rick and Oliver's relationship was not improving.

'Well, why don't you tell him all this?' she said.

'I do.' Rick's voice travelled despairingly down the telephone wires. 'I keep telling him, but he doesn't listen. I might as well speak to the wall.'

'Well.' She could well believe it. Oliver, for all his politeness, was so controlled; and Rick, for all his vanity, all his selfishness, so foolhardily open. But it was not, she reminded herself, her problem. She had decided when the telephone rang that if it were Rick, she would give him fifteen minutes, and it was now seventeen. 'I'll tell you what.' It could not be healthy for the two of them to spend so much time together in the dark apartment, with Rick not working, and Oliver not being kind to Rick. 'We're having a friend of Susan's to dinner tomorrow, why don't you both come too? Get you out of the house a bit.'

'Well, OK.' His voice brightened slightly. 'That might be nice. What sort of friend?'

'Oh, some English publishing type. Oliver'll like him.'

'Yeah.' Annoying though he could be, it was touching how easy it was to cheer Rick up. 'They can be uptight together.'

'And you and I'll have a good time.' Eighteen and a half minutes. 'Look, Ricky, I really have to run. But I'll see you tomorrow around 7.00, OK?'

'OK. Bye, Joanna. Thanks.'

It was quiet in the evening without Susan. She had looked so nice when she had left, positively pretty, almost girlish. What a waste, what a shameful, shameful waste. Joanna stretched — she really would have to visit the health club tomorrow and then there was her hair cut to think of — poured a glass of wine, and went to sit in the evening sun before she started the curry.

As she left the front door, a familiar yellow Volkswagen drew up, and Kathy got out.

'Hello,' said Joanna. 'What a nice surprise.'

'Surprise, yeah; nice, I wouldn't bet on.' She was wearing her office clothes, and looked hot, uncomfortable, and bad-tempered. 'I'm really not fit for human society.'

'So you came to see me instead. How flattering. You look like you could use a glass of wine.'

They went inside and sat at the kitchen table. Kathy looked around at the sunsoaked wood, the rack of vegetables, the shelf of spices, and her frown lifted a little.

'This is a nice kitchen,' she said. 'Wish I had a decent one. When I write my play, it'll all be set in the kitchen. Thanks.' She took the glass of wine Joanna handed her. 'God, I need this.'

'Had a rough day?' asked Joanna.

'God.' The frown lowered again. 'I hate offices. Hate 'em, hate 'em. They're squeezing the soul out of me. I'm thirty years old, Joanna, I'm too old for this.'

Abruptly, she stopped, pulled a paper clip from her pocket, and sat twisting it between her fingers, her lower lip pouting. Joanna watched, her heart heavy for her.

'I know,' she said. 'I do know. You deserve better.'

'Thirty years old. Thirty, and typing dumb letters for dumb men in suits about . . . Do you know who I'm working for this week? A company that imports novelty toilet tissue. Novelty toilet tissue. And I'm thirty.'

'Oh, dear. But you know, lots of people do make it after they're thirty.'

'Yeah. And lots more don't. Well.' She shook herself and gulped again at her wine. 'Where's Susan?'

She clearly wanted diversion, so Joanna gave it to her.

'Gone to Westwood. To see a friend of hers who's over.'

'Oh. That's nice for her.'

'Well, it is and it isn't.' Damn Susan's privacy, decided Joanna. 'Listen, don't mention this to anyone or anything, but he's not just her friend, he's her boyfriend.'

'Well, that sounds even nicer.'

'Yes, it would be. If it weren't for the little matter of his wife and three kids at home.'

'Oh.'

'And she went out of here looking so nice and so happy

and . . . well, like you, she deserves better.' She paused, looked into her own wine glass. Maybe not the most tactful thing to remind Kathy of her own happiness, but thinking of Susan, she could not but be aware of it. 'I don't think I could bear it if I weren't the one Mike comes home to.'

'What happened about that doctor Eileen was fixing her up with?'

'James, oh, don't, it was a disaster. And he was perfectly sweet, too.' An idea struck her. 'Would you like to meet him?'

'No way.' Kathy shook her head. '*No* way. I'm off men for ever.'

She had finished her wine, and Joanna poured more. 'Someone been treating you bad?'

'Yeah.' She thought about it, frowned again, and sighed. 'Kind of. Well, yeah. *Yeah.*'

'Oh dear, poor you. It's a jungle out there, isn't it?' She thought back to her own single days, the days before Mike. The memory, in contrast with what she had now, was tiring, lonely, sore; and then she had been seven years younger and seven years stronger, too. 'I don't know how you stand it.'

Kathy laughed. 'Me either. Well, it beats being married to Wayne, I guess. But you know, when I married him, I thought I'd left all that behind.'

'I don't miss any of that,' said Joanna. 'Boyfriends and stuff. I wondered if I would, but I don't at all. It was more trouble than it was worth. You know, sometimes I look around me, and I think about Mike and me, and I get really quite frightened at how lucky I am.'

'You deserve it all,' said Kathy. 'All of it and more. Jesus, I wish I was lesbian, it'd be so much simpler.'

'Oh, Kathy!' said Joanna. 'Stay for supper, I'm cooking curry. Do you want to borrow a dress? You look really uncomfortable.'

'I have to go. I said I'd meet Mark from my acting class.'

'I thought you said you were off men for ever.'

'He's not a man, he's Mark from my acting class. So I guess I'll see you at softball, right?'

'I suppose so. Oh, Susan's friend and Oliver and Rick are coming to dinner tomorrow, why don't you come too?'

'I don't know.' She looked down at the paper clip, now pulled into a straight, rigid line, and flicked at it, sending it spinning across the table. 'Can I say I might?'

'You can say anything you like, and we'll all still love you.'

'You're putting on weight.'

'I hate you, bitch.'

When Kathy had gone, Joanna sat alone at last in the kitchen, thinking of her, and Susan, and Rick, and her own vast good fortune, and wondering what she would cook for dinner the next day.


Susan did not stay the night, but took, ridiculously, but typically, a taxi home, arriving shortly after eleven, with her eyes still sparkling and some gin and rather a lot of wine on her breath. An anonymous black and white film was on television, of the sort that nobody watched but Mike: he was glued to it, his gaze darting envy and admiration for who knew what at each corner of the small, night-filled screen. The cousins went into the kitchen to talk.

'I gather,' said Joanna, 'that you had a good time.'

'A very good time.' Susan was by no means slurring her speech; but she was, undeniably, picking it with slight care. 'A very good time. I do like Felix, you know, I like him very much. I know you'll like him too, Joanna. You will.'

The next evening while Joanna was chopping vegetables for a risotto, she pondered the conversation and wondered whether Susan could possibly be nervous about their meeting.


Susan, meanwhile, was in the hotel lobby, introducing Felix to Mike.

'Would you like a drink?' asked Felix.

'Yes, please,' said Susan promptly. Joanna, she was sure, was glad to be rid of them for a bit, and the martinis yesterday had been good.

As if by magic, the same dazzling waiter appeared, and they ordered. Two martinis and a beer.

'Beer?' Felix raised an eyebrow. 'I thought you all drank Perrier and lived to be a hundred out here.'

'You'd have to ask my wife about that,' said Mike. 'Me, I'm just aiming for my next birthday.'

There was a pause while the two men exchanged polite, appraising glances from the corners of their eyes.

'How was your day?' Susan asked Felix.

'Terrible,' said Felix. 'The man . . . ' He turned courteously to include Mike. 'I had an appointment with a professor at UCLA, and the man had the brain of a pea and the sense of humour of a pneumatic drill. He seemed to regard me as being not too distantly related to God. His first words to me were, "Mr Grahame, sir, it is a great honour and a privilege to meet you, and I am certain that we will enjoy working together." I said, "My good man, how on earth can you know?" and he looked particularly blank.'

Mike laughed, and Susan spotted relaxation on the horizon.

'Felix finds Los Angeles very strange,' she said.

'Lots do,' said Mike. 'I did myself at first.'

'Really? You're not a native, then?'

'Ain't no sich critter.' Mike, gratifyingly, appeared to be already enjoying himself. 'I'm from Chicago. Whereabouts in London do you live?'

'Oh, God.' Felix raised his eyes. 'The inevitable question. I sometimes wonder, when I'm in America, whether I'm a man or a walking tube map. And all on the basis of two days on their way to Paris-Rome-Athens. Do you, in fact, know London?'

Mike shot at Susan a brief, questioning look of surprise. 'In fact,' he said, 'I lived there for two years. In South Kensington, and then in Highgate. And my wife is English.'

'Of course she is.' He smiled, quickly apologetic. 'Of course. Do forgive me, that wretched professor has set my every nerve on edge. In fact, I don't live in London at all, I commute from Oxford.' The drinks arrived, and he raised his glass in salutation. 'And my wife is English, too.'

Was it by comparison with Mike, Susan wondered, that he seemed so much ruder than usual? And was it her imagination, or had the knowledge that Mike had lived in England brought not only apology to his tone, but increased respect?

By the time they reached the house, the lavender summer evening had set in, and Rick and Oliver were already there, sitting in the living room, sipping wine. Rick, as they entered, looked up with a quick smile, and Susan found herself wondering whether anyone, even Oliver, even Rick himself, ever grew hardened to the way Rick looked.

'No sign of Kathy,' said Joanna, after introductions had been made. 'Probably means she's not coming. That's a pity, because she seemed fed up yesterday, and I don't think she had anything much planned for tonight.'

'I'll call her,' said Mike. He went into the kitchen to telephone, shutting the door on the noise behind him.

'What part of England are you from?' asked Oliver.

'Yorkshire, originally,' said Felix. He caught Susan's eye, and she saw that she had been wrong, she could not be fully friends with Oliver after all. 'Do you know it?'

'Only from books, unfortunately. It was one of the places I missed while I was there.'

'It's a beautiful part of the world,' said Joanna. Just beautiful. And the City of York, too. I do miss England, sometimes.' But as she spoke, her eyes looked contentedly enough out through the front door at the jacaranda tree, and the road from which you could see the Ocean.

'Me, too,' said Mike, coming back to join them. 'Let's all go live there.'

'No luck?' said Joanna.

'Answering machine. I left a message.'

'She's probably out pounding the streets,' said Rick. 'Looking for work.' He smiled. He was almost luminous tonight, as if a candle had been lit inside his head, to shine behind his eyes, and through his clear olive skin.

'Rick has some exciting news,' said Oliver. 'Haven't you, Rick?'

'Have you?' said Joanna. 'Tell us.'

'Well.' Rick blushed. 'It might be, it might not. But I met a guy last night at a club, Alan, a guy I know slightly.'

'Alan's a fan,' said Oliver.

'No, he's not! Anyway, he directs *The Van Der Meers*, you know, that television show about the family, and I was telling him how unhappy I was, not being able to find work and stuff, and just this morning he called.'

'And imagine,' said Oliver. 'They just happen this very week to be casting the long lost son everyone thought was drowned in the Amazon years ago.'

'Ricky!' said Joanna. 'How marvellous!'

'Well, I haven't got the part yet. But he did say, I mean, he did seem to say, that if I did an even halfway good reading . . .'

'Congratulations!' She flung her arms around him, and kissed him. 'I'm so proud of you!'

'Yes,' said Oliver, watching Rick's blushes through narrowed eyes. 'We're all very proud of him.'

'Well,' said Joanna. 'Since everyone who's coming seems to have come, shall we all sit down and eat?'

They sat and passed dishes, nut brown rice, spangled with vegetables, speckled with herbs, wholemeal bread, a crisp salad glistening with vinegar.

'What a very Californian meal,' said Felix.

'Is it?' said Joanna. 'I just thought after all that hotel food, you might like something simple. And the vegetables here are so good.'

Between gold coloured corn and peppers of ruby and emerald, Felix speared a small cube of white substance.

'What's this?' he asked.

'Tofu. You know, soybean curd. Don't you have it in England? It's marvellous stuff, you get all the protein of meat, and none of the fat.'

'I've heard of it,' said Felix. He looked at Susan, who looked, deliberately, away from him.

'Isn't Yorkshire quite far from London?' said Oliver.

'I actually live in Oxford,' said Felix.

'Ah, Oxford. The city of dreaming spires. Now, there I did go.'

'Really,' said Felix.

Oliver raised his eyebrows, and said nothing.

'Terrific risotto, Joanna,' said Rick. 'You must give me the recipe.'

'For next time you feel moved to cook.' Oliver turned to him. 'Whenever that might be.'

Rick's eyes widened. 'I cooked Tuesday,' he said.

'You scrambled eggs.'

'Have you been to the movies out here, Felix?' asked Joanna. 'You really should try to. It feels quite different, seeing them in the town they were made in.'

'An American film?' said Felix.

'I haven't been to Hollywood proper yet,' said Susan quickly.

'You haven't missed much,' Joanna told her.

'I like Hollywood,' said Mike. 'When I was growing up, it was like *the* place. Glamour. Magic. The movies. Still is. And then you go there and it's this seedy little strip full of cheap hookers.' He smiled, an Irish grin that made his eyes disappear. 'I like that,' he repeated.

'I'll like it a lot better,' said Rick, 'when I get my star on the Walk of Fame.'

'Well, you're on your way now,' said Joanna. 'Isn't it exciting?'

'Yes, he's well on his way,' said Oliver. 'Pretty soon, he'll have forgotten us completely.'

'Oliver, what a thing to say! Of course I won't forget you.'

'No.' Oliver smiled and helped first Susan and then himself to more wine. 'No, you won't forget me, anyway. I'm far too unpleasant to you. Wasn't it a countryman of yours, Felix, who said that women and elephants — and I have a feeling our Rick, too — never forget an injury?'

'He was Irish,' said Felix.

'An Irishman, then.'

'Yes, but please don't confuse the two.' Felix, Susan knew, had strong feelings about the IRA. 'Englishmen, on the whole, tend to be literate.'

'Yeah,' said Mike. 'Unlike Swift, Sheridan, Shaw and Beckett.'

'*Touché.*' He turned from Oliver to raise a glass to Mike, his foot under the table nudging Susan's as he did so. She withdrew her own foot sharply. He was being more rude than she had ever seen him, and she would not let him think she in any way approved. Oliver, at least, was only ever rude to Rick.

'I hate people like that,' said Rick. 'People who forget their friends. I'd never do it.' He smiled over his wine glass at Joanna. 'Especially good friends like I have.'

'Yes,' said Oliver. 'You have some very good friends. Haven't you, Ricky?'

'We all have,' said Joanna firmly. She raised her own glass to no one in particular. 'Here's to friendship, it's one of the most important things we have.'

Through lowered lashes, Susan watched Felix looking from Oliver to Rick to Joanna. Mike was looking at his plate.

'Yes, Oliver,' said Rick. 'I have some very good friends indeed.'

'And here's to them,' agreed Oliver. 'And isn't it heartening to know how far, in the friendship stakes, a pretty face will go to compensate for almost any other deficiency?'

'All right.' Joanna laid down her fork. 'All right. That's enough from both of you. I'm ashamed of you both, I really am. If you want to fight, you can bloody well go and do it in your own home, you do not do it around my table. Do you understand?' She jumped up, and, although Felix had not quite finished, began to clear the plates. 'Rick, if you're going to stay, you can help me with these. And when I come back, I want absolutely everyone to be absolutely pleasant to everyone else.'

She stalked out, followed by a humbled Rick.

Mike refilled the wine glasses. 'How long did you say you were here for?' he asked Felix.

'Just a couple more days,' said Felix. 'Unfortunately.'

Only Susan knew him well enough to know that the brightness in his eyes came not from the wine, but from pleasure.

The baking, brick oven heat of high summer had set in. Plants languished, grass gasped for water, and even the Mexican children next door were listless and quiet. It was too hot to sit indoors, too hot to sit in the sun, too hot, Joanna decided, to do anything but lie in the lounger under the jacaranda tree, and read a whodunit, and wait until the breeze came whispering up from the Ocean in the evening. How Susan could work in this weather, she had no idea; but the whirr of the electric fan from the garage was often joined by the irregular clatter of the typewriter, so something must be going on in there. Joanna doffed a mental cap to her.

It was a classic whodunit, an English village, a vicar, an eccentric busybody, and a growing number of corpses, and she tried to throw herself into its Englishness, to see rain dripping from leaves on to lichen-covered walls, to feel herself, rain-softened, picking roses in a lush garden between showers, shivering, chilly damp. It was difficult, however, to concentrate with Mike around. He was still on his break between synching and editing and paced in and out of the house like a great dog, restive, purposeless, ubiquitous. Joanna hated him when he was like that.

'This what you do every day?' he asked now, briefly recumbent under the water sprinkler, its droplets falling and sparkling on his bare legs.

'It's what I do today,' she replied. 'Why don't you go out somewhere?'

'My Mom used to do housework in the morning.'

'Your Mom had two children and a big house to take care of. And no great useless husband lying under her feet all day long and never leaving her in peace. That's a hint, by the way.'

He looked at her with faint curiosity. 'You haven't painted for a bit, have you?'

'Oh, Susan would like that, wouldn't she? Excuse me, Susan, just shift your bed and your books while I get my smelly stuff out and splash it everywhere.'

'But you haven't,' he pursued. 'Have you?'

'No.' She stretched languorously. 'I haven't.'

'Gettin' lazy, kid,' he mumbled, turning himself over on the damp delicious grass.

'I know,' she agreed. 'It's disgraceful, isn't it, and reading novels in the morning, too. Or trying to. That's another hint. Oh, look. It's Nancy.'

It was indeed, stepping out of her shining family Cadillac, make-up intact, every hair in place.

'Go away,' said Joanna, hauling herself up to kiss her. 'You look far too posh to talk to.'

'Posh!' She flicked a hand at crisp white shirt and well-cut khaki shorts. 'I'm a wreck. I just dropped the horrors off at the beach, do you guys want to come and sit by the pool?' She sighed ecstatically. 'Just grown-ups, if you can imagine such a thing.'

'Now, that,' said Joanna, 'sounds like the best idea I've heard in a long time. Are you coming, Mike?'

'Nah.' He rolled over again, and sat up. 'I think I'll look in on Kathy, see how she's doing. Should we tell Susan we're all going out?'

'Her? She wouldn't notice. She's like you, all wrapped up in her own little world. Give me two ticks, Nancy, and I'll be with you.'

He waited until they had gone, laughing together about ladies who lunch, and then climbed into his own car, and drove to the anonymous office block, a grey oblong on a street full of grey oblongs, near the freeway, where Kathy was working. The imports firm was on the fifth floor behind an uncompromising wood door, and as he waited for her in reception, the cool conditioned air around his legs reminded him that he was still in shorts. The only non-trade magazine on the table, *People*, was several weeks out of date. Mike frowned. It was a cheerless place, and he did not like to think of Kathy unhappy.

'Hi, Mike.' She had arrived; she looked less comfortable than ever in tight brown skirt and businesslike shoes, and somehow dimmed, wan, as if the place were draining her of her very blood.

'Hi. Just stopped by. You free for lunch?'

She thought, shrugged. 'Sure. Just wait a minute.'

She disappeared, and returned with the one thing that was recognisably Kathy, a garishly striped canvas carryall bag. She had only an hour, so they went to the bustling coffee shop across the street: he ordered a hamburger, she a salad.

'You didn't turn up last night,' he said. Turn up. Another Anglicism; he would really have to watch them.

'Yeah, well, I was tired, I went to bed early. How'd it go?'

'Fine. Well, OK. Oliver and Rick . . . ' He stopped, decided not to tell her about Rick's news. 'Well, you know Oliver and Rick. You OK?'

'Yes.'

He looked at her.

'No,' she said. 'No, I'm not. It's the job, well, what else? It's not what I want to do, and I've spent too long doing it, and I can't see that I'll ever not have to do it.'

The waitress arrived and set their food in front of them. Kathy picked up a lettuce leaf, examined it, put it down again.

'I'm forgetting how to act, Mike.'

'Bull.' But to spend hours of the day in that office. 'Can't you take a couple of weeks off?'

'Can't afford to. Well. How's *Marina*?'

'OK.'

'You still resting?'

'Yeah.' But he might, it occurred to him, just have some heartening news to give her, and God knew, she could use it. 'Listen, don't put too much into this, but that woman at the studio the other evening?'

Her head jerked up. 'Celia?'

'Yeah, Celia. Well, she's quite interested, in a movie, I mean. Of course, that's a bit down the line, wouldn't be till after Christmas at least. But it's something to think about, right?'

'Great.' She looked down at her salad, would not meet his eyes. 'That'd be great.'

'Never know, kid, we might be stars yet.' He paused. 'Hey,' he added softly.

'Yeah?'

'Celia.'

She looked up then, and at him. But he had to tell her: she knew already.

'I screwed her.'

She nodded. 'I figured.'

'Does it bother you?'

'Why should it?'

'Why shouldn't it?'

'Well, we're not married, are we? If I was Joanna, it'd bother the hell out of me. But I'm not Joanna, am I?' For an uncontrollable second, her mouth twisted. 'You going to . . . to screw her again?'

'Dunno. Maybe not. Probably. Why?'

'Just curious.'

'You look terrible in those clothes.'

'Thanks.'

'What time d'you get off work?'

'Five. Jesus. Four and a half hours.'

'OK if I come by at 5.30?'

'Well.' She looked at her plate, closed her eyes, sighed, and then, irrepressibly, began to smile. 'Yeah. Yeah, that'd be great.'


Carefully, Felix poured wine into their two clear glasses.

'I thought you said,' he remarked, 'that everyone was always so nice to everyone else.'

Susan raised her glass sharply towards herself and drank. She should have been feeling better disposed towards him on this his last evening, but there it was, she was not.

'Everyone is,' she said. 'Usually. And you didn't have to be quite so rude.'

'Rude?' His lips lifted in amusement. 'I was perfectly charming. In that dry British way they all love.'

'I know what you were thinking.'

'My dear Susan, I was having a thoroughly delightful time.'

'I know you were.'

'That sad couple shooting barbs at each other across the table. And the splendid Michael O'Connor, blissfully unaware of it all.'

'I wouldn't lay bets on that.'

'And unquestionably top of the bill, the *cousine sans peur et sans reproche* herself, cracking down among them like a veritable governess. "I'm ashamed of you!" I quite expected her to rap them over the knuckles and send them upstairs without pudding. And the husband just smiled, and that pretty boy — perfectly ridiculous, *no one's* that pretty — I thought he was going to burst into tears.'

How ugly he looked, she thought, as she had when she first saw him, how unwholesome, how grey; but she thought it, this time, without pleasure. She said nothing.

In the silence, his eyes softened.

'More wine?'

'Yes, please.' She smiled as she proffered her glass; it had not been kind to think of him as ugly, and he was going away in the morning. 'No work tomorrow, so I can get as drunk as I like.'

'No work? What will you do, then, *Susanna mia*?'

'I don't know. Last week, I went to the beach.'

'Skipping along merrily with your bucket and spade?'

'Not exactly skipping, it's a bit like Piccadilly Circus down there.'

'Your favourite London haunt. And was everyone having a wunnerful, wunnerful time?'

'Not everyone.' She had not yet told him about the shooting: the right moment had somehow not arrived. It was probably not the right moment now; but she decided to tell him anyway. 'I saw a man shoot his wife.'

He had raised his glass to drink, but set it down untasted. 'Good God.'

'In a side street.' She was right: it was not the right moment. But then, she suddenly thought, would the moment ever be right? 'There was a lot of blood.'

'I imagine there would be. What a distressing experience.'

'I was rather relieved, actually. Oh, not for the woman, of course. But there is violence here. Passion. It's not all sweetness and light, like you think it is at first.'

'Well.' He smiled. 'Like it was last night, for instance.'

'Oh, well.' What had she hoped to achieve by telling him that, what to make him see, to make him understand? Whatever it was, he had misunderstood: worse, had not even bothered to examine closely enough to decide whether it merited understanding. She took a sip of her wine, distancing herself from him, wondering whether it was the Los Angeles air that presented him in so unattractive a light.

He saw her annoyance, and, perversely, prepared to be more annoying.

'And on Sunday?' he asked. 'Does Michael O'Connor go to Mass? I couldn't help noticing the crucifix over the nuptial bed, so erotic a touch I always think.'

'His mother does,' she snapped. 'We three have a standing engagement to play softball in the park.'

His silence scored higher than her words.

This was wrong. It was not how it should be for them, together for their last evening in this foreign land; they should be drawing closer, not further apart. Suddenly, and most unusually, she felt she could almost cry. She swallowed, lit a cigarette, tried for something they could agree on. *Emma*. Dear, familiar *Emma*, which they both loved, in the same way, for the same reasons. They had barely touched on her work, her so surprisingly productive work this surprising summer. She opened her mouth to talk of Highbury.

'Well,' he said then. 'At least when I go home, I can say I've eaten tofu.'

It was the final straw.

'At least,' she said, as she had never before said to him, 'you've met my cousin. Which is more than I can say about your wife.'

He raised an eyebrow. She wondered what it would be like to shoot him, to watch his face turn pale, and surprised, and then to twist in agony as the messy blood spurted over his pristine white shirt front and dripped down his narrow, well-pressed trousers.

'Would you mind,' he asked, indicating the empty wine bottle, 'if we ordered just a couple more glasses rather than a full bottle? I have to be up quite early for my flight.'

Rick would have preferred to share a bedroom, but Oliver insisted on separate rooms, so he woke up this morning, as every morning, alone. He woke slowly to the sweaty heat of the day, and the sound of Oliver, who always rose first, moving in the kitchen next door, and lay awhile in his tangled sheet, remembering who he was, and where, and why, and finally, what the two matters were that were uppermost on his mind that weekend. One of them was purely pleasant; a tingling certainty that, although nothing definite would be heard until Monday, there had been that in Alan's voice as he bid him goodbye that had told him that, stumbled line, missed cue (but he was allowed some nervousness, was he not?), and all, the part was as good as his. The other was slightly more ambivalent. It was a distinct feeling that had been growing in him over the last couple of weeks that he and Joanna were falling in love.

Rick while growing up had had few doubts about his homosexuality. He had been, by nature, and encouraged by the example of his sisters, a feminine child; and by the time he was old enough to realise that others of both sexes were attracted to his good looks, it was to his own sex that he had perfectly naturally gravitated. He had never questioned it, never wondered why: it was simply the way he was. But who, he asked himself now, was to say that that was how he was meant to be? Joanna was so kind to him, much kinder than Oliver, rejoicing with him over his good news, even defending him against Oliver that other night when they were there for dinner. If he were not homosexual, he was sure he would have fallen in love with her long ago.

And there was another point; a small point, but one which it was as well not to ignore. *The Van Der Meers* was a popular show, widely viewed all over the country: if the part were indeed to go to him, he would become almost immediately rather famous. (Rick, alone in his bed, hugged himself at the prospect.) There were, of course, many famous actors who kept their private lives hidden. But that involved pretence; and would it not be sweet if Rick, when his time came, did not have to pretend? All of life with Joanna would be sweet. Mike was a lucky man.

Meanwhile, it was grossly unfair that he, who everyone said was such a survivor, should this morning be lying in bed listening to Oliver crashing bad-temperedly around the kitchen, brooding almost audibly about Alan (foolish Oliver, who did not even know who his real rival was), while in other houses other people were waking up with Joanna.

The noise from the kitchen grew louder. Oliver disapproved of his staying too late in bed. Rick stretched, shelved his speculations, and prepared to face the day.

It was too hot for a strenuous game of softball. They played for as long as they could, the sweat gathering and trickling down their backs, and then Nancy, up for batting, threw down her bat.

'I've had enough,' she said. 'I can't take any more. Let's go get a drink.'

'Wimp,' said Mike.

'Yeah, Nancy,' agreed Kathy. 'What's the matter with you, you sound like a girl. Walk like a man, talk like a man, walk like a man, my so-o-o-on . . .' She straightened her shoulders, squared her elbows, and loped in from the pitcher's mound.

Rick laughed. 'You make a good man,' he said.

'Thank you,' said Kathy. She had flinched a little on hearing his news, but had congratulated him firmly. 'So do you.'

'We got a lady dying of thirst here,' said Bill. 'Can we get her to a bar, please?'

They piled into cars and drove to a nearby bar, a cool, cavelike interior, with Mexican posters on the whitewashed walls, and saucers of fiery red *salsa* on the table to dip hot *tortilla* chips into. Beer came, icy cold and amber in tall, cold glasses, and Joanna raised hers.

'Here's to good news tomorrow, Rick,' she said, and they all drank. The first draught was gelid paradise.

'How're the kids, Nancy?' asked Kathy.

'Don't ask,' said Nancy. 'Barbara never stops eating, and Alex has decided he wants to be an actor.'

'Put 'em in the Army,' said Mike. 'Straighten 'em up a bit.'

'Oh, right, I can just see Alex in the Army. Have you been in that kid's room lately?'

Rick, sitting next to Joanna, turned to her, quietly. 'Thank you for the toast,' he said.

'Well, let's hope it works out,' she answered.

He moved a little closer to her, cutting the two of them off from the others. 'Oliver's taking it bad, you know.'

'Oh, dear.' She grimaced. 'Is he?'

'Yeah. He's sure that Alan and I . . . you know?'

'Oh, dear.' She watched powerlessly over his shoulder as the general conversation began to drift away from them. But Rick did look so unhappy. 'But he can't seriously be, can he?'

'Yeah. Oh, yeah. You don't know Oliver. And if I get this part, it's going to get even worse, isn't it?'

'Oh, dear,' she repeated. It was, after all, unkind of Oliver so to cloud his success.

'Oh, dear,' he mimicked her, gently. 'Ew dee-ah.' He dropped his voice. 'I might have to move out.'

'I'm not kidding.' Across the table, Mike laid a hand on Bill's shoulder. 'This guy only has to look at a dollar, and it turns into twenty. Why else d'you think Nancy married him?'

'Mike!' said Nancy.

'Ignore him.' Joanna moved slightly away from Rick, entering the general conversation. 'Maybe he'll go away.'

'Now, my own wife,' said Mike, 'married me for pure love.'

'How touching,' said Susan.

'That,' agreed Joanna, 'and his rich friends.'

'I mean it.' Rick nudged her, drawing her attention back to himself. 'If it doesn't get any better, I might have to move back to my own place.'

'Your own place?' This was the first time she had heard of any dwelling of Rick's own.

'You know about my place, don't you?'

'Mike's first words to me,' came Susan's measured voice across the table and into a burst of laughter, 'one rainy Thursday morning on the steps of the British Museum, were, "So *you're* the one who thought *Mr Smith Goes To Washington* was made before *Mr Deeds Goes To Town*."'

'You do know about it,' Rick said, again. 'Don't you?'

'Well, actually,' said Joanna, 'no.'

'Well, what did you think I was, some kind of hanger-on?' He paused, moved back towards her, blocking her again from the others. 'Do *you* think I should move out?'

'Do I . . . Ricky, what a question! How should I know?' Momentarily, she caught Nancy's eye.

'I have an idea,' said Nancy. 'Why don't we all go lie by our pool?'

'What is it with your pool?' said Mike. 'Every time we meet, you try to take us there. You charging an entry fee or something?'

'Nah.' Bill shook his head. 'That's dumb. What we charge is an exit fee. Which, for you, we'll waive.'

'It sounds like a marvellous idea,' said Joanna. 'Doesn't it, Rick?'

'I probably shouldn't get too tan,' said Rick. 'The show's supposed to happen in New York.'

'We have umbrellas,' said Nancy. 'Come on, let's go.'

'I don't think I'll come,' said Kathy. 'I haven't finished my drink.'

'Oh, go on,' said Joanna. 'Don't be so unsociable.'

'I haven't finished my drink,' she repeated. 'You guys go on, I might look in on you later.'

'Oh, Kathy.'

'Oh, Joanna.' She smiled. 'I'm OK, I promise. I like it here.'

'I don't think I'll come, either,' said Susan. Enough of Nancy and Bill was, after all, enough. 'Would you drop me at the beach, please?'

How Californian she was growing, it struck her, not only accepting favours, but actually asking for them.

'Stay and have a drink,' said Kathy. 'I'll drop you.'

Susan considered: she had, until then, been perfectly happy in the bar. 'All right.' she said. 'Thank you.'

As the others left, Kathy looked after them wistfully.

'They are such good people,' she said. 'Nancy and Bill. I wish I could be that good.'

'Do you?' said Susan. 'I don't.'

'No.' Kathy looked at her. 'No, you probably don't. Listen, I've had enough beer, how about a margarita?'

They ordered from a stocky waiter who smiled at them with a gold tooth, and sat back to wait.

'Nervous without your cousin?' said Kathy.

'Hardly,' said Susan.

'Hawdly. Well, I would be, all alone in a foreign country. When I first met you, I didn't think you were at all like her, but now I think you are, a bit.'

'Thank you. We were sorry you didn't come on Thursday.'

'In-choy.' The waiter set down the drinks and scurried off.

'I meant to,' said Kathy. She drank with gusto. 'That's good, a real drink. I wanted to meet your friend. But when it came to it, I was too depressed, you know? I wouldn't have been any fun. He still here?'

'No.' Susan tasted her own drink, icy, salty, puckering with lime. 'No, he left yesterday morning.'

'Pity. He enjoy himself?'

'Quite. It was a business trip really.'

'He's married, isn't he?' she said suddenly.

Susan looked at her in surprise.

'Sorry.' She shook her head. 'Sorry, I shouldn't have spoken. I just . . . Oh, shit.'

She had knocked her drink over; it flowed in a sticky stream over the table and on to the reddish stone floor.

'Shit,' she repeated, as the waiter ran over with a damp cloth. 'Shit, shit. Yes, another, please. Did I splash you? Sorry, I'm just real nervous today.'

'It's all right,' said Susan. She had seen what was about to happen, and had moved out of the way in time.

'You ever get days like that? You don't look like you do, but I guess you must.'

'We all have them.'

'I guess.' Her drink arrived, and she attacked it with enthusiasm. Susan watched her, wondering how politely to lighten the conversation. It was an unfortunate side effect of being Joanna's cousin that Joanna's friends tended to unburden themselves to her, and in England she was skilled at discouraging the tendency. But these people were foreign, she did not quite follow the rhythm of their speech, could not quite command the flow of their conversation.

'Nice drink,' she attempted.

'Yeah.' But it was wrong and too late: Susan wished she had gone straight to the beach after all. 'Rick doesn't help, you know.'

'I'm sorry?'

'Rick. You know, sitting around preening about that part.' She drank again. Although she had had a healthy amount of the first glass, the level of liquid in her second was already lower than Susan's. 'I mean, it's not the sort of thing I'd have wanted to do anyway — Jesus, can you imagine what it must be like? —although I probably would, because you do, don't you?'

Susan did not attempt a reply. Kathy, evidently taking her silence for encouragement, went on.

'It's just that it's what he wanted.' On the table was a small basket of toothpicks. She picked one out and began systematically to shred it. 'And he got it. And he wanted Oliver, and he got him. And I'm a nicer person than he is, and I don't get anything I want, and it's not fair.'

'But,' despite herself, Susan could not help pointing out, 'you wouldn't have wanted Oliver either.' A thought struck her. 'Or would you?'

'God, no!' She threw her toothpick down; then picked it up

again. 'Well, now I think of it, yeah. Oh, not Oliver *Oliver*, you know, but wouldn't Rick just fall in love with someone who was secure, and available, and fell in love with him . . . Listen.' She lifted her glass again with a hand that shook: she was, it seemed, less accustomed to hard spirits than was Susan. 'I'm sorry I brought it up about your friend, your married friend, but the reason I did is that I'm kind of in the same situation myself.'

By now, Susan could have been at the beach, and alone.

'Really?' she said.

'Well, obviously, I don't really know what your situation is, but I've been kind of seeing a married man, and,' she looked away, 'it's getting kind of serious. Another drink?'

'I was going to the beach.'

'It's too hot and too crowded.' She caught the waiter's eye. 'Two more, please.' She turned back to Susan. 'It's no life, is it? Being the other woman?'

'Isn't it?' said Susan.

But Kathy missed her tone. 'How long have you known your friend?'

It was none of Kathy's damned business how long she had known her friend. But the waiter was already bringing the drinks from the bar, and there would be no escape until they were finished.

'Five years,' she said.

'And can you stand it?'

'Actually, it works out rather well.'

'It does? Jesus, you must be made of iron. I . . . Oh, thanks.' The drinks were on the table and she gulped eagerly at hers. Susan addressed her own with an appetite: not having chosen a second margarita, she nevertheless intended fully to enjoy it.

'You think you're so tough, don't you?' said Kathy. 'You think you've got it all figured out, think you'll just have a little fling, know what you're letting yourself in for, won't really change anything. But, of course, it doesn't work out that way.

Except for the guys it does, and that's not really fair, either. Do you know your friend's wife?'

'No.'

'Never met her?'

'No.'

'Don't you want to?'

Susan shrugged.

'Well, that's probably better. I know my guy's wife quite well. Well, I mean, really well. I mean, she's a friend, she's a terrific person. I love her.'

Susan said nothing.

'I *do*. And I don't feel badly about screwing her husband, because they've been together ever since I've known him, and in fact, this sounds crazy, but it was being married to such a nice lady that was one of the things that turned me on to him in the first place. Is that a really dumb thing to say?'

'Probably not.'

'You know what really gets me? It's that I don't feel jealous of him with her, I really don't. I mean, if I was her, and I knew about us, I'd kill both of us, but I don't know if she knows or not, and anyway, I don't have the right to feel that, right? Not about them. Not about anyone. But a couple of days ago, I saw him with another woman. Not me, not her, someone else. And it killed me. It really killed me. Isn't that something? I'm cheating on his wife, and then I get mad when he cheats on me. I mean, on her, but not with me. It wasn't supposed to be like that.'

'I'm sure it happens all the time,' said Susan.

'It's shit,' said Kathy. 'Shit.' The toothpick was in pieces, and she reached for another. 'I wasn't supposed to fall in love with him. He's not in love with me, and I don't even know if he's in love with his wife, he seems to be, although he cheats on her a lot.' She gulped again at her rapidly disappearing drink. 'I wonder if she knows. I've never been able to figure it out. You think she can't possibly, and then you think to yourself, she can't possibly not.' She frowned at the shreds of wood on the table, and then looked up at Susan. 'Do *you* think she knows?'

'Who?' said Susan.

'Well, Joanna, of course. Shit.' She grimaced. 'Hadn't you guessed I was talking about Mike?'

Susan, who had raised her glass, set it down untasted. Mike cheated on Joanna. Mike cheated on the woman with whom he cheated on Joanna.

'You hadn't,' said Kathy. 'Well, I'm glad I've done such a good job of hiding it, then. But the truth, if you must know, the truth is that I've been pretty much in love with him for about a year now. And I knew he wasn't in love with me, because he's married to Joanna, and that was OK, well, it wasn't OK, it was pretty much hell, really, but I always sort of thought I was second best, and I was getting on OK, living with that. And then I saw him leaving the studio with her, and I thought, maybe I'm not second best at all, maybe I'm third, fourth, seventeenth best, and I don't know that I can take that. And I can't even ask, because if you're not first best, it doesn't matter what you are, anyway, does it? I mean, is the guy in love with Joanna? And would he be in love with me if Joanna weren't around? And I'm damned sure he's not in love with *her*, but she was the one he was leaving the studio with. God, life's confusing, isn't it?'

Susan said nothing. It had darted through her, with the speed of the arrow that darted through Emma Woodhouse that day, that Mike must be in love with no one but herself.

'How long's she been here, anyway?' said Mike.

'Two? Two and a half weeks.' Joanna, stretched by the pool in a swimsuit borrowed from Nancy, kicked lazily at the blue water. 'It's really nice to have her here. And she seems to be enjoying herself, which is nice. Alex, cut it out.'

Alex had sent a spray of water splashing over her; he swam, guffawing, to the other end of the pool.

'Does she enjoy herself?' said Nancy. 'Every time I'm at your place, she's locked in that garage, working. Alex, if you can't behave like a human being, go inside.'

'She likes working,' said Joanna. 'Always has. She's a worker of the world. Like Mike.'

'She works up a storm,' said Mike. 'There's this like cloud of concentration hanging over the place. Now, my wife here hates to work.'

'Not true,' said Joanna. 'I love teaching.'

'Sure you love it, you get to spend half the year lying on the sofa watching game shows on TV.'

'Yes, I adore game shows. And I'm usually eating bon-bons, at the same time.'

'Right. Keep forgetting those bon-bons.'

'I've never seen Joanna watch a game show,' said Rick from the shade.

'Thank you, Rick.' She splashed water at Mike. 'At least someone appreciates me.'

'Joanna's a teacher,' chanted Alex. 'God made the bees, the bees make honey; we work hard, and the teachers get the money.'

'Alex, that's enough,' said Nancy. She jerked an authoritarian head. 'Go inside, see what Barbara's eating, and tell her to stop.' She waited until he had splashed indoors before she relaxed her face. 'Barbara'll be excited at your news, Rick, she's a big *Van Der Meers* fan.'

'Barbara!' scoffed Bill. 'You mean, you are.'

'Only when Jack Wordsworth's on. Hey, this means you'll be working with him, right?'

'Ooh! Ooh!' Raising his voice to a falsetto, Bill clasped his hands to his heart. 'Brett Van Der Meer!'

'Beautiful Brett,' squeaked Mike.

'Darling Jack.'

'That reminds me.' Carefully ignoring them, Nancy turned to Joanna. 'Those videos, that special Cary Grant package, I got it. Come over one day next week, and we'll watch them.'

'Smashing. I'll bring the bon-bons. Which films are they, anyway?'

'I told you. Cary Grant films.'

'Jesus.' Bill shook his head at Mike. 'The women we married.'


It had happened, the unthinkable, the inevitable. The part was Rick's. Alan called him early on Monday morning, person-ally, before he had even spoken to his agent, and told him what to expect: things, it seemed, in television moved fast. He was to report to the studio the next day for wardrobe fittings; rehearsals began at the end of the week; within the month, he would be known all across the country as Rick Morrison of *The Van Der Meers*. He sat at the breakfast table, nursing his coffee cup, his lungs and heart and stomach cosily aglow with joy.

'Well,' said Oliver. 'You're really on your way, then.'

The glow dimmed just a little. 'You might,' said Rick, 'at least try to sound pleased.'

'I am pleased, of course I am. You're going to be Rick Morrison, the famous actor, whom I once knew when he was poor and struggling. Why shouldn't I be pleased?'

'Oliver!'

'I'm sorry.' Oliver sipped at his own coffee. Oliver was not always unkind to him, had, in fact, on occasion been very kind indeed. 'Believe it or not, I am sorry. How about we start again? You got the part? Great! Terrific, congratulations, I always knew you had it in you.'

'Thanks.' The glow returned full force, and for the joy of it, he prepared to go through it one more time. 'See, Alan as good as told me I had it on Friday, but he couldn't confirm it. But I knew he'd pull it off. I have a feeling Alan pulls off most things he wants to.'

Which, he realised too late, was foolish, foolish.

'Ah, yes,' said Oliver. 'Alan. I'm quite sure he does manage to pull things off, and how is he anyway, did your agent happen to mention?'

Rick sighed. 'He's fine. And you know perfectly well that that was him on the telephone.'

'That was Alan!' Oliver gave an exaggerated start of surprise. 'But surely it's more usual in these cases for the agent to break the glad tidings?'

'Well, in this case it was Alan. Oliver, I keep telling you you don't have to worry about him.'

'Now why would I worry about him? Simply because this is the guy you're going to be working with day in, day out, the guy whose tongue just happens to hit the carpet every time you flash your lovely brown eyes at him . . .'

It was true, he could not but know it, could not but take pleasure in it. He tried not to grin, not to blush. 'I can't help that,' he said.

'Of course you can't. Well.' He replaced his coffee cup neatly in its saucer and stood up. 'I have to finish that article.'

Oliver had not published an article since Rick had known him. Where his money came from was a mystery — not that, since he never seemed to be short of it, Rick had ever particularly thought to enquire. He described himself as a journalist, but apart from half a dozen pieces — a guide to Sonoma County wineries, a review of a gay theatre festival — in magazines no longer new in the bookcase, there was small evidence of it. All there was was the closing of the study door, coldly exclusive, a sign that he wanted to be alone and, especially, to be alone away from Rick.

'I think I'll call Joanna,' said Rick now, as Oliver made for the study. 'Maybe take her to lunch to celebrate.'

'Do,' said Oliver vaguely before he disappeared.

Rick sat for a while, watching the closed door, and feeling the hot coffee and the hot joy inside him. Poor Oliver, he thought, again. Getting himself all excited over someone who didn't really matter, and at the same time handing his real rival to Rick on a plate.

★

The weekend was over, and at last, Mike could allow himself to start editing. He slouched alone in the wide projection room, watching hour after hour of the same slight story, angle after angle of the same scene, Kathy's face, Kathy's hands, Kathy's body, walking, stopping, talking, crying, all with the wide, cruel afternoon desert behind her, and the remorselessly blue sky above. It was a bleak film. All Mike's films were bleak, which often surprised those who had met him socially, but there it was; as cheerful as his life's experiences had so far left him, there was yet that in his Irish soul, which, even after all these generations, still eschewed gaiety, craved pain, and sorrow, and tears, and this was the part of him that was his film maker's vision. Even so, this was a particularly gloomy effort. Kathy said it was his gloomiest yet.

Perhaps, thought half his mind, as the other half, riveted to the screen, intently compared long shots, sorted close-ups, he should lighten up just a little for the next, force in a single strand of joy, if only to emphasise the desolation of the rest. It would be months, of course, before he could even begin seriously to think of the next project; but already, and especially since he had met Celia, embryonic ideas were drifting through his brain, like the tumbleweeds that had drifted through the filming of *Marina*. Structure would be more important next time, he decided, and irony, an East Coast irony, even a European, like Susan's. How different physically was Susan from Joanna, he suddenly thought, a shot of Kathy's stumbling dusty legs bringing to his mind's eye both Susan's brown severity and his wife's lush curves, grand-daughters of the same seed, but different, so different. Perhaps there was a movie in that.

The door of the projection room opened, shut, someone came in and sat next to him. It was Celia. She raised a hand in greeting, but did not speak; was, in fact, an impressively non-intrusive presence as he ran reel after reel, reran, made notes, reran again, while again and again, Kathy's face, Kathy's legs,

Kathy's voice, Kathy's sighs, Kathy's sobs filled the darkened room. At length, he switched off the machine, stood up, turned the lights on, and stretched mightily.

She watched with unconcealed admiration the play of the muscles under his greyed T-shirt.

'Nice stuff,' she said.

He grunted. He was by no means sure that he wanted her here, grafting her desirable self on to the train of his thoughts, disrupting the pattern of his morning's concentration.

'Someone told me you were in here,' she said. 'If you'd minded, you should have said.'

'No, that's OK,' he said. Her behaviour had been faultless. 'Don't you have work to do?'

'Somebody cancelled an appointment. My next isn't till 3.00. Buy a girl lunch?'

'Uh-uh.' Tall and slim and dark as she was, his mind and body today belonged to *Marina*. They left the projection room; she watched while he shut and locked the door.

'I'm going for a drive,' he said. 'Clear my head.'

'Where are you going?'

'Home. Pick up a sandwich. Maybe say hi to my wife. Want to come?'

'I don't think so.'

They walked together through the dark corridor.

'That Kathy,' he said. 'She is hot. Hot.'

She looked at him sideways in the gloom.

'You think so?' she said.

'You saw her.'

'What do I know?'

'Know it. She's good.'

She shrugged. 'If you say so. I've been looking at some figures, we have more money than I'd thought.'

'Congratulations.'

'I'll be talking to your agent soon. I'm sure you could find some way to use a bigger budget.'

A bigger budget. A bit more time; a slightly more elaborate

setting; extra actors; possibly an assistant for post-production. So he was on his way then. He sighed.

'Yes,' he said regretfully. 'Yes, I guess I could.'


Susan laid down her Biro, and with it all pretence of working, leaving Emma — since she had been looking at a late portion of the book — to her misery, while she herself concentrated on her own. She had looked at the situation from all angles, and try as she might, could reach no other conclusion but that which had struck her the previous day. She was in love with her cousin's husband.

That it was real love was beyond question. Never having been in love before — no, not even with Felix, she now realised, as cavalierly as she had assumed that what she felt for him was what most people meant by the term — she recognised it here, unconditionally, as a mother knows the freak to which she has given birth, as the woman on the beach had received the bullet that killed her. It was love: not the frothy, flighty thing that some women knew, it had nothing to do with bunches of flowers, with pretty dresses, with moon, spoon, June, and all the joyous paraphernalia that songwriters must have plucked from somewhere to sing to the majority of people. This was Susan's version of love, the only version she knew; it was painful, it was not pretty, and it would be with her for ever. She loved Mike.

How and when it had happened, she had no idea: at a look of mutual amusement that had passed between them, perhaps, or perhaps during one of those evenings when they had both stumbled, work-numbed, into the twilight under the jacaranda tree. Perhaps she had been always in love with him, even since that London morning of rain and illuminated manuscripts, perhaps it had been with her always, a precious secret she had kept even from herself, that only the last weeks' contact had forced her to acknowledge. She did not know, would never know, and the knowledge anyway would have brought no comfort. She loved the man who belonged to Joanna.

But that, as she had known for the last twenty-four hours, was the point, was the surprisingly left open door through which these new feelings had so surprisingly rushed. He did not belong to Joanna after all. He belonged to Joanna, and to Kathy, and to still another woman, to, possibly, as Kathy had hinted, many other women. He was on the open market, a philanderer, fair game. Joanna was married to a philanderer.

The question she could not escape, that even though her desolation fascinated and slightly appalled her, was, how far was Joanna aware of Mike's behaviour? She could not, as Kathy herself had suggested, Kathy with whom Susan had suddenly so much in common, not know. Could she? But then again, she could not, surely, in human self respect, simply know, and do nothing. Could she? Were Susan married to Mike, or even involved with Mike . . .

But that, at least, was one cold consolation in this sorry state of affairs. She was not, and would never be, involved with Mike. True, he obviously liked her. He was affectionate towards her, appeared always pleased to see her, listened and responded to most of the things she said, teased her with a gentle, and wholly charming, flirtatiousness. But so he treated most women, even his mother, even, good God, Nancy. As a potential love object, he was about as aware of her as he was of a fly on the wall, a hummingbird in the tree.

And how much better it was that it was so. Because it was one thing to appropriate the husband of an anonymously dowdy woman in an Oxford suburb; but to do the same to her earliest friend and closest living relative . . . and yet it was Mike who was involved, Mike whom she suddenly realised she desired, Mike whom, given the opportunity, she — selfish Susan, who had so rarely not taken what she wanted — would unquestionably, unquestioningly, take for her own. So that it was as well that she was not to be given the opportunity.

She could, of course, leave. She could pack up today, catch

the evening flight back to London, and stay with a neighbour, or a colleague with a spare room, or even Aunt Betty,
who, she knew, would be delighted to have her. But then
again, she reflected drearily, what difference would it make?
There would be no escape there, thoughts of Mike would
only follow her, as they would follow her wherever she
went. Susan had recognised this love for a bare day; but even
so, she knew it was hers, her, she knew she would be marked
with it for life. For the rest of her life. No, there would be no
escape in London. So she might as well stay here, while she
could, here where at least she could see him, speak to him.
And *Emma* was going so well here, and it would be a pity to
disturb it. And it was not as if she posed any extra threat to
Joanna's marriage.

But she could not help reflecting, as she returned to her
notes, on what a different book it would have been if it had
been John, instead of George, Knightley with whom Emma
had fallen in love.


It was curious, she thought later at suppertime, how things
could change so utterly, and yet remain so utterly the same.
Here they all were, sitting around the same kitchen table,
eating the same sort of food, making the same sort of jokes as
they had every other evening, with the only obvious difference in the world being that since Joanna had been out to
lunch, the meal was somewhat later than usual. And yet,
knowing what Susan now knew, of herself, and of Mike, and
of Joanna, it would never be the same again.

'The service in this place is terrible,' said Mike. 'Don't get to
eat till nearly midnight because the cook's been out to lunch
with television stars.'

Joanna set the salad bowl on the table, and slid down behind
her plate of plump shark. 'If you know a better hole,' she said,
'go to it.'

'Nah.' Mike shovelled a healthy forkful of fish into his

mouth. 'Get my kicks being kept waiting by a friend of the famous.'

'What an interesting condition,' said Susan. 'Have you told the medical journals?' She sounded the same herself. But she had sounded the same after her parents had died, for that full year, she had sounded so much the same that those who had not known about it had not even suspected that anything unusual had happened. She had the gift for concealment.

'Rick was funny,' said Joanna. She was still flushed, and had about her a faint, sweet smell of champagne. She pushed her too long hair back from her forehead. 'I told him to wait till his first pay check came in, but he insisted, he had to do it today. He's so excited about it, he's like a little kid.'

'He's growing up, then,' mumbled Mike.

'Oh, don't be so rotten about him, he's really very nice, you know. And I did feel a bit sorry for him . . .'

'Now, there's a novelty,' interjected Susan.

'Shut up, the pair of you.' She shook her head. 'I did feel sorry, and you can both stop sniggering because I'm going to finish this, I did feel sorry, because here he was, it was his big day, and where was Oliver?'

'Susan,' said Mike. 'Where was Oliver?'

'I give up,' said Susan. 'Where *was* Oliver?'

'Well, Oliver wasn't there,' said Joanna, 'that's where Oliver wasn't, and I think it was mean of him, because he should have been. There. It should have been him, not me. Poor Rick.'

'Yes,' said Mike. 'He's had a rough couple of days.'

'Oh, well, if you're both determined to be so funny.' She helped herself to more salad. 'But listen, Susan, I meant to ask you, how was Kathy about it? She was so nice when he told her, but if it had been me, I'd have wanted to kill.'

'Well,' said Susan, 'she seemed a bit fed up. With life.' She looked at Mike, but could read no expression in his eyes.

'She's having a bad time,' nodded Joanna. 'There's some

man around who's messing her up. It's such a shame, because she's so sweet. She deserves someone lovely.'

'She's a good kid,' agreed Mike.

'Kid! I hate that expression, Mike, she's not a kid. She's thirty years old.'

'OK,' said Mike. 'She's a good crone, then.'

'Honestly, you men!' Joanna turned to Susan for support, but Susan's eyes were fixed on her plate.

Again, with that strange suddenness, Joanna was struck by that irritation with Susan, Susan who if she only had a normal relationship with a reasonably acceptable man, would be meeting her gaze, would be exchanging smiles, shakes of the head, rolls of the eyes. But it was not to be. She was wedded to her little portion of the insufferable Felix as firmly as Joanna was wedded to Mike: they two would never laugh together over their men as once they had over parents, and teachers, and Girl Guide leaders.

'Aren't we getting old,' she said.

'Been there for years,' Mike reminded her.

'You may have. It's my birthday at the end of the month. Another year gone.'

Susan looked up at last from her plate. 'What are you going to do?' she asked.

'Have a day off,' suggested Mike. 'You've earned it.'

Was Joanna imagining an edge to his voice?

'I think you're jealous,' she said. 'Because I'm having a lovely lazy summer doing nothing. Let's see, what shall I do? Will you take a day off, Susan, and do it with me?'

'If I can,' said Susan. 'What about you, Mike?'

'Him?' Joanna snorted. 'My last birthday, he was locked in the studio till 9.00 at night, and came staggering in, cross-eyed, and belching up that disgusting Cola stuff.'

'Some of us,' said Mike, 'have to work. Even in the summer. Even on our wife's birthday.'

'Well.' Joanna shrugged defeat, and turned to the happy thought. 'What shall we do? We could go up the Coast, or . . .

no, I know.' A sudden inspiration struck her. 'I'll have a party.'

Mike groaned. 'You just gave a party. For Rick.'

'No, I mean a proper party. In the garden, with balloons and music and lots of people.' Enough people, in fact, to make it inconspicuous if James were of their number. After all, Felix had gone, and Susan would still be there for two weeks afterwards. 'Lots of people,' she repeated firmly.


The next afternoon, she set about making telephone calls. Nancy and Bill would love to come to the party; Kathy's machine was on, which was unfortunate, since she had been hoping to speak to her personally, but she left a message, anyway. Oliver told her that since Rick was at a wardrobe fitting, he could not speak for him, but that he himself would be delighted to attend. As always, his manner towards her was charming; as always, his voice impassive. But there was that, lurking at the back of his tone, which made her, unexpectedly, forgive him for his behaviour of the previous day, made her, even, putting the telephone down, wonder, briefly, what had prompted it. Then she telephoned Eileen.

'Are you busy?' She did not usually telephone her mother-in-law at work, but this was a call that could only be made during the daytime.

'No more than frantic.' Eileen's voice betrayed a momentarily elderly quaver. 'Something wrong, honey?'

'God, no!' Joanna assured her. 'Absolutely not. No, I wanted to invite you to a party.'

'A party.' Her voice firmed, became young again. 'Well, that's nice. When?'

'A week from Friday, my birthday, you know. Just to let you know to keep the date free, before your other beaux come battering on your door. Although, if you want to bring Dr Weintraub, do.'

'I might just at that, young lady, to embarrass you.'

'Do!' She paused. 'Oh, Eileen?'

'Yes?'

'Why don't you invite your friend James, too?'

There was a silence.

'Really?'

'Bugger Susan. It's my birthday, and I liked him.'

'Well, fine.' There was a faint noise in the background. 'In fact, he's here now, why don't you ask him yourself?' Her voice receded slightly. 'James, there's someone here wants to talk to you.'

This was not what she had planned: if he had decided never voluntarily to speak to her or her family again — and remembering some of the expressions on Susan's face, she could not altogether blame him — she had infinitely rather hear it through Eileen. But Eileen's voice had already been succeeded by another, male and questioning.

'Hello?'

'Hello, James.' She paused, wishing herself elsewhere. 'It's Joanna, Eileen's daughter-in-law, you know?'

'Oh. Hi.'

His voice had warmed, which was encouraging. She plunged on. 'I'm having a party in a couple of weeks, and I wondered if you'd like to come?'

She shut her eyes, crossed her fingers, and hoped. If he rejected her outright, she could not blame him; if he was actually rude, she would make herself toast and honey.

'That'd be great,' he said.

She opened her eyes, and expelled her breath.

'Really?' she asked.

'Really. I haven't been invited to too many parties here . . . Will your cousin be there?'

'Susan? Yes, she'll be here for another month or so.'

'Good! I enjoyed talking to her, you know. She's so funny.'

Alone in the living room, Joanna emitted a silent whoop of joy.

'In fact,' he continued, 'I was wondering, if I could get my courage up, if I might call her and ask her to dinner. What do you think?'

What did she think!

'Well,' she said casually, 'you could always try.'

She put the telephone down, and, in imitation of Mike, raised a clenched fist of victory in the air. Then she lowered it, remembering Susan. But Susan could not truly prefer even what Joanna had seen of Felix to even what they had both seen of James: it was preposterous, inconceivable. If only she would give James a chance. Give herself a chance.

A car's engine stopped, a door slammed, footsteps hurried up the path, and it was Rick.

'Enter,' he announced dramatically, 'Mister Cary Grant.' He pranced through the living room, head held high, like a model. 'Fresh from his wardrobe fitting, which he completed in record time, because he has such a perfect body, it was no trouble to fit him at all.'

Joanna laughed. 'Come and have some tea, Cary,' she said. She led him into the kitchen, found iced tea in the refrigerator and cookies in a jar, while he followed, bubbling with excitement.

'It was great! Just great. They kept saying how handsome I was, and how tall, and what great bones I had, and Alan was there, and he's really pleased, *really* pleased I've got the part, and hey, that old hooker who plays my mother was there too, and she was just drooling over me, it's a bit sick, she's over fifty, you know.' But he did not look sickened. 'And I have a script here, look, and I have to learn my lines, not too many of them this week, thank God, and rehearsals start on Friday — rehearsals, can you believe it? — and they're going to do a paragraph about me in *TV Guide*, and oh, Joanna, isn't it great?'

She smiled at him over her tea, but something was preventing her from fully joining in his glee. Then she remembered Oliver's voice: it was quite possible that Rick was not even aware that he might be hurting him.

'Have you told Oliver all this?' she asked.

'Oliver?' His smile faded: he dropped to a chair, and raised his glass to her. 'Why should I tell him? He doesn't give a shit what I do.'

'Oh, don't say that, Ricky. Of course he does.'

'Does not, either. He's been writing another dumb article the last two days, hasn't said a word to me.'

'Well, I spoke to him this morning, and he sounded rather upset.'

He frowned. 'Why were you talking to Oliver?'

'We do speak occasionally, you know, if it's all right with you. Actually, I was inviting you both to my birthday party, a week from Friday, so don't forget. But listen.'

'Your birthday!' He jerked upright. 'I didn't know. What do you want?'

'Oh, don't be daft. Rick, about Oliver.'

But he had shut his eyes, and was counting on his fingers. 'You're another Leo, then. No, you're not, you're Virgo. Well, that's OK, we're supposed to get on. What sign's Mike?'

'Will you shut up about birthdays!' She had used her schoolmistress tone; and the tone, if not the words, had finally reached him. He stopped talking, and looked at her expectantly: sometimes, it was disturbingly like dealing with one of her pupils. 'I want,' she continued, 'to talk about Oliver.'

'Well,' said Rick, 'I don't.'

'Rick! He really did sound quite lonely and miserable, you know. I think he's feeling a bit left out.'

'Good.' He reached for a cookie.

No, she decided, he should not be allowed to carry on like this. 'It's not good, and you know it. Listen.'

'No, I won't listen. I'm sick of listening about Oliver. I'm sick of Oliver. I don't need him any more. You listen yourself.' He looked at her over his cookie, his eyes dark, watchful, the childishness quite gone from them.

'What?'

'I might move out.'

'Oh.' Oh dear, she thought, oh dear. 'Don't talk like that.'

'I mean it. I might.'

'Ricky.' But gay relationships were not, she knew, as heterosexual: the best of them were rarely expected to last as she expected her marriage to last. And that between Rick and Oliver was all too far from the best. 'Is it really that bad?'

'Really.' He was still watching her, that curious expression still in his eyes. 'How would *you* feel?' he asked. 'If I moved out?'

'Me?' she said. 'Don't be so silly, it's not up to me, is it?'

'But how would you feel?'

His eyes were still on her, and he waited for an answer. She thought about it, and tried to think honestly.

'Sorry,' she said finally. 'I'd be sorry.'

'Only sorry?'

'Only?' He obviously wanted more; so she thought more. 'Well, obviously, if — if, mind you, *if* it was what was best in the long run, then I'd agree that's what you had to do.' He was still waiting. 'And of course, you know I'd always love you, no matter what happened.'

Which at last seemed to satisfy him, so they returned to the story of his wardrobe fitting.


They were still there when Mike came home, laughing over their tea as Rick imitated the wardrobe master, paying outrageous court to the woman who would play Rick's mother while surreptitiously slipping Rick his telephone number.

'So this,' he said, tramping thick-headed into the centre of the levity, 'is the man who's leading my wife astray.'

Rick, caught in the middle of his imitation, looked up at him, startled.

'Taking her to lunch, getting her drunk on champagne.' He took the next to last cookie, leaving the last lying sad and alone on the wide plate. 'What's for dinner?'

'Nothing.' Joanna raised her face for a kiss. 'I thought that since last night was such a terrible experience for you, we'd eat out tonight instead.' She turned to Rick. 'I was an hour late with dinner, and you'd have thought he was the entire Third World.'

'So tonight we go out. My wife the millionairess.'

'Anyway, I think we should be taking Susan out a bit more.'

He pointed an accusing finger at Rick. 'Your fault,' he said. 'Teaching her expensive habits.'

He took the last cookie, and went into the garden, dropping on to the sun lounger as their two mingled laughters followed him from the kitchen. Beneath his grumbles lay, in fact, genuine annoyance. Food was important to Mike, and while he did not too much mind on occasion eating later than usual, or at a restaurant instead of at home, he did, when those occasions arose, like to be given notice of them if possible. It was not, of course, reasonable to expect a regularly run household when Joanna was at work all day; but the fact was that right now, she was not at work, she was at home. At home and doing, openly, very little. And that annoyed him more than anything else.

Just what he had hoped she might do with her summer, he could not precisely say. Paint, perhaps; but she had done so little of that lately, and besides, she herself had pointed out that with Susan here, it was scarcely feasible. Housework; but the house was so small, and she had always done most of that anyway. But he knew that most people did do things with their time. He himself, finished with one project, would immediately start a new one; his mother, widowed, her children grown, was devoted to the hospital; even Nancy had her classes. But on the other hand, maybe he should count his blessings: at least Joanna did not occupy her time with prying into his hours away from her.

The garage door opened, and Susan, a walking counterpoint to her cousin, stalked stiffly out, to drop on to the hot grass at his feet, and turn her face to the sun. He laid a bare, broad foot on her thin, bare leg.

'Gettin' brown,' he commented. She was almost as brown as he, he noticed, but not with his masculine leatheriness; it was more a honey with the faintest tint of lemon, that lent a sparkle to her teeth and blue to the whites of her heavy-lidded, unmade-up eyes.

'So it seems.' She lowered her eyes to look down the length of her body. 'Emma would think I was a gypsy.'

He grunted, comfortably, and they fell into an end of the day silence that was broken by two laughs from the kitchen.

'Who's that?'

'Rick.'

'Oh.' She lowered her voice. 'How is he?'

'Doing great. And we're going out to dinner. To a restaurant. Joanna says we don't appreciate her enough.'

'Don't we? Well, that'll be nice, anyway, a bit of local colour.'

Joanna was right, he thought. They could be taking Susan out a bit more.

'We haven't shown you round much, have we?'

'Well, I did go out a bit when I first arrived. And since then I haven't wanted to, actually. I can't really think of anything like relaxing till I've finished this blessed introduction. Till then, I'm just a . . . a working stiff, is that it?'

He nodded his approval. 'Coming along.'

She stretched, yawned.

'But what I would like to do, one day, is go to Hollywood. I've been here so long, and haven't even seen the Hollywood sign yet: I'm beginning to feel a bit of an ass.'

'Ass.' He laughed. 'I wouldn't say that in mixed company around here.'

She frowned: then blushed faintly, and smiled. He watched her in enjoyment: he had never seen her blush before.

'Hey,' he said. 'You should come and see *Marina*. Soon.'

'Thank you,' she said. Her skin returned to its normal colour. 'I'd like that.'

157

'Right. Take a few hours off, if you can, see the real Hollywood. Some poor sucker tearing his brains out, trying to make a movie.' He yawned. 'God, it's killing me.'

'You work a lot, don't you?' she said. 'I mean, Joanna never mentions you being out of work, like most people here seem to be.'

'I guess I do. Yeah, I guess I do. Knock on wood.' As he reached behind him to the jacaranda tree, he thought of Celia, not Celia the rambling rose, but Celia the business-woman. He had not yet mentioned Celia to Joanna; but Susan had asked, and Joanna was in there laughing with Rick. And they were going to a restaurant. 'Listen, don't mention this to Joanna, or anyone, but I might just have the backer for my next.'

'Really?' Her face lit up. 'But that's marvellous!'

'Yeah, well, it's still up in the air. But they're more dentists, and I think they may have more money to throw around than Mac and his pack. Hell, think, I know they do. So if it came off, it'd be a bigger operation all round. And they'd still let me do what I wanted. Goin' up in the world, cousin.'

'You don't sound very excited about it.'

'Don't I?' She was sharp, was Joanna's cousin. 'No, I guess I don't. It's just . . .' He paused, then decided to confide in her. 'This may sound crazy, but I'd be kind of sad to leave all the boring stuff behind. *Is* that crazy?'

'When I was a child,' she said, 'I hated maths. Hated it. Boring. Tedious. I mean, who cared what $x$ equalled to the point of $\gamma$? But, you know, I've never in my life — in my *life* — had quite so much pleasure from reading as I did on those evenings when I'd open a good book straight after my maths homework.'

'You both look serious.' Joanna came towards them, a glass of wine in her hand, Rick trailing behind her. She gave the glass to Susan. 'For the wandering scholar. I thought I heard your voice.'

'Joanna.' Susan took the glass gratefully, and drank from

it. 'You are a *cousine sans peur et sans reproche*. Mike says we don't appreciate you enough.'

'Uh-uh. I said *she* said we didn't appreciate her enough. Different thing.'

'Well, I'm glad you cleared that up, Mike, we couldn't have her confused about that, could we? Susan, this came for you.'

She handed her an envelope, with Felix's handwriting and a Maine postmark. He must have written it on the plane, and mailed it during the stopover. Susan took it, postponed wondering what was in it, and slipped it into the pocket of her shorts.

'He also says,' she said, 'if I understand him correctly, that we're going out for dinner.'

'Well done, Mike! You see, you two *can* communicate when you try.'

'Can I come too?' said Rick.

Susan and Mike exchanged alarmed glances; but Joanna was in control.

'I don't think you should, Ricky,' she said.

He stuck out his lower lip; not for the first time, Susan wondered how Joanna stood him.

'Why not?' he said.

'You know perfectly well why not,' said Joanna. 'You've got to go back to Oliver.'

'Oh, Joanna.'

'And now that you mention it,' she continued, 'I think you should go now. Go on, shoo.'

'Joanna!'

But she hustled him down the drive and into his car. Then she returned to the garden.

'I don't know what to do with him,' she complained.

'Have a T-shirt made up,' suggested Mike. 'To read, "I am not your mother."'

She looked down at her generously swelling breasts. 'I think it's what's under the T-shirt,' she said, 'that's confusing him in the first place.'

Mike rose from the sun lounger, and grabbed at her. She sidestepped him neatly, then reached up to pull at his coarse black hair. 'Look at this,' she said. 'It's in a worse state than mine, we look like a couple of hippies. Come on inside and I'll cut it before we go out. Want to watch me play hairdresser, Susan?'

'No, thanks,' said Susan. 'I think I'll just sit here and stare at the sun.'

She watched them go in, laughing together, and then took out her letter and sat for a while, turning it in her hands, wondering what on earth he could possibly have to say that was so important that it could not wait until he had returned to London. The possibilities that sprang to mind were three. It might be that he wanted to reassure her that, despite their coolness at parting, he still cared for her. Which would be sweet, touching even; but how far did this new Susan care for Felix? It might, less sweetly, be that he wanted to break off the relationship. She examined this prospect for a little, wondering if it would hurt, and how much, and for how long. Or... Or it was even just barely within the bounds of possibility — or no less likely, at least, than that she should have fallen in love with Mike O'Connor — that he had decided, here on this foreign ground, inspired who knew when, or by who knew what, that it was her, and not his wife, whom he really loved. Now, there would be an interesting turn of events. She lit a cigarette, and had smoked it halfway through before she opened the envelope.

'My dear Susan,' the letter began, conventionally enough. It went on to describe his situation: the plane, interestingly; the other passengers, amusingly; the food, disdainfully. It said that they were passing over the vast central flatlands; that he had tried to sleep and could not; that the movie was breaking whole new frontiers of banality. It said that it trusted that she, whatever she was doing this presumably fine Saturday, was enjoying herself rather better than was he. It said it looked forward to seeing her in London, and signed itself, affectionately, Felix.

She read the letter a second time, folded it, and returned it to its envelope. That was it; that was all there was to it. He had been bored on the aeroplane, and since there was small point in writing to the wife whom he would be seeing in a few hours, he had killed some time by writing to her instead. She had been sitting, a few yards from the man she loved, with her stomach churning and her imagination afire, and all over a device to fill thirty empty minutes. Looking at his handwriting, familiar under the unfamiliar American postmark, she realised that if he had wanted to end things, she would not have minded very much at all.

'If,' came Joanna's exasperated voice from indoors, 'you could bear to keep your head still for a minute, I might just have a sporting chance of not blinding you.'

And she had thought she would not envy Joanna again. Joanna who had so frivolously let her precious gift for painting slip away, who, as far as Susan could see, had not even the grace to regret its passing — as, after all, why should she? Since it had been replaced by the so much more precious gift of Mike's love. Mike's love, his life, his hair to cut, his supper to cook, or, if she felt like it, not to cook. But as she thought it, the thought returned, deliciously cold in her hot envy, that Joanna did not have his love exclusively; that, lovable as she was, more lovable, far, than Susan was or would ever be, she could not — or was it, would not? — command his fidelity. And to that thought came a new, chill extension, whose words she formed to herself as she finished the icy wine her cousin had poured her. 'He would not,' she thought, deliberately, precisely, 'be unfaithful to me.'

The telephone rang, and a minute later, Joanna's head appeared through the front doorway.

'Phone call,' she said. 'We're in the living room, so I've put it in the kitchen.'

Susan knew no one in Los Angeles, and it was too late for a call from London. 'Who is it?' she asked.

Joanna shrugged and disappeared.

Susan went around the house to the kitchen where the telephone, a squat snail trailing its lengthy extension cord, lay on the table. She lifted the receiver.

'Hello?' she said. She hoped it was not Nancy fulfilling at last the threat of the coffee *klatsch*. But if it were, Joanna would surely have said so.

Anyway, the voice that answered was male. 'Hi, Susan. Remember me?'

'I'm sorry?'

'James. Eileen's friend.'

James, Eileen's friend, was telephoning her. The impertinence struck her, momentarily, numb.

'How you doing?' he asked.

'Fine, thank you.' She heard the stone in her voice, and remembered that Joanna had suggested more graciousness. 'And you?' she added.

'Oh, doing fine. Say, I wondered if you'd care to come to dinner one evening this week?'

Oh, he did, did he, James, Eileen's friend. She opened her mouth to tell him, graciously or no, precisely what to do with his dinner invitation. As she did so, another burst of laughter from the other room was cut short, melting into a silence whose meaning she determinedly did not pursue.

'Yes,' to her most utter astonishment she found herself saying into the receiver. 'Yes, that would be very nice, actually.'

After all, as Joanna herself had said, he seemed a perfectly nice man.

'Well?' said Joanna when Susan went into the living room, Mike having mysteriously vanished. 'Who was it?'

Susan looked at her, and two plus two became four. 'You know,' she said. 'You know perfectly well who it was.'

'Oh.' She pulled a guilty face. 'Do I?'

'Yes you do.' And four plus four became eight. 'You know who it was, and you know what he wanted, too. My God, Joanna.'

'Oh, dear.' She hid her face in her hands, peeping between her fingers. 'I'm sorry. Do you think I'm terrible?'

As a matter of fact, Susan did think she was terrible, and she should not clown her way out of it, either. 'Yes,' she said coldly. She sat, looked briefly over at her, and then down at the little pile of Mike's dark hair clippings on the floor. 'Yes, I do.'

'Oh.' She dropped her hands. 'I am sorry, Susan, really I am.'

Susan shrugged.

Joanna sat for a minute, then sighed, fetched a dustpan and brush from the kitchen, and began to sweep up the hair on the floor.

'I didn't ask him to phone you, you know,' she said.

'Good.'

'Oh, don't be so . . . ' She finished her sweeping, and laid the pan on the table, the hairs in it black against the cheap yellow plastic. 'Listen, do you really like Felix all that much?'

'Not that it's any of your business,' said Susan. 'But apparently I do.'

'Well, he's not good enough for you.'

'Well, I'll write and sever the relationship, then. Got a stamp?'

'Oh, stop it. Look, Susan, Felix is married.'

'No! Really?'

'Well, if you're just going to be sarcastic about it. But what sort of man would . . . I do think it's wrong, you know, what you're doing. And I remember the nuns at the convent when Daddy was alive saying that when you do wrong, you hurt yourself as much as you hurt anyone else. I didn't know what they were talking about then, but I do now.'

'I remember you at that convent,' said Susan. 'I remember you were always convinced you were catching leprosy, and you had nightmares about being burned at the stake.'

'Oh, yes, you would remember that, wouldn't you? Look, all I'm saying is that, whether Susan Barnes likes it, or whether

Susan Barnes doesn't like it, the way of the world is that people were made to go in twos. And Felix simply isn't available for that.'

'And James is.' Susan reached over, picked up a hair clipping from the dustpan, and quickly dropped it. 'And I am. And that makes the two of us automatically perfect for each other. Do you have the faintest idea of quite how insulting that is?'

'OK.' Joanna raised her hands in defeat. 'OK, I'm sorry, I put my great clumsy foot in it, and I was wrong. I'm sorry. But I happen to think you're rather special that's all. And because I'm a smug fat married cow, I can't help thinking that you'd be happier if you were together — properly together — with someone as special as you are.' Briefly, her spirit returned to her. 'And I just bloody hope you were a bit more polite to James this time than you were last time.'

Susan rose, and made for the door. 'As a matter of fact,' she said, conscious of a rather neat exit line, 'I'm having dinner with him tomorrow night.' At the door, she turned and raised a warning hand. 'Dinner,' she repeated.


Celia at last had contacted Mike's agent, so his meeting with her this morning was strictly business; but somehow he had still not mentioned to Joanna even her existence. And yet, he realised, sitting steaming in the agonised crawl of traffic that lay between his home and the Beverly Hills hotel, he had told Susan all, or all he would ever tell, about her. Curious, how he had got into the way of telling Susan things. He would miss her when she left.

His agent had been delighted with the figure Celia had mentioned; Mike was becoming successful. His father would have been proud at last. But his father had been successful: he had worn suits, and dined with the right people, and not, Mike suspected, although they had never discussed it, invariably questioned too closely the worthiness of each of his clients' claims. His father had died early of a heart attack. Mike did not intend to die early; there were many ways in which he did not intend to be like his father. But the alternative to success would mean that he lacked talent, and that he could not bear. His father had been talented; that much, at least, was beyond dispute.

He was sorry his father had not met Joanna, he would have liked her. But everyone liked Joanna, even her mother-in-law. Eileen herself had hated her own mother-in-law. Alone in his car, Mike laughed, remembering raised voices, slammed doors and telephone receivers, high drama. He sometimes rather missed that drama.

He passed the fountain at the intersection of Santa Monica and Wilshire Boulevard, watching with envy as a couple of teenagers, their nondescript clothing proclaiming them to be from out of state, dipped joyous feet into its bowl, and cut through the richly grassy sidestreets that led to the hotel. He handed his keys to the valet parker, and strode, comfortably oblivious, since he was not going to the Polo Lounge, to the glances his workaday jeans were attracting, to the coffee shop where she was waiting.

'How d'you find Sam?' he asked, when the coffee had been brought, and the doughnuts lay in a golden, cinnamon-smelling heap in front of them. 'He live up to your idea of an agent?'

'Not quite.' She watched, amused, as he tore into the sweet, doughy flesh. 'He seemed almost like a human being.'

'Yeah, he's a good guy, is Sam. That's why he's down dealing with losers like me.'

She laughed, and put her elbow on the table, the side of her face resting on a strong, long-fingered hand. A plain gold ring winked on her little finger. Mike was reminded by contrast of Kathy's small hands. Kathy bit her fingernails. Well, there was something nice he could do for Kathy here.

'I'll get you a script by Christmas,' he said. 'I have a good part in mind for Kathy, Kathryn Schneider, you remember? Get her to mature a bit.'

'Ah, yes,' said Celia. 'Your little protegée.'

He frowned at her tone.

'She's a hell of an actress,' he said.

'And a good friend, too. Apparently.'

'She's become one. I really hope she'll be free in January.'

'Well.' She shrugged a slim shoulder. 'You're the director of course.'

'Yeah. I'm the director.' He reached for another doughnut. 'Hey, it's my wife's birthday, a week from Friday. We're having a party, why don't you come?'

She stared at him.

'Really. Meet Kathy properly . . . Meet my wife. Gonna have to do it sooner or later, kid.'

'Yes,' she said. 'It looks as though I shall.'

It was not a long meeting, since she had an appointment scheduled for mid-morning; by soon after eleven, Mike was back in his car and in the very middle of the rush of people flocking to the beach for the day. He had not, reviewing the conversation, quite liked how some of it had gone. It was not that she had said anything specific, but there had, especially when he had mentioned Kathy, been that in her voice, that in her look . . . She had money at her disposal, and that, he appreciated, put her in the more powerful position; but she should not suppose that, by buying his talent, she was buying him. If that was the price of success, it was too high by far.

He sat, frowning and drumming his fingers on the steering wheel, until he reached the turning for his studio; but when at last he did, he somehow found himself turning, not left towards his own place of work, but right, towards Bill's office.


'Don't you ever go to work?' Bill greeted him. He nodded at Mike's clean, unfrayed shirt. 'What's with the fancy duds?'

'Had a meeting,' Mike told him.

'Yeah? Something interesting?'

Mike shrugged: it was bad luck to talk about these things until they were fully settled. Yet he had told Susan.

'Might be. How's Nancy?'

'Expensive. Now she wants to send Barbara to a camp for fat kids, poor kid. It's only a few pounds. Oh, and Alex is to take fencing.'

'Fencing?'

'For when he plays Hamlet. I don't like the way he's sticking to this one.'

'Yeah, it's been almost a week.'

'He's heard about Rick, and he says if Rick can make a living at it, he's sure as hell he can. Says he's a better actor than Rick is, now.'

'He probably is.'

'Thanks, you're a big help.' He shook his head. 'Damn, I wish Rick hadn't got that part.'

'You wish. *I* wish he'd quit following Joanna round like a lost sheep. She won't get rid of him, either.'

'Maybe he gives her something to do,' said Bill.

So Bill, too, had noticed Joanna's inactivity, had he? Mike watched him thoughtfully, while his secretary brought in a small pile of letters and waited for him to sign them. For the first time it occurred to him that it was just possible that, secretly, Bill approved of Joanna as little as did Mike of Nancy. It was odd to think of someone disapproving of Joanna; odd, but by no means discomforting.

'Nice legs,' he said, after the secretary had left the room.

'You couldn't afford her,' said Bill.


Although the heat was still fiercely upon them, Mike had been looking unusually spruce when he left. Joanna wondered if he were going to meet Mac, although he had not mentioned it to her. But delightful as it was to have Susan around, it had been making private conversation a little difficult lately. She hoped Mike was not feeling neglected.

She took her plate and coffee cup, laid them in the sink, and wandered through the living room to the garden. The hummingbird was back in the tree, and the cat from next door sprawled, prone, in the shade of the fence. Joanna crouched on the doorstep, put her chin in her hands, and wondered what she would do with the day. It was really quite disgraceful to have so laid waste to a summer of the prime of her life; Mike did not like it, she knew, and even she was beginning to feel ashamed of herself. It was just as well that school was starting again in a couple of weeks.

She could, of course, her conscience inconveniently suggested, draw something, if only to keep her hand in. The cat, perhaps, or the bird at the jacaranda blossoms. She wondered if she could unearth her sketch pad and pencils without too much disturbing Susan; and even as she did so, felt her thoughts dilly-dally downstream to the greener fields of Susan and James. What a funny old thing Susan was. After all she'd said about James, about the situation, here she was agreeing to have dinner with him. Maybe there was hope after all.

She was shamelessly planning the wedding reception when the telephone rang, and it was Rick.

There was a lot of noise in the background.

'Where are you?' she asked.

'In Santa Monica,' he said. 'I've been shopping, and now I'm having morning coffee. Come and join me.'

'Oh, dear. I'm not sure that I can.' She had, she rather thought, seen as much of Rick that week as was good for either of them.

'Oh, please. It's my last week, and it's only ten minutes away, and I'll treat you. Why not?'

She thought. Why not. 'OK,' she said. 'I'll see you in twenty minutes.'

When she arrived at the small coffee shop, he was in command of a booth, a mug of coffee and the *Hollywood Reporter* shining in the sun on the Formica table in front of him.

'Have some cheesecake,' he said. 'They do it great here, I've been waiting for you to order.'

'I mustn't.' She slid on to sunwarmed orange plastic. 'I've just had breakfast.'

'Me, too. Two cheesecakes and another coffee,' he told the waitress, a motherly coffee shop waitress, with a weary face and swollen dishpan hands, who smiled fondly at him, as middle-aged women always did.

Cheesecake in the morning. How positively decadent she was becoming this summer.

'What have you been buying?' she asked.

'Oh, everything. Look.' His side of the booth, she then noticed, was piled high with bags, expensive, creamy paper carrier bags, with stores' names on the sides and silky tassels at the top. 'Jeans, shirts, shoes, well, I'll show you later. I mean, if I'm going to be a TV star, I have to dress the part, right?'

'Right.' The coffee and cheesecake arrived, and she raised her cup smilingly to him as the waitress waddled off on her fallen arches. 'Now that you're my rich and famous friend.'

'I am, aren't I?' Over his own coffee, he laughed for the pure pleasure of it. 'I mean, I will be soon.'

She took a mouthful of cheesecake: it was too rich, and too sweet, and quite delicious. 'People will be staring and pointing and hounding you for autographs.'

'And we won't even be able to go out in public in peace. Oh, Joanna, won't it be fun?'

'Well, just so long as you don't have the *paparazzi* hanging around our house while Mike's picking his nose.' Yes, she decided, she would remind him that he had a partner. 'How's Oliver, by the way?'

Rick's face closed, and he shrugged. 'How should I know? He's still writing his article.'

'Oh, dear. Haven't you talked at all?'

'No. Oh, when I got home, he said, "What's for supper?" and I said, "I don't know." Well, you guys went out for supper. So he made himself a sandwich and went back into his study, and then at midnight he came out and said good-night. And that was it.'

'Oh dear, oh dear. And what about this morning?'

'This morning, I got it together and got up even earlier than he did, and when he got up, he said, "Good-morning, Rick, you're up early," and I just walked out without answering. Why should I talk to him?'

'Oh, poor Oliver,' said Joanna.

'You always say that.' He did not attempt to hide the resentment in his tone.

'Yes, because I mean it. I don't think he's finding any of this easy at all.'

He looked at her, brown eyes blank. She wondered, in a gust of irritation, what went on inside his head, and whether it ever occurred to him to wonder what went on inside others.

'I know,' she went on carefully, knowing that to express her impatience would be the reverse of productive, 'it's not my business. But I can't help feeling he really could use some cheering up, you know.' She noticed again the parcels beside him, and had an idea. 'I know. Why don't we go and buy him a present?'

'Oliver? A present?' It was, she reflected, as if she had burst into fluent Swahili. 'Why?'

'Because,' she began, and stopped. Because, in terms that he could understand, why? 'Because it might just make things easier. And I think it would be a nice thing to do, I really do.'

He had stopped listening, and was stirring extra sugar into his coffee. 'I'm sick of talking about Oliver,' he said when she finished talking. 'Let's stop thinking about him. What do you want for your birthday?'

She sighed and abandoned the effort.

'World peace,' she said.

'No, really. Come on, tell me. Hey, why don't we go and buy it now?'

'Oh, Rick.'

'Come on. I'll leave my junk in my car, and we'll go to the mall. I'm coffeed out anyway, aren't you?'

After all, he could afford it now, and the alternative was to sit here and eat the other half of the sinful cheesecake. 'All right,' she said. 'If you finish my cheesecake first.'

They left the coffee shop, locked Rick's purchases in his car, and strolled through the down-at-heel alley that was the old shopping mall to where the new mall rose, its whitewashed walls agleam with glossy promise. Rick extended his arm, and Joanna took it.

'Seen in Santa Monica,' he said. 'Rick Morrison of *The Van Der Meers*, with curvaceous English blonde beauty, Joanna O'Connor. Mike'll be jealous.'

She laughed. 'I think Mike can learn to live with it.'

He looked at her curiously, as he had lately whenever Mike was mentioned.

'Do you get on OK?' he asked. 'You and Mike?'

'What do you mean?' she said.

'Well, do you?' he said. 'You always seem to, but do you really, Joanna?'

There was that odd look still in his eyes; perhaps he was envious of what he perceived as their idyllic relationship.

'We have our problems,' she said. 'Of course we do.'

'Big problems?'

'Sometimes. Yes, sometimes quite big. It isn't only you and Oliver, you know.'

Which seemed to cheer him considerably, and they walked for a few minutes in silence. Halfway down the mall, stuck among the Mexican cinemas and cut price clothes stores, was an art bookshop, and she stopped out of habit, to check the window.

'If I had a lot of money,' she said, 'I'd pretty well move into this shop.'

'Oh,' he said. 'But you don't want a book for your birthday, do you? They're too serious for birthday presents.'

He had a point there. 'No,' she said. 'No, now that you mention it, I don't think I do.'

They walked on through the old mall, and into one of the department stores in the new. It had been a long time since Joanna had been shopping, not shopping for groceries or toothpaste, but blatantly, frivolously shopping, shopping in the morning, shopping for something new, and pretty, and thoroughly inessential. She began to feel rich, a lady of leisure, like the leather shod women who had sauntered through Dickins & Jones, that student summer when she had had a job on scarves.

There were scarves in this store, billowing cool in the conditioned air, and deckle-edged notepapers, and sweet smelling soaps, and snakeskin belts, and frippery scraps of strappy high heeled shoes. And jewellery. She had a weakness for jewellery, although besides her wedding ring, her service-able tank watch, and her gold stud earrings, she rarely wore it for everyday. But there was the party to consider, and her favourite blue dress, beautifully though it matched her eyes, could use a little new in the way of decoration. She looked through necklaces and brooches, and then she saw the earrings. Long and gold, just angular enough to flatter her round face, they would droop against her jaw under her upswept hair, changing her at their touch from a pretty, plump pigeon to a lovely swan.

'Look, Rick.' With one hand, she drew her hair above an ear, with the other held both on their cardboard square to her lobe.

He looked; he looked again. 'They're gorgeous.'

'Aren't they.' Having already optimistically checked the price, she put them back on the stand. 'One day.'

'Let me see.' He picked them up, turned them over, looked at the price ticket on the back. 'You should have these.'

'Sure.' From the jewellery department, she could see through to the bags. 'I'll tell you what, I could use a new beach bag.'

'No,' he said seriously. 'You should have these.'

'Well, one day when we're both millionaires maybe.'

'You should have them now.'

'Rick!' Enough daydreaming was, after all, enough. 'Come on, let's go and look at the bags.'

He held them to her ear. 'I want to get you these.'

'Oh, don't be daft. Come on.'

'No, I mean it.' He did, she realised then, actually mean it. 'I want to give you these for your birthday.'

'Well.' On the verge of annoyance, she raised her eyes. 'I don't want you to, so let's go.'

'Let him give them to you, honey,' said the shop assistant, watching them. 'I wish my guy would.'

'You see?' he said.

'Rick.' Joanna lowered her voice in embarrassment. 'Will you please stop being so silly, because I won't accept them. You've seen how much they cost, it's more than a day's salary.'

'Not my salary. Please, Joanna.'

His brown eyes soft with pleading, he looked into hers. From the corner of her vision, she caught sight of two girls, trying on plastic bracelets at the other side of the counter, staring at them in undisguised envy; and suddenly, on that rich summer morning, she saw herself as they saw her, an unremarkable looking woman being begged by a beautiful young man a good decade her junior to accept a ridiculously extravagant gift of jewellery.

'Rick!' she said, but her tone had changed, and they both knew it.

'Please, Joanna. Please, please.'

She sighed.

'I'm your rich and famous friend, you said it yourself. Please.'

'Oh.' She sighed again. 'All right, then.'

'Really? Oh, Joanna, thanks!'

As he enveloped her in a hug, she saw, and was not above

enjoying, the glance the two girls exchanged with the shop assistant.

'Put them on now,' he ordered, as soon as he had paid.

'Now?' She looked down at her T-shirt and faded cotton skirt. 'Aren't they a bit dressy?'

'I don't mind.' He caught himself. 'But if you don't want to.'

'No, I do, actually. If they won't look too silly.'

In front of the small, slanting mirror, he watching intently, she took out her gold studs and replaced the others, watching in delight as on first one side of her face and then the other, the eyes became larger, the jaw more defined, and cheekbones appeared.

'What d'you think?' she said at last.

'You're gorgeous,' he said.

'*They*'re gorgeous. Thank you so much, Rick. I shouldn't have let you, but thank you.'

'Daon't be darft,' he mimicked her. 'They are pretty, though, aren't they? Hey, you know, we should do something to celebrate.'

'Oh, sure. Let's go and buy a car.'

He laughed down at her, and then his laughter turned to a smile. 'I know what we could do,' he said. 'We could go buy that present for Oliver.'

'Really?' She stood on tiptoe to kiss him. 'Oh, what a lovely idea!'

'Yeah,' he said. 'It is a good idea, isn't it?'

They left the store, she inches taller and pounds lighter, floating like the airy bits of solid gold that dangled down her neck and brushed against her face, and went into the mall proper.

'What shall we get him?' she said.

'I don't know. What do you think?'

'Well, what does he like? What about a book?' She laughed at him, teasing. 'If you don't think that's too serious.'

'No, I don't.' He smiled back at her, strong teeth white

against his brown face. 'It's not his birthday, and I can't buy him earrings, can I?'

'You could try.'

Laughing at the thought, they walked through the mall. There were not many other shoppers there; it was too early for the lunchtime rush, and the teenagers who would swarm in in the early afternoon were, for the most part, still stumbling blissfully through the mid-morning breakfasts of the school holidays. Almost alone, Joanna and Rick walked under the escalator, past the fountain, and along the main aisle of shops, clothes shops, shoe shops, card shops, the place a warren of consumerism. Joanna tried to remember whether Susan had yet been into a shopping mall. She thought not: Joanna would take her one day when she wanted to shock her.

At the end of the aisle was a bookstore, the sort of bookstore that malls spawn, a brash link in a commercial chain, its wares laid out screaming for recognition. They went in.

'Isn't this a horrible bookshop?' said Joanna.

'Shall we go somewhere else?' he said.

'No, the books are OK. It's just the place is horrible.'

They wandered around racks of best sellers, new fiction, and show business biography. In the humour section, Joanna's eye was caught by a book of cartoons called *How To Live With An Impossible Man*, and idly, she opened it. The first cartoon showed a couple sitting up in bed, disgruntled expressions on their faces. 'It might be easier,' the man was saying, 'if you weren't the sort of butch ballsbuster who was always putting down my sexuality.' Joanna laughed.

'What's that?' said Rick.

She showed him. 'It's cruel,' she said. 'But it's funny.'

Together they flicked through the book. Most of the cartoons were funny; some were kinder than the first; many were less kind. Rick laughed louder at each one. 'I think,' he said at last, 'I'll get this for Oliver.'

'Oh, yes,' said Joanna. 'He'd love that, wouldn't he?'

'No, I mean it, I think I shall.'

'Oh.' She took the book from him, and looked through it more carefully. 'Really?'

'Don't you think I should?'

'Well.' Well, she was not, she reminded herself, his mother. 'I don't know, it's your relationship, not mine.' But the book was so cruel. 'I don't know, I really don't.'

'Well, you keep saying we should laugh more together.'

'Do I?' Susan was right: she was bossy.

'Yes, you do. And you think this is funny, don't you?'

'Oh yes.' Having pointed it out, she could hardly deny it. 'Yes, it's funny, all right.'

'Then he'll think so, too, won't he?'

And it was not, she repeated to herself as he took the book from her, marched to the cashier, and paid for it, her relationship. And she was still not his mother.

Outside the store, he took her hand, and hustled her out of the mall.

'Come on,' he said. 'I want to see the earrings in the sunshine.'

She stood on the steps and posed for him, the gold shining just on the very outer circle of her vision. 'How do they look?' she said.

'Terrific. Just terrific. Come back and show Oliver.'

'Oh.' And watch the presentation of the book. 'No, I really can't.'

He frowned. 'Why not?' he demanded.

'Rick, I do have things to do here, you know.'

'What do you have to do?'

'Well . . . ' She scanned her plans for the day. 'Well, for one thing, I have to cook something bloody nice for Mike's supper tonight, and cook it on time, too, or he'll divorce me, and sue *you* for alienation of appetite.'

'Mike, Mike. It sounds as if he could use this book, too. It's not even noon, Joanna.' A cloud crossed his face. 'Don't you want Oliver to see the earrings?'

She would regret it; but it was, after all, not even noon.

'OK,' she said. 'But I'm not staying for lunch, so don't ask me.'

His face cleared. 'I wasn't going to,' he replied.

They walked to the other end of the mall, found their cars, and drove in tandem down Santa Monica Boulevard, its inland bound traffic now clear of its morning jam. A little too clear, thought Joanna, watching the back of Rick's undistinguished blue Honda lurch steadily under the dry late morning sun from one light to the next: had the traffic been heavy, she would have felt justified in turning off down one of those long straight roads, Sawtelle, say, or Sepulveda, that led so tantalisingly south towards her home. She was sure that Oliver would not enjoy the joke of the book. And yet, and yet — she slowed as a pampered ivory limousine, its windows luxuriously shaded against sun and prying eyes alike, cut between her car and Rick's — it was Rick who shared his life, who might reasonably be expected to know what would amuse, and what would hurt. Oliver might just find it funny. She could only hope so.

Curious how her sympathies see-sawed between Rick and Oliver, Oliver and Rick. They were each as bad as the other, of course, and yet she would be sorry if they did indeed break up. For love to go to waste would be wicked, wanton; and she was sure that, in their own way, they did love each other. Granted, they did not present to the world quite so united a front as, for instance, herself and Mike; but that was just that, a front, such as all couples forged hiding who knew what in the way of private compromises, intimate pains, a shell to protect the privacy of their love. She hoped that Rick realised that: there had been that in his tone as he had questioned her about her relationship with Mike that had faintly disturbed her. She hoped she had been able to set him straight. Then she smiled as the limousine ahead turned off down one of the fat Beverly Hills roads that led to the security patrolled estates up in the canyons. False as his picture of her marriage was, it was undeniably flattering.

Her smile died as they drove into the parking space under the building, and she saw Oliver's car by its accustomed pillar. She had rather hoped he might be out.

Rick himself appeared to have no doubts of his welcome, bounding through the apartment door into the living room, dark in the bright daytime, and calling Oliver's name. Not your relationship, Joanna told herself yet again, wondering nevertheless as she followed him in whether he could possibly have forgotten the terms the two had parted on just a few hours before.

'Good-morning, Rick, for the second time.' Oliver appeared from his study, the dressing gown he wore to write in thrown over his clothes, glaciers in his eyes. 'I see that . . .' he noticed Joanna, and his face became that of the Oliver she knew. 'Joanna! What a nice surprise!'

'It's practically a case of kidnapping,' she told him. 'Rick simply wouldn't let me go home.'

'Well, come and give me a kiss, anyway. Don't you look well! Summer must be agreeing with you. Stay for lunch.'

'Thank you, and no thank you. I can't stay.' She stepped back from his warm indoor arms. 'I just came to show off.'

'Show off?' He considered her. 'Show off what? New hairdo? No: in fact, you could use one.' He tweaked at her hair, then picked up her hand and sniffed at it. 'And you haven't been painting either, so it's not that.' Oliver was one of the few people in Los Angeles who regularly asked about Joanna's painting.

'Oh, Oliver!' Rick broke in impatiently. 'Isn't he hopeless, Joanna? Can't you *see*?'

Oliver looked at Rick, and splinters of ice returned to his eyes. 'No,' he said. 'I can't see.'

'Well, don't tell him. Make him guess.'

'Oh, shut up, Rick,' said Joanna. 'Don't you notice anything different, Oliver?'

'Unpardonably unobservant of me, Joanna, but . . . Unless you maybe lost some weight?'

'Oh, God, of course she didn't! You see what I have to put up with?'

'Thanks, Oliver, but you were closer with the hair.' She pulled her hair back, and turned towards him one ear, and then the other. 'Rick's birthday present.'

He looked. 'Very nice,' he said slowly. 'They're very nice.'

'Aren't they? Much too nice, I told him not to buy them, but he insisted. I think success has gone to his head.'

'They're beautiful.' He reached out, and gently touched one dangling triangle. 'Real gold. And you know, it's better that I didn't notice them at first.'

'Oh, yes. That would be awful, wouldn't it? Here she comes wearing her earrings. But these are . . . just . . . '

'Perfect,' he said.

'Oh, look,' said Rick. 'I brought you a present, too.' He handed it to him. 'Go on, open it.'

'A present?' Oliver's voice softened. 'That's kind.' He took the package, their hands touching, and Joanna watched him open it, wishing it did not look so cheap, so flimsily paperback in its plastic bag. She watched Oliver's brows rise as he read the title. '*How To Live With An Impossible Man.*'

'It's very funny, isn't it, Joanna?' Rick moved towards Oliver, leaning over his shoulder to turn the pages. Oliver turned away. 'Look at page seventeen, go on, just look at it. Isn't it us?'

Oliver looked. 'Very funny,' he said.

'Isn't it, though?'

'Yes, isn't it? Well.' He laid the book, cover side down, on the table. 'I'll look at it properly later. Thank you, Rick.'

'Well, you shouldn't really thank me. Joanna found it.'

'Yes,' said Joanna quickly, 'but you were the one who thought of Oliver. I wouldn't dare give it to Mike, he'd skin me alive.'

Oliver smiled at her. 'I doubt it. But what hosts we are, you'll have a cup of tea at least, Joanna? Coffee? Wine?'

'No, and I mean it. I honestly just looked in to show you, I have a million things to do at home.'

'Well, it was delightful to catch even a glimpse of you, and I'll look forward to seeing more at your party.'

'By which time, Mr Oliver Clever Beauchamp, I shall have a whole, spiffy new haircut, so there.'

'And between that and the earrings will be looking, if one can imagine such a thing, even more radiantly beautiful than ever.'

'Hard to imagine, but yes.'

'Come on,' said Rick. 'I'll walk you to your car.'


Susan wore the same cream silk shirt that she had worn to meet Felix, but with it a skirt, a long, pale skirt that skimmed close to her flat stomach and swirled around her brown slender calves. The sort of skirt, it could not but be obvious to her as she checked her reflection in the shower-steamed bathroom mirror, that, were Joanna to wear it, would make her look like no one so much as Mrs Pepperpot. Although of course Joanna would never attempt such a skirt: she was too well aware of her body's shortcomings for that. Susan herself had never been anything but slim.

She took a last look at herself in the mirror, smeared to make more subtle the touch of green eyeshadow that brought out the green in her eyes, and, skirt swinging, feet arched in high heels, skin alive with sun and shower and smelling faintly of coconut oil, stepped into the living room.

Mike whistled.

'Susan!' said Joanna. 'You look lovely!' She herself was still wearing the day's old cotton, evening tired now, and on the brink of grubbiness. 'Doesn't she look lovely, Mike?'

'Terrific,' said Mike.

'Thank you,' said Susan. She did look good and she knew it, felt it deep in her bones and glowing from her face. The pity of it that it was for the wrong person.

'Don't you feel old?' Joanna asked Mike. 'Sending her out on a date while the old folks stay at home?'

'Yeah,' said Mike. 'What's for supper?'

'He's so romantic,' Joanna told Susan.

Susan smiled.

There was a knock on the door and it was James, rather taller than Susan had remembered, and with a little grey in his beard that she had not noticed before.

They shook hands. He refused a drink, saying their table was waiting at the restaurant.

'Bring her back by midnight,' Mike threatened, relaxed and able to joke as no one had been with Felix.

'Yessir,' he replied promptly and respectfully as he ushered her to the door, returning the feeble joke as Felix would not have dreamed of.

The restaurant was near the beach and not far from the house, a long room, dimly lit, with a pianist quietly noodling in the corner. He lifted to her a glass of perfectly flinty Northern Californian wine.

'I'm glad you came,' he said.

'Thank you,' she replied.

'I kind of thought you might not. We got off on a bit of a wrong foot there, didn't we?'

So it was in the open. She was glad that he had brought it up; glad, too, she realised on a different level, that she had made an effort with her appearance for this rather smart restaurant. Susan liked smart restaurants, and apart from the dining room of Felix' hotel, she had not been to one here.

'Yes,' she said. 'We kind of did.'

'I walked into it, too,' he said. 'Just the way you did.'

'Did you?' She was pleased to hear that, and pleased that he had seen it necessary to tell her. 'I wondered.'

'Well, I did. That Eileen.' He shook his head. 'Great lady. Terrific lady. But . . . '

Susan smiled. 'One to be reckoned with.'

'Right. She scares the pants off us at the hospital.'

'Does she?' But in fairness, the guilt must be shared. 'Well, we mustn't only blame her, because Joanna was in on it, too. As I discovered, to my fury, yesterday.'

'She was? That's why she . . .' He stopped.

'She what?' asked Susan.

'Well.' He stopped again, shook his head again. 'I guess I have to tell you now. Or maybe you know already. She asked me to her party.'

'She . . .' No, this was too much. 'Bloody hell.'

'I guess you didn't know.'

Their eyes met, and they both laughed at the same time.

'Susan Barnes,' he said. 'I'm James Biggin. I'm delighted to meet you.'

Sitting, she bowed. 'Pleased to make your acquaintance, Dr Biggin.' Which was, she realised, on this occasion, no more than the truth.

'And,' he added as their glasses clinked, 'this time around, you won't have to hear the story of my trip to Dorsetshire.'

'Dorset,' she corrected. It was the least she could do.

'So,' he continued after the waiters had taken their order, 'how are you liking Los Angeles?'

An excellent question: how *was* she liking it? Two weeks ago, she would have known the answer; but since then, she had changed. She had witnessed a murder; she had fallen in love.

'It's different,' she said eventually.

He nodded agreement. 'It's different than everywhere. Much different than back East.'

'Yes?' For the first time, she wondered just who he was, and where he came from. 'How long have you been here?'

'Couple of months. My marriage broke up, and soon afterwards I was offered the chance to come here, so I took it.'

'That's a lot of changes to make at once.'

'Yeah, well, if you're going to make changes, you know.'

'I suppose so. What about you, do you like Los Angeles?'

He thought, laughed. 'Yeah, that's a tough one, isn't it? It's weird, you know. When I first came out here, I was completely freaked. It was like, what *is* this place? There was no order, no pattern, no . . . But if you stick around, you find there is an order after all. In a strange kind of way.'

Susan thought of the shooting on the beach, of the sunny Saturday afternoon that had turned blood red as the meek little man had pulled the gun from his pocket and had used it.

'It's a savage order,' she said.

'Exactly. It's savage. I mean, look at this place. This restaurant. It's real nice, real pleasant, everyone looks good, we're all having a good time. And yet we're all sitting here knowing that any second — any *second* — we could all be swallowed up in a major earthquake.'

Susan looked around at the other diners, the glossy haired women, the tall men, and tried to imagine the scene if the earth started to move under them.

'It's not very polite here,' she commented.

He laughed. 'Not very polite, no. People are friendly, though.'

'Oh, yes.' It was, in fact, the most satisfactory conversation she had yet had about the city. 'They're very friendly.'

The waiter arrived with their food, and she found herself smiling, exclaiming with delight over plain grilled fish and rice as if it were ambrosia. She was changing more than she had realised: perhaps loving an Angeleno was turning her into one.

'Are you really all frightened of Eileen at the hospital?' she asked.

'Terrified.'

'Well, I can see that you would be. She's a — what do you say? — a feisty lady.'

'She is that. I like her, though.'

'Oh, me too,' said Susan quickly.

'She's a good person, you know? Solid. And she worships her kids, which I always think is sort of cute.'

Her kids. Susan's heart, so rigorously controlled at home, broke free here and pounded and thudded into her throat at the thought of the only one of Eileen's kids she knew.

'So I'd noticed,' she replied.

'You don't really like her at all,' he said. 'Do you?'

'I . . . ' she paused, poked at her fish, and finally shrugged. 'I'm afraid I'm your classically repressed Englishwoman. I'm not awfully good at a lot of raw emotion.'

'You don't seem repressed to me. And we have repressed Americans, too.'

'Thank you, and yes, of course you do. And to be fair, Joanna's just as English as I am, and she and Eileen get on very well indeed. Which is just as well, isn't it? For Joanna.' And that, of course, of dull joyless course, was all that mattered, was how it was for Joanna.

'Just as well,' she repeated.


The expensive car drew up quietly at Joanna and Mike's front lawn.

'There's someone, isn't there?' he said.

'Is it so obvious?' she asked.

'To me. Pity. For me, I mean. He's a lucky guy, whoever he is.'

'Thank you. Well, I suppose I'll see you at the party, won't I?'

'You bet. Do you mind if I don't ask you out again?'

She kissed him on the cheek, and prepared to get out of the car. 'Thank you for a lovely evening,' she said. 'You'll find someone soon.'

He laughed. 'Hope so,' he muttered, as the car sprang to smooth life.

It had, indeed, been a lovely evening, she thought as she tripped up the path, a meal, compliments, a flirtation, the sort of evening she had not had since she had taken up with Felix. What a shame, what a heartbreaking, crying shame that the person she had shared it with had been the wrong person. If only, if only, the man sitting watching her under the flattering lights, pouring her wine, bending to light her cigarette, had been not James, but . . . At the front door, she paused, listening to the cheerful crickets in the tree, and feeling, suddenly, angry with Mike. Her life until Sunday had been running perfectly adequately after all; it had yielded fully her fill of joys and sorrows, of controlled hopes and not devastating disappointments. It had been — despite Joanna's opinion — perfectly satisfying, perfectly enough. And now, here came Mike, lumbering North American, to force open her soul's magic casement on to a whole sea of messy emotions, of sharp pains, of joys ever unattainable, always in limpid view. And she, foolish, sunsoaked woman that she had become, had been so careless as to let him. She should have heeded the advice of the lady in the old Scots ballad, the poor, abandoned lady, shivering with her bastard in the cutting East Wind of all those centuries ago; she should have locked her heart in a case of gold and pinned it with a silver pin.

The house was in darkness, ostentatiously so, although it was barely midnight. Joanna's doing, probably, making sure they should not seem to be waiting up for her. Or perhaps they had taken advantage of a night alone, and retired to bed early, for other purposes. Two of them, together, pleasuring each other under the bleak, black crucifix.

She brushed her teeth hastily, and tiptoed through the kitchen door to her own narrow bed in the garage.


'Well, I think you're jolly mean,' said Joanna. 'You go wafting off, dressed up like the dog's dinner, you come wafting back in at God knows what hour, and now you won't even tell me what happened.'

Susan smiled at her, relishing her frustration, and stretched herself, lazily, into the late Friday afternoon. 'I've already told you what happened,' she said. 'We had dinner at a restaurant, and talked. We had brandy at a bar, and talked some more. Then he drove me home.'

'I hate you sometimes. Come on, tell me honestly now. Do you like him?'

No, after the way Joanna had behaved, she deserved to dangle a little.

'Of course I like him,' said Susan. 'He's a nice man, you said so yourself.'

'Susan!' Joanna made strangling motions with her hands. 'I'll try again. Are you going to see him again?'

'Yes.'

'Yes!'

'At the party to which you so officiously invited him.'

'Yes, well.' She had, at least, the grace to blush. 'But not till then.'

'No.'

'But he is coming.'

'Yes.' She poured her second glass of wine, and decided to put her cousin out of her misery. 'And you can take that hopeful look off your face, because yes, he's a nice man, and yes, we had a nice time, but there's nothing there, and there won't be.'

'Oh, Susan! Why not?'

'Because there isn't.'

'Well, he does like you, you know. I do think you might give it a try.'

'Yes, but why should I?' She looked at her drink, away from Joanna. 'There'd never be anything big there. And it's all pretty pointless without that, isn't it? Without the real thing. Well, *you* know that. And you must know that, next to it, everything else seems pretty well second best.'

'Do you know,' said Joanna after a moment, 'you've never talked about Felix like that before. I hadn't realised quite how much he must mean to you.'

It had been barely half a glass of wine, the dregs of the bottle. Susan rose and went to the refrigerator for another.

'Well,' she said, returning, peeling off the green foil that sealed the cheap cork. 'It must have been nice for you two to have me out of your hair all evening.'

'Aaah.' As Susan sat down, Joanna reached over to pinch her cheek. 'Our little girl was all grown up and out on the town and we old fogeys sat at home and talked about the old days. Oh, Mike's got some news.'

'Oh, yes?'

'Yes, he might have found a backer for his next. Some other dentists or something. It won't be for months, though, and it's still a bit up in the air, so don't say anything, OK?'

Don't say anything to Joanna, Mike had said on Wednesday. He had told her himself on Thursday; but on Wednesday he had told Susan, and had said, don't say anything to Joanna.

'OK,' she said.

'I mean, I'm sure he wouldn't mind you knowing, but just don't say anything, all right?'

'I'm silent as the grave.'

'Oh, and talking of Mike, after you left last night, he said how nice you were looking.'

'Did he?' She would not react now; she would store the thought away to pore and gloat over later, when she was alone. 'That's nice.'

'I thought I'd mention it, because he never ever, ever notices how people look, so it's quite a compliment.'

'Well, I'm flattered.'

'Well, so you should be. And talk of the devil.'

Mike's car roared and racketed up the street, and drew to a stop outside the house.

'My women.' He stamped through the living room into the kitchen, his masculinity bringing sex into the air, making them women, where before they had been simply people. 'My harem. My witches' coven.' He kissed first Joanna, and then Susan.

'Would you like some wine?' said Susan.

'Nah. Going straight for the hard stuff here.' He reached into a drawer for grass, and sat down at the table to roll himself a joint.

187

'Hard day at the office, dear?' asked Joanna.

'Uh.' He grunted, and took his first puff.

'I haven't smoked grass,' said Susan, watching him, 'since I was an undergraduate.'

'No? Had some great grass in London. Have some.' He extended the joint to her, and she laid down her cigarette and took it.

'Not bad,' she said.

'Not bad! You should be shot. It's great. *Primo. Numero Uno.*'

'If you say so. Joanna?'

'No, thanks.'

She puffed again before she handed it back, and watched sweet smoke mellowing the tobacco haze she had already left in the air. 'Friday evening,' she said.

'Oh, God,' said Joanna. 'Does that mean I'll have you two hanging around the house all tomorrow?'

Mike looked at Susan and shook his head.

'Hell for her,' he commented.

'And we thought,' agreed Susan, 'the early Christians had it rough.'

'Hanging around the house,' continued Joanna, 'and being very funny indeed. I think I'll go back to England. Actually, you know, Mike we've been terrible hosts, we haven't taken Susan anywhere for ages. How about Santa Barbara? Or if we got up early, we could make Mexico.'

Susan yawned, and retrieved the joint from Mike. 'You can tell,' she observed, 'who's on holiday here, and who's been working all week . . . Although, if you are offering an excursion, I still haven't seen Hollywood.'

'Good idea,' said Mike. 'I'd like to show you Hollywood.'

'Well, how very organised of us,' said Joanna. 'We've made a plan.'


But when they were sitting at the breakfast table the next morning, the telephone rang. It was Eileen.

'Hello, Eileen,' said Joanna. 'How are you?'

'Fine. Listen, honey, I have a problem.'

'Oh?' Her throat tightened at the word: Eileen was no longer young. 'What is it?'

'It's my darned car, it won't start. Just sitting there. And I promised to take that stuff across to the nuns this morning, and would one of you two drive me?'

'Oh.' She first breathed out in relief, then twisted her face in vexation. 'Yes, sure. No problem. I'll do it.'

'You will? Good. Well, why don't you all come, then I can take you to lunch?'

'Well, I don't think we all can, actually, Eileen. You see, we were planning to take Susan to Hollywood . . .'

'Honey, you have plans, forget it, I'll take a cab.'

'Oh, don't be silly.' Mike, across the kitchen, fluttered his eyelashes and simpered into an imaginary receiver; she curled her lip at him. 'I was going to say, Mike can take Susan to Hollywood and bore her stiff about films, and *I'm* still open to lunch invitations.' She mouthed bloodcurdling curses at Eileen's car down the telephone.

'Oh, you. But I don't want to spoil your day.'

'But you won't. I've seen Hollywood, and I've heard Mike's speeches, too.'

Mike lobbed at her an imaginary hand grenade.

'Well . . .' Eileen paused, wavered. 'I'll let you do it on one condition. You all stop by for coffee, and I'll walk to the corner store for some pastries to set you on your way.'

'We'd love to,' said Joanna. 'We'll see you in about half an hour.'

'What,' asked Mike suspiciously, as she replaced the receiver, 'would we love to do?'

'Just stop by for coffee, just for half an hour, on the way. Look, I'm sorry, I can't come with you, her car's broken down, and she needs a lift to the convent. Sorry about this, Susan.'

Susan shrugged. 'It's not your fault. And we don't have to go to Hollywood today; we could do it another time.'

But Joanna could tell that she wanted to go.

'Of course you must,' she said. 'It'll be fun: you two can talk about how awful I am, and Eileen and I can talk about how awful you are. The only thing is, she was getting a bit upset, so I did say we'd look in for coffee. Hope you don't mind too much, Susan?'

'Not at all,' said Susan.

She was, in fact, it struck her as the two cars together pulled up outside the apartment block, almost looking forward to seeing Eileen. Eileen, too, was different from when they had last met; she had grown, had become not merely Eileen, but Mike's mother. It would be interesting to see how far she changed when seen in this new light.

Not that she seemed much different, as she bustled with coffee pots and plates of pastries, only perhaps a little faded under the strong morning sun that made even more garish the religious pictures on the walls.

'What's wrong with your car, Mom?' asked Mike, through a mouthful of sugar.

She swatted him with the back of an adoring hand. 'Much you'd know, Michael Francis O'Connor. It wouldn't start, and there's no answer from James' telephone, and the nuns need the stuff by this afternoon.' She indicated a pile of cardboard boxes filled with old clothes, and turned to Susan. 'I hear you and he had a good time the other night, dear.'

'Yes, thank you,' said Susan. 'It was very pleasant.'

She was even prepared to go into further details, but they were not asked: Mike's mother or not, Eileen was still Eileen.

'Joanna,' she said. 'You need a haircut.'

'So everyone says.' Joanna pushed her too long hair from her eyes. 'I'm getting one next week.'

'Good. You want to show off that cute face. Well, everyone, how do you like the pastries?'

They were simply pastries, and Susan's breakfast had been perfectly adequate. 'They're very nice indeed, thank you,' she said. 'May I have another?'

Eileen may not have changed, but what on earth was happening to Susan, she wondered as, under the other's positively approving eye she started on another pastry. The sun moved full on to Eileen's face, and Susan suddenly felt pity for her, an ageing woman whose husband was gone and would never return, who did not see enough of her son. Who was Dr Weintraub, anyway, a serious suitor, or merely someone Joanna teased her with? She wondered just how lonely it really was to be Eileen.

'Why don't you two come back this way?' said Eileen. 'We can all have supper together.'

'That,' said Joanna firmly, 'would be lovely. Wouldn't that be lovely, Mike, Susan?'

Susan had not changed quite so far as to be able to agree.

There was a shameful, but unmistakable, holiday spirit in Mike's car as they left Joanna and Eileen to their good work and headed down the busy freeway.

'Joanna is nice to do that for Eileen,' said Susan.

'Really nice,' said Mike. 'You and I'll have to have her fun for her.'

And they did have fun: Mike knew his Hollywood. They saw old deserted studios; quiet streets of stucco houses where early film crews had lived; fadedly grand hotels where stars had danced and flirted and fallen in love in public; mournful apartment blocks where the formerly famous had drunk or dosed themselves to a quiet death. They lunched on small, sweet fish called sand dabs and excellent wine in a darkly cool restaurant where writers homesick for the East once used to drink more than was good for them, and stumbled into the afternoon sun to pick their way through the joyful sleaze of Hollywood Boulevard, to stand outside the Chinese Theatre, and exclaim over the size of the footprints, and imagine search lights, and jostling crowds, and frenetically gabbling interviewers in movie premières gone by. At last, they found a hotel, once elegant, then shabby, now elegant again, and collapsed on to overstuffed armchairs in the airy lobby to share a pot of tea.

'That was fascinating,' said Susan. She had not realised how far the myth of Hollywood had permeated her world view, how potent was its pull on the strings of her romanticism. 'I didn't know how much I knew about this place.'

'No? But you went to the movies when you were a kid, didn't you? Joanna did.'

'Did I? I suppose I must have.' She frowned, trying to remember. 'I think Joanna might have gone a bit more than me, though. Aunt Betty likes a nice film.'

'And Aunt Joan didn't?'

Aunt Joan. Susan never talked about her parents, rarely thought of them: it had always seemed simpler that way. But now, with him beside her, she could remember that she, too, had once been a daughter; and how sweet, how sinfully sweet, the remembrance was. Oh, he would be good for her, damn him, would this man.

'I don't know,' she said. 'Maybe she did. She never mentioned it.'

'You got on better,' he said, 'with your Dad.'

He was right: she did. She thought of her father, as she always used to think of him, in his study, a book in his hand. Then she thought of her mother, but not of the woman she remembered, rather, an earlier memory, of her mother and Aunt Betty as almost girls, bright in the full-skirted summer frocks of the 1950's, giggling together as her mother had never giggled with her father or herself. It occurred to her, too late, that she had quite possibly not known her mother very well at all.

'Much better,' she said. 'Poor Mother.' Then she thought of Eileen's dead husband. 'What about you and your father?'

He shrugged. 'We got along well enough. He and my Mom had a real strong marriage, she thought the sun shone out of him. She had quite a difficult life, you know, before she met him.' Vaguely, Susan remembered Joanna's once saying something about Eileen's family and the Depression. 'That's why she can be . . . ' He stopped, met Susan's eyes, and they both laughed.

'Joanna's very good to her,' she said. 'Isn't she?'

'Real good. Shit.' He glanced at his watch. 'We should be heading back over there. No, damn it, there's something I want to show you first. Finish your tea, we have to leave now.'

They left the hotel, found the car, and drove into the hills above Hollywood Boulevard. Set implausibly at the top of a steep, winding lane was a restaurant masquerading as a Japanese palace, with a pagoda in the grounds, fish in a pond, and a bar looking southwards across the city. Mike found them a table by the window and ordered drinks, and together they watched in silence as within the space of half an hour, the sky turned from pale blue to lavender to molten copper, and the lights on the streets began, first a twinkle, then a glimmer, then row after row of fairy-tale brilliances, some moving, some standing still, stretching in all directions, as far as eternity.

'My God,' said Susan at last.

'Best show in town,' said Mike. 'No question. Some people prefer the Ocean. Joanna does. Says the only reason the sunset's so terrific here is because of the smog. And she's right, it is.'

'And *you* think,' said Susan, raising her nearly empty glass to him, 'that's half its charm.'

'Yeah,' he said. 'Now you mention it, I do. Damn, I wish we didn't have to go to Mom's. Let's have another first.'

He ordered; Japanese beer for himself and a martini for her, and the waiter brought the drinks promptly: waiters, she was noticing, tended to with Mike.

'Shouldn't really have this,' he said, flourishing his glass, 'but . . . to cousinhood.'

'Cousinhood,' she echoed, clinking her glass against his.

He settled back with a sigh. 'Damn, it's good here. I could stay . . . She's a good kid, Joanna. Sorry, good woman. Makes my life hell sometimes.'

Susan sipped her drink slowly: she had not the faintest intention of hurrying. 'When we were at school,' she said, 'there was this repulsive girl. Margaret Mason. Ugh. Nobody liked her, and nobody had any reason to. And Joanna used to invite her to tea. On days when she'd invited me. My God, she used to make me cross. Not that, I suppose, it was Margaret Mason's fault she was repulsive. But she was.'

'What was she like?'

'Margaret Mason? Haven't the foggiest recollection. But she was repulsive. To everyone but Joanna.'

'Joanna.' He smiled, then frowned into his beer. 'Hey.'

'Yes?'

'Do you know what she *does* all day?'

Susan thought: wrapped as she had been in her own work, the question had not occurred to her.

'I have no idea,' she said.

He continued to frown, looking, for the first time since she had known him, actively disapproving.

'I don't think she does anything,' he said.

'Well, she's a teacher,' said Susan. 'She's on holiday.'

'Susan.' He shook his head. 'She's been on holiday — as you call it — since June. Most teachers do something with their long vacation, don't they?'

'I suppose so.' Susan paused, pretending to consider, in reality allowing herself, if ever so briefly, to savour their complicity. She herself had never been offended by Joanna's laziness: Mike obviously was. Besides, it was true: most teachers did find some occupation for the summer. 'Yes, of course, they do.'

'Right,' he said. 'Right. Well, *you're* writing your introduction. And she's just . . . She doesn't even paint any more.'

'What happened,' asked Susan — treacherously? sincerely? how could she know? — 'to her painting?'

'God knows.' He stabbed a finger of agreement at the question: he had, she realised, very probably had no one to have this conversation with until now. 'What happened? She could have worked on that this summer, she could have . . . She sits, you know. In the garden. Or she has coffee with Nancy. Or she goes to buy earrings or whatever the hell they do, with Rick. What she's really doing is nothing. Can you imagine that? Three months of doing nothing.'

'You don't,' she said, and this was treacherous, thrillingly so, there was no question about it, 'like people doing nothing, do you? Anyone?'

'No,' he said. 'No, I don't. People in Europe don't do nothing, do they? They do things. This crazy place, either you're doing twenty things at once, or . . . Corrupted the hell out of Joanna. So.' He looked up at her, and his face lightened. 'How about you? What do you think of it here?'

She sipped again at her ice cold, fiery tasting drink.

'Actually,' she said, 'I'm liking it more than I thought I would.'

'Yeah?' He softened into a grin: he was unquestionably fond of her. Damn him, she reminded herself. 'How'd you think it would be?'

'Oh, you know.' Despite herself, she smiled back at him, feeling her tanned skin crease in the cool evening air. 'People munching beansprouts, and' — she remembered Felix's joke of all that long, long time ago — 'surfing to their analysts and no "there" there.'

'That's Oakland,' he said.

'I'm sorry?'

'Oakland. City up north. Gertrude Stein said there was no "there" there, and people are always quoting it about Los Angeles. Or was it Alice B Toklas? Anyway, it's Oakland, not LA.' He straightened his chair, aping a professorial manner. 'It's a common mistake.'

So on top of everything else, Felix had made a common mistake.

'Well, anyway,' she said, 'it's not like that at all, is it?'

'You're getting the feel of the place,' he said. 'Faster than I thought you would. To be honest, I thought . . . ' He stopped.

'Go on,' she said. 'Say it. You thought I was a stuck up English prig, and I am!'

'No, you're not.' He looked at her; looked closer; reached

over, and gently tweaked a lock of hair at her temple. 'You're going blonde.'

'Am I?' She did not move away from his touch, but did not move towards him, either. 'You see, before your very eyes, I'm turning into a Southern Californian.'

'Get you that lobotomy yet, kid.'

They both laughed, not quite awkwardly, and returned to their drinks. After a moment, Mike looked again at his watch.

'We should go,' he said.

'Mm.' Susan had not finished her drink, and made no move to.

'Really. Pity, but.' He nudged her leg with his foot. 'Come on, kissin' cousin, drink up.'

They drove back quietly, the car's lights now one of the lights they had seen sparkle from the hillside, the Saturday evening traffic rumbling excitement, parties, sweaty palmed first dates.

'I must say,' said Susan, 'that this car is one of the more disgusting I've ever had the honour to experience.'

'The time will come,' he told her, 'when this type of car will be the only car to be seen in. Probably the year I buy a new Ferrari. So how d'you like Hollywood?'

'Very much. Very much indeed, thank you. I'll think about it next time I go to the cinema.'

'Right. Next time you rush to see an American movie. Hey, you really must come and see *Marina*, you know.'

'I want to,' she said. 'I've never seen — what d'you call them? — dailies before.'

'They're not so interesting,' he said. 'Go on for hours, can't drag Joanna near them. But you should see some. Well. Here we are.'

They had arrived, surprisingly quickly, and he parked under a palm tree that loomed piratically black out of the blue, velvet night. Neither of them got out immediately.

'That was a lovely day,' she said. 'Thank you very much indeed.'

'Yeah,' he said. 'It was good, wasn't it? Thank *you*.'

They sat on for a moment.

'Well,' she said eventually.

'Yeah,' he said. 'Well.'

'Well,' she said. 'Thanks again.' And leaned over to kiss him, politely, like a cousin, on the cheek.

And of course, the kiss was neither polite, nor cousinly, nor was it on the cheek; but it was the kiss that since that morning it had been inevitable that would happen that evening, then, there.

They both at last drew apart; and looking at him, she knew— and in one terrible instant wondered both how she could bear to know, and how she could have borne not to know before—that it was not just a kiss, that her love could love her, too.

'Wow,' he said. Then, 'Shit. Christ. Shit.'

She smiled, a grim little smile. 'I couldn't have put it better myself.'

'Christ,' he said. He rubbed his face with his hand. 'So what happens now?'

'I don't know,' she said. 'Believe it or not, I don't often find myself in this situation.'

'Christ,' he said. 'I want you. No, I don't. You're Joanna's cousin, you're Susan, I can't want you. I want you.'

'I want you,' she said.

He reached for her; she pulled back.

'Shit,' he said.

They both sat back and she saw them as an outsider might, two adults with lust in their hearts, sitting side by side and apart, staring into the dark night. Was it a comical vision, or only a sad?

'Well,' she said. 'We can't just sit here all evening, can we?'

He looked at her quickly. 'What do you suggest?' he asked.

She set her lips, shut her mind and body. 'I suggest,' she said, 'we go in before they start to send out search parties.'

He was still looking at her; she could not look at him.

'Really?' he asked.

'Really,' she said.

'OK then. If that's what you want. But it's not what you want, is it?'

'Mike.'

'Sorry. OK, then. OK. We'll go in. Susan?'

'Yes?' she asked, warily, wearily.

'This is some shit,' he said.

'I know,' she said. And it was only at its beginning. 'I know.'


'Where the hell have you guys been?' asked Eileen when they presented themselves, carefully apart, at the door. 'I thought you must have gotten lost.'

'Sorry, Mom,' Mike bent to kiss her. 'No, we weren't lost, the traffic was bad.'

'I told her,' said Joanna from inside the apartment. 'I said you couldn't get lost in Hollywood if you tried.'

'Right,' said Mike. 'Hollywood was no problem. Trouble started with the drive home.'

'What lovely flowers,' said Susan hastily. 'Were they there this morning?'

'They're always there,' said Joanna. 'Doctor Weintraub sends them every week. Doesn't he, Eileen?'

'Ah, don't listen to her nonsense.' Eileen flapped a hand at her, and turned back to the door. 'Well, don't just stand there, you two, come in and tell us all about your day.'

So, in a flurry of laughter, of proffered drinks, snacks and ashtrays, and the aroma of good cooking, they set themselves about the business of a companionable evening.


Rick and Oliver sat in silence at the table, its top littered with cardboard cartons, dragons stamped on the outside, and inside all manner of mixtures of shrimp and pork, ginger, broccoli, cashew nuts, the fierce, the bland, the spicy, the sour and the sweet, the crunchy, the chewy, and the soft. Rick had sprung for Chinese food, and was digging in with an appetite, heaping new combinations on to his plate, sprinkling soy sauce, driving his fork through rice and fish and meat and pancake. Oliver, chopsticks clenched in white knuckled fist, toyed with a chicken salad.

'Would you like some pork?' said Rick at last.

'No, thank you,' said Oliver.

'You're not eating very much,' said Rick.

'You appear to have forgotten,' said Oliver, 'that I'm not especially fond of Cantonese food.'

Rick shut his eyes: he had completely forgotten.

'You could have reminded me,' he said, 'before I left.'

'I don't recall,' said Oliver, 'being consulted.'

It was impossible. Rick shrugged and withdrew into himself, where, indeed, he had plenty to occupy him in remembering yesterday's rehearsal. And what a pleasurable memory that was. He had had little himself to do in the way of acting, one small scene, and not more lines than he could comfortably remember, and had had, consequently, more time simply to enjoy the being there, the being on the set, the being part of it all. Pleasure had followed pleasure: the introduction to the cast, the faces familiar from television screen and magazine covers smiling at him, asking how he was, declaring themselves pleased to meet him; the lunch in the commissary, all of them at one table while other studio workers, secretaries and their out-of-town guests, surreptitiously craned their necks to see *The Van Der Meers* in the flesh; the delivery to the set, when he returned from lunch, of a chair with his name on it. And if the rehearsal ever became boring, with scenes repeated over and over from storylines which affected him not at all, then he could just sit back in that chair, switch off, and think about Joanna.

It really did appear that, whether she knew it or not, she was falling in love with him. She had as good as told him that she was having problems with Mike; had accepted the earrings from him; had laughed with him over the book. Oliver had not found the book amusing: but then, Rick and Oliver had

199

not laughed together for some time. Once — but this was long, long ago, a time he could barely remember, although it could not be more than a few months — they had laughed, Oliver had thought him funny, charming, sweet. But the laughter was dead now, even its echoes had died, suffocated in the heavy, tasteful walls of the dark apartment. Joanna's house was full of light, and there would never, he was sure, be a time when he and she would not be able to laugh.

Imagine Rick thinking this way about a woman. But then again, he asked himself, why shouldn't he? He had loved women before, he had loved his mother, and he supposed he loved his sisters. Other men fell in love with women: why should not Rick Morrison of *The Van Der Meers*?

Oliver laid his chopsticks neatly on his plate, went into the kitchen, filled the tea kettle, lit a gas ring, and took one cup from the cupboard on the wall.

'Can I have a cup, please?' said Rick.

Oliver took another cup from the cupboard, and laid it next to the other on the shiny Formica surface.

'I'm sorry,' said Rick. 'Oliver, I'm sorry. I really had forgotten. I'm sorry.'

'Don't be,' said Oliver. 'It's just typical of you, that's all.'

'Well.' Rick sighed at the sheer hopelessness of it all. 'Would you like me to cook you something? Something else? There's eggs and mushrooms, or if you could wait for rice . . .'

'No, thank you,' said Oliver. 'I wasn't very hungry anyway.' He poured the tea into the two cups, and returned to the table, stopping to place one in front of Rick.

'Is there anything you'd like me to do?' said Rick. 'Anything that might make you happy? Anything at all?'

Oliver's eyes flicked once over him. 'I really can't think of anything,' he said.

There was silence.

'Would you like me to move out?' said Rick.

Oliver said nothing, staring at the two fortune cookies that lay, golden glazed and unopened, in the middle of the ruins of the meal.

It was a little cooler than it had been for the previous week's softball game, but not much.

'Do we have to play?' said Nancy. 'I'm pooped just walking from the car.'

'Iced tea,' said Joanna. 'By your pool.'

'Really? Do you want to?'

'We play,' said Mike. 'We came to play, and we play.' He turned to Bill. 'Pair of wimps we married.'

'Letting us down,' agreed Bill. 'In front of my staff.' He had invited some of his employees to join the game, and they stood together in a group, T-shirts just a little too clean, laughs just a little too eager.

'Grounds for divorce there,' said Mike. 'Come on, guys, let's play ball.'

They split into two teams, Mike and Bill, as the tallest and strongest, going to opposite sides. Mike took Susan to his side, and Kathy and Ted followed; Bill took Nancy, Joanna, Lauren, and Rick. The people from Bill's office reluctantly divided themselves between the two. Mike's team was first in to bat.

Susan sat on the bench in the sun, waiting her turn. Mike took a drink from the cooler, and sat next to her.

'We need to talk,' he muttered.

Susan looked, not at him, but down at the yellowing summer grass.

'I'm not at all sure we have very much to talk about,' she said.

'Shut up,' he said. 'We don't have time for crap. We need to talk.'

'I don't talk crap.'

'Hi.' Kathy sprawled at their feet and smiled up at them, a sun visor shading her eyes, casting a scarlet glow on her tanned face.

'Hi, Kaz,' said Mike.

201

Susan smiled, politely.

'So how's it going?' said Mike.

'Oh, you know.' Kathy shrugged. 'How've you been? I came by the studio in the week, but you weren't there.'

'Right. Went to the desert for the week.'

'Batter up,' called someone, and Mike kicked Susan.

'You,' he said.

He watched as she walked to the batter's box, and bent her angular British body into the classic American batter's stance, narrow bottom stuck out, thin arms aggressively akimbo.

'She's getting good,' he said.

'Yeah. So — any news about the movie?'

'It's doing OK. Lot of stuff, but I'm getting through it.'

'I meant the new one.'

'Oh.' Susan cracked the ball a respectable distance, and ran for first base. 'All right, Susan! No, no news there. You got any news?'

'No.' She scrabbled her stubby hands among the dry grass. 'Mike?'

'Yeah?'

'Where were you Thursday morning?'

'God knows.' The next batter took his stand. 'Go for it, Eric! . . . Eric. Who's called Eric?'

'Were you with Celia?'

'Maybe. Dunno. Yes.' He looked at her for the first time, then back as Eric hit the ball, ran to first base, and then to second. 'Why?'

'Just bugging you,' she said hastily. 'About getting me a job. I'm a pushy actress, remember?'

He twanged affectionately at her visor. 'We'll get there, kid. Shit!'

Eric was run out, and Susan with him, making it the end of their innings.

'Sorry about that,' said Eric, as the teams changed sides.

'Ach.' Mike shook his head, pinching his wife's waist as she passed. 'This bunch haven't a prayer. They've got

202

Joanna *and* Nancy.'

Joanna pulled a face at him, and went to sit on the shady side of the bench. Her legs were white under her white cotton shorts, but not the dead white of the cloth, a living white with shades of pink and blue and mauve, like the colours of Granny Forrest's garden swirled together. Next to them appeared two strong legs, deep brown, and furred with black hair. It was Rick.

'Those,' she told him, tapping a knee, 'are not New York legs.'

'Legs don't show,' he said. 'It's the face I have to watch.' He was wearing the sort of shady straw hat her mother wore for gardening, and his skin glistened faintly. 'I have an inch of sunscreen on here. So — how did Mike like the earrings?'

'Oh, he loved them. Of course. Rick, they really are lovely, thank you so much.'

'Oh, you deserve them.' He paused. 'And I'm happy someone's happy. Oliver didn't like the book at all.'

'Oh, dear.' Her heart sank: it was so hot. 'Didn't he?'

'No, he didn't. We're having problems, Joanna.'

'No!' A forlorn hope was that she might jolly him out of it. 'You and Oliver are having problems? Surely not!'

'Don't laugh at me.'

'Sorry.' Lauren, up for batting, struck at the ball, and made it just in time to first base. 'All right, Lauren!' cried Ted, absent-mindedly, forgetting team loyalty. Joanna wished either that it was not so hot, or that they were not playing ball, or that Rick had not chosen her as his, apparently, sole confidante. 'I am sorry, really. But it's such a lovely day, please let's talk about something nice instead. How did the rehearsal go?'

'Oh, terrific. That was terrific. Really. We talked about moving out last night.'

'Are you guys playing?' said Bill, suddenly standing over them. 'Or just shooting the breeze?'

'Sorry, Bill,' said Joanna. 'Who's up?'

'Rick. Now. Get out there, Rick, go get 'em, tiger.'

'Will you look after my hat, Joanna?' asked Rick, preparing to go.

'Talk to you later, Ricky.' Joanna, taking the hat, could only hope the relief did not show too clearly in her voice.

'You guys playing or having a Tupperware party?' roared Mike from out field.

Bill sat down by Joanna, and watched pessimistically as Rick took his stand. Rick was fast and reasonably powerful, but his judgment was notoriously poor. 'Guy's going to dream his life away,' he said. 'And worse — the game with it.'

'He's got a lot on his mind,' said Joanna. 'The series. And he and Oliver are having problems, you know.'

'Yeah, Nancy told me. Do you believe that?' Rick had sent the ball skimming far to the left of Mike, who had retrieved and returned it as neatly as if it had landed at his feet. 'The man's an ape. Hey, O'Connor, you throw like a girl.'

Mike smiled, and calmly raised his middle finger.

Joanna laughed. She loved Bill, who had loved Mike before she had even known him. 'Am I up yet?' she asked.

'After my wife. If there is an after my wife.'

Which, it turned out, there was not, since Nancy was caught out on her first ball.

They changed sides, Kathy now going first to bat. Susan dawdled in from her position on first base, stopping to return to Nancy the glove she had lent, to kick at the grass, to examine the fence, until Mike seemed well established in a conversation with Eric and someone who might or might not have been his girlfriend. Then she sat down, far away from them, on the bench.

Almost immediately, he was beside her.

'We have to talk,' he said again. 'Alone.'

'You see,' she replied carefully though the chaos of love and anger that surged inside her, 'I don't think we do. I don't think those five minutes in the car really happened, and I don't think we have anything to talk about.'

'How d'you sleep last night?' he asked.

She bit her lip as the anger rose to swallow the love. How, rather, had he slept, with his wife beside him, his mother's meat loaf in his stomach, and the image of the man in agony twisting above them? But to ask the question aloud would be to enter into a dialogue, and that she must not do.

'Very well, thank you,' she replied.

'Your nose just grew,' he said. 'About six and a half inches.'

'You're up, Mike,' said Eric.

'You guys playing?' shouted Bill from the field. 'Or having a Tupperware party?'

Susan watched as Mike rose to his feet and lumbered, ursine, to the box. Kathy, on second base, looked from Susan to Mike, and back to Susan, and her eyes narrowed, and her head ached in the sun.

In the end, it was Nancy, again, who called a halt.

'I know you guys think I'm a wimp,' she said. 'But I just can't go on. I can't.'

'You're not a wimp,' said Joanna, dropping next to her on to the bench. 'I think you're jolly brave, saying what we're all thinking, but we're all too afraid of Mike to say.'

Mike and Bill, standing over them, exchanged glances of disgust.

'Want to do a trade?' asked Bill.

'Nah.' Mike shook his head. 'They're all alike in the dark, anyway. Want a drink, lady?'

'Yes,' said Joanna. 'Yes, yes, oh, yes.'

In the car, she turned to Mike and Susan. 'Do me a favour, OK? When we get to the bar, would one of you sit on one side of me, please, and one on the other? Just don't let me get stuck with Rick. OK?'

'Aha.' Mike chuckled over the steering wheel. 'Course of true love not running smooth, is it?'

'Oh, shut up, Mike. He's very sweet, and he's not very happy, and it's just that . . . Oh, you know. Just today. It's so hot. Please?'

'What d'you think, Susan? Should we?'

Susan shrugged. 'Why not?'

'Bless you both. You'll go to heaven.'

The bar was as cool as it had been the previous week, the table as welcoming, the beer as icy cold.

'Thank you, Nancy,' said Joanna, raising a glass to her, 'for standing up for the slothful rights of all of us. God, it's good to stop playing.'

Sitting next to her, Mike turned to look down at her. 'You know,' he said, 'pretty soon, you won't be doing anything at all. Won't even get up in the morning.'

'D'you think so?' she smiled, sunnily, up at him. 'Well, I'm safe tomorrow anyway, because I've got to go and have my hair cut.'

'You do?' said Nancy. 'So do I. Come to my guy with me.'

'Oh, sure thing, Nancy. I just happen to have a couple of thousand dollars saved.'

'Go on, I'll treat you. He'll do your nails, too.'

'No, really, thank you. That's very sweet, but I like the girl I go to.' She leaned forward into a stage whisper. 'And she's cheap, too.'

'I don't think you need a haircut,' put in Rick, sitting disconsolately across the table.

'And thank you, too, Ricky, but I think I do. I want to show off my earrings, don't I? He bought me some lovely earrings for my birthday.'

'How're the Van Der Meers?' asked Kathy.

'Terrific,' he said. 'Just terrific.' He beamed around the table. 'It's so good to be working.'

'It must be,' said Kathy.

'Wait till you guys see Kathy in *Marina*,' said Mike. 'She's great — better than she's ever been. Even better. There's one scene — and I hardly have to do anything to it, so it's all her — and every time I see it, I just want to cry.'

For a split second, unseen by anyone but Mike, there raged across Bill's face that wild, quickly controlled jealousy. 'How's *Marina* coming, anyway?' he asked.

'Comin' along. Got a long way to go, though. Which reminds me.' He turned across Joanna to Susan. 'When are you going to come and see it?'

'I'm sorry?' said Susan.

'*Marina*. You said you wanted to come and see it, didn't you? Well, how about tomorrow evening?'

'Tomorrow?' She took a slow sip of her beer. 'I honestly don't think I can, you know. I've got a whole sub-section to finish, and by the time I have, I'm afraid I'm pretty sure I'll be too tired to do anything. Thanks all the same, though.'

'Tuesday, then,' said Mike. 'You can come on Tuesday.' He jerked his head at Joanna. 'Give the cook a night off.'

'Go on,' said Joanna from in between them. 'Go with him, he won't give you a moment's peace until you do.'

'All right, then,' said Susan. 'Tuesday it is.'


Mike stopped the camera and sucked on his can of Cola : for the first time, he was having difficulty in concentrating on his work. Kisses, and more, outside his marriage were far from a novelty to him; but what had happened on Saturday was something more. Something that might just possibly change his entire life.

He had been unfaithful to Joanna since before they had married. He had never discussed his infidelity with her, nor had it ever seriously occurred to him not to practise it, monogamy being simply a part of the marital deal which he had from the start disregarded as inapplicable to his own case. He knew quite well that this was wrong, that he was doing her wrong, and was rarely, if ever, free from that knowledge; but when the guilt had threatened to overwhelm him, he had always, until now, managed to comfort himself with the reminder that it was Joanna whom he loved, that faithful or unfaithful, in her arms, or Kathy's, or Celia's, or any of the numberless arms over the years, it had been always she who was his woman, his wife.

But that was before last Saturday, when he had kissed her cousin. Susan. Like Joanna, but not like; a Joanna stern, uncharming, and more than that, an entity of her own, a person unlike any other, capable, it now appeared to him dreadfully capable, of arousing in him feelings unlike any he had known. He could not, of course, be falling in love with Susan; he was married to Joanna, his luscious, laughing Joanna, had been for seven good years, longer than many marriages lasted in this sweet city, seven years strong enough, he had always assumed, to carry them through the years that lay ahead. Why, then, was it Susan's voice which now echoed in his head, Susan's face he now saw, as on the previous afternoon, eyelids drooping as they watched Kathy, and why did he feel again so vividly the tense thrill of seeing the knowledge in the cold eyes underneath? Jesus, she would make his life difficult, would Susan, would make demands that Joanna would not even dream of. He would have to shape up for her, it would all change, change utterly. Shit, he thought to himself. Shit. And she wasn't even pretty.

'Boo,' said a voice from the door.

He jumped. It was Celia.

'You were miles away,' she said. She came in, closed the door, and reached up to kiss him. 'I didn't know you daydreamed on the job.'

Instinctively, he turned his face, so that her mouth met not his lips, but his cheek. 'I guess you do it all the time.'

She raised her eyebrows, but did not comment on his action. 'You should see the fantasies I get doing root canal. How about a drive to clear your head?'

'A drive where?'

'Up the coast? I have a friend with an apartment in Malibu. Private beach.'

She would have. 'You have a lot of time off, don't you?'

'I have to be back by 5.00. Evening surgery. Say forty-five minutes each way, gives us three and a half hours there.'

After all, he was accomplishing little enough in the studio. 'Why not?' he said.

Her car was parked outside, a small, silver import, elegant without ostentation, its interior fresh smelling and free of clutter. Mike hunched inside, too big and too dusty, his bare knees folded towards his chest, particles of studio grime, dead skin, debris from his own car flaking and spreading over the clean beige seat as they sped down the freeway towards the Ocean, and disgorged themselves on to the Pacific Coast Highway. They drove up past the public beaches, too many people crammed into them like currants in a too rich fruitcake, past the wild stretch where the Ocean thundered almost on to the road itself, past fishing tackle shops, and bikini shops, and Malibu Pier, and into a quiet road smelling of salt and sand and the country. She parked under a building high on stilts above the sand, and led him up stone steps to an apartment furnished in cream, its vast windows gazing directly on to an untouched indigo Ocean and an empty beach pale as a fading suntan.

'Make yourself at home,' she said.

'Whose home?'

'A friend's.'

He sat at a burnished yellow wood table, and looked out of the windows. A seagull swooped; a pelican perched on a rock; far in the distance, a lone man walked a large dog. It was cooler here than in the city, and the only sound was the unending suck and thump of the waves almost beneath them. After a moment, she joined him, carrying two slender glasses, and a slim bottle of cold white wine.

'Your patients will like that,' he said.

'I'll have worked it off by then.' She poured the wine, and held out her glass to clink. 'To the movie.'

'The movie,' he agreed. It was not his teeth she would be working on.

'We're all very pleased with the deal,' she said. 'My associates want to meet you as soon as possible.'

'Terrific,' he said, and, of course, it was. But even on that today his mind refused quite to focus, hearing the words through a fog, as if he had a head cold.

'I thought so,' she said.

'You thought right. You done good, kid.'

She looked into her glass, running her slim finger around its narrow rim. 'There's just one thing, before you start working on the script.'

'Oh, yeah?' She had caught his attention at last: that tone was there again, the tone he did not like.

'We've been talking,' she continued. 'And some of the others think . . . Well, in fact, we've been rerunning your stuff. And frankly, we don't much like the girl.'

'Girl?' What girl?

'The actress you use. Well, the one you were talking about. The one I met. What's her name?'

'Kathy? No, you can't mean her. She's good.'

'Well, unfortunately, some of us don't think she's quite good enough.'

'Well.' Mike finished his wine, and unceremoniously helped himself to more. 'Unfortunately, I don't give a damn. I pick my actors.'

'Of course you do,' she said quickly. 'Of course you do. For most of the project. But we do all feel . . . '

Light dawned on Mike. 'When you say we,' he asked, 'who d'you mean, exactly?'

She looked him full in the eye, with just a glint of a grin in her own. 'OK. I mean, I.'

He looked back at her, and at the same time the laughter erupted in both of them.

'Nice try, lady,' he commented.

'No dice?'

'No dice.'

'Pity.' She poured more wine for herself. 'Did we just have a tiff?'

'I believe we did.'

'Want to kiss and make up?'

The wine was hitting Mike's stomach, and the waves roared on to the beach beneath the two of them. She was beautiful.

Susan was almost plain. With a curious mixture of fury, and fear, and elation, he realised that, although he was tempted, he would, for the first time in his life, choose not to yield to the temptation.

'I think,' he said, 'I'd rather go for a walk.'

'Sure.' She leaned over, and traced his lips with a long, light finger. 'We'll look for shells, and you can teach me to skim stones.'

He did not move, did not respond to her closeness, but sat still until she drew herself, her beautiful, dark, pale, sweet-smelling self, away from him.

'I mean it,' he said. 'Do you want to go for a walk?'

'No,' she said. Her eyes were hard. 'I don't want to go for a walk. In fact, I think I'd just as soon drive back to the city now.'

'Sorry, kid,' he said.

'Me, too.'

She did not speak again until they were well on the road back to Los Angeles.

'She must mean a lot to you,' she said then.

'What?' Mike, wrapped in his own thoughts, new thoughts, newer even than that morning's, was startled.

'Sarah Bernhardt.' Her knuckles were tight on the steering wheel, but her tone had softened slightly. 'She must mean a lot to you.'

'I guess she does.'

For a moment there, he had almost forgotten that he and Kathy had had an affair at all.


Kathy had left the office, but her answering machine was on at home, which was a nuisance, since Joanna had wanted to ask her the recipe for the fish dip which was her only culinary boast. However, Joanna could confirm, catching sight of herself in the small living room mirror, that it was a thoroughly satisfactory haircut, the style not changed, but

211

trimmed, so that what had been shaggy was now simply thick, what had been verging on a frizzy mass was now dozens of little curls covering her suddenly smaller head, and curving around her neat ears. It would show the earrings off to perfection.

She was looking forward to her birthday. She liked parties and was good at them, enjoyed mingling close friends and teachers and film people over wine and fellowship and, later on in the night, barefoot dancing on the cool grass. And it would, she felt, do all three of them good to have some merriment. Susan had been quiet lately: Joanna hoped she was not working too hard. Or perhaps she was simply missing Felix, about whom she had spoken so surprisingly just the other day. Poor Susan, thought Joanna, now that she understood what her cousin really felt, to feel so much for someone not her own. A party would cheer her up.

Mike could use some cheering up, too: he had not been the easiest he had ever been to live with, baiting her about being lazy, about doing nothing with her days, as if he himself had not been the one to suggest she take the summer off in the first place. And it was unfair of him, too, because he simply did not realise quite how much energy was involved in being a hostess, even to Susan. It was too long since she had had an evening alone: how pleasant would tomorrow evening be, with both of them out of the house, and herself free to stare into space over leftover salad and a sandwich. What good luck that they both got along together so well. She wondered what would be on television. Perhaps she would walk to the grocery store and buy a *TV Guide*.

And of course then the telephone rang, and of course it was Rick.

'Aren't you supposed to be at work?' she said.

'I am. I'm calling from my dressing room. What are you doing?'

'Nothing much. I was just admiring my new haircut.'

'Haircut? Oh, yes. I hope they haven't taken too much off. Have you seen how the earrings look?'

'No, I think you'll still recognise me, and of course I have, and they look lovely. Are you really calling from your dressing room? How posh.'

'Well.' He sighed. 'It's not real good to call from home right now.'

Joanna glanced at her watch. Ten minutes, she told herself. 'Oh, dear,' she said. 'Is it still that bad?'

'Well, we talked again last night. And we're talking tonight. But.' He paused, heavily. 'It's looking more and more as if I'm going to move out.'

'Oh, Ricky.'

'Probably tomorrow.'

'Oh, *Ricky*.'

'Yes.'

'Oh, dear.'

'Yes.'

There was silence while she tried desperately to think of something to say.

'Is there anything,' she asked at last, and feebly enough, she felt, 'I can do?'

'Well.' Very slightly, his voice lifted. 'You could come round to see me tomorrow. To my place. If you felt like it.'

'Tomorrow?' She opened her mouth in a howl, and raised imploring hands and eyes to the heavens.

'I don't have much stuff to move. I'll just be a bit lonely, is all.'

'Well, you know,' she said, 'maybe after you talk tonight, you won't move out after all.'

'I think I will. Will you come?'

What could she say?

'Yes, of course I'll come. Ricky, I'm most terribly sorry about this, you know that, don't you?'

'Thanks, Joanna. So — tomorrow, then?'

'Yes, of course, tomorrow. And love to Oliver, and specially lots of love to you.'

'Yes, you, too. See you tomorrow, Joanna.'

She put the telephone down, and groaned long, loud, and deep.


Together, the two cars drove along Lincoln Boulevard to the entrance to the Santa Monica Freeway, where with a hoot and a wave, they parted, Mike and Susan to join the freeway traffic itself, while Joanna turned off down Olympic Boulevard.

'She doesn't do freeways,' commented Mike. 'Take her an hour or more to get to Hollywood this time of day. But she won't use them. Love 'em, myself. Sometimes, when I want to think, I get on one and just drive.'

Susan, thin in her seat, her eyes fixed on the palm trees rushing past against the purpling sky, said, as she had since she had got into the car, nothing.

'Am I being paranoid?' said Mike. 'Or am I picking up a certain hostility here?'

He waited for an answer.

'I don't think,' said Susan, 'that this is an especially good idea.'

'You,' he returned, pleasantly enough, 'are full of shit.'

She shrugged, and crossed her legs away from him.

They reached the studio and walked through endlessly unwelcoming corridors, dotted with uncomfortable chairs and cork boards pinned with indecipherable notices. In a couple of doorways, stubble faced men leaned, glinting-eyed, against cheap doors, staring intently at nothing that anyone could yet see. Susan had not seen such a concentration of ill-nourishment since she had arrived in Los Angeles.

'Some of these guys never go home,' said Mike, as they at last arrived at his work room.

'Do they have homes?' she wondered.

He thought about it, and laughed. 'Dunno,' he acknowledged. He took a Cola from the refrigerator, and began to collect reels, large, pale grey wheels with his name taped to the sides, displacing to reach them a cache of empty plastic coffee cups, battered felt tip pens, and wrappers from chocolate bars. Watching him, Susan suddenly saw, like an archaeologist stumbling on a new layer of a complicated site, the trace of a younger Mike, a Mike who had been before Joanna brought to his life polished wood floors and a balanced diet, an untidy bachelor shambling at his own gait through a world of dingy sheets and windows the sun never shone through, towards his own, glorious, kaleidoscopic, celluloid dreams.

He turned, caught her eye on him, and she looked sharply away.

'Show time, kid,' he said.

They crossed the corridor to the projection room, where, carefully, his brows drawn down in concentration, he fitted the reels to the projector. When they were done to his satisfaction, he left the projection booth, and joined her in the room proper, its rows of seats and large screen somehow tawdry with the light full on, like the morning after a party which no one has bothered to clear up. He perched himself on the back of the last row of seats, and looked full at her.

'Now', he said.

She looked back at him; she was still standing.

'Now what?' she said.

'Now we talk.'

'About what?'

'Maybe you don't want to talk,' he said. 'That's OK by me.'

He rose and came towards her, the man she loved, love in his own eyes, his arms reaching for her.

'Don't do that!' she snapped. Then she sat down on top of the seats, searched for and found a cigarette, and lit it. 'OK,' she said. 'We'll talk.'

They sat in silence until her cigarette was smoked half through.

'Last Saturday,' he said at last.

'Mike,' she said. 'You're Joanna's husband. Joanna's husband.'

'I know,' he said. 'Shit, isn't it?'

'Absolute shit.'

They looked up at the same time, their eyes met, and they quickly looked away.

He picked up his Cola can from the floor, peeled back the ring, but did not drink.

'I've never been faithful, you know,' he said. 'Never.'

'So I rather gather,' she said. Then, despite herself, 'What, never?'

'Not really, no.'

'Does she know?'

He shrugged. 'Dunno.' He thought, shrugged again. 'Dunno.'

She looked at the glowing end of her cigarette moving nearer to her brown fingers. 'It's not very good, is it?' she said. 'I mean, I don't want to judge — my God, I'm not in a position to judge — but it's not. Is it?'

'No,' he agreed. 'It's not very good. It's not very good at all.'

The conversation was wrong, wrong and dangerous, but having started she lacked the strength to stop.

'Then why do you do it?' she asked.

He grimaced, yet with something of a relief in it: this, too, she realised, was a conversation he·could not often have. 'People keep saying — well, keep saying, they sometimes say, no, often say, really — that we have such a good marriage. And we do. In some ways, we really do. But it can't be that good, can it, if I'm doing this?' He raised the Cola can halfway to his lips, and lowered it again. 'I think about that sometimes.'

'Does it bother you?'

'Sometimes.'

'Sometimes?'

'Sometimes. Shit sometimes.' He shook his head. 'Susan, sometimes I tell you things I . . . If you want to know, it bothers me all the time. If you want to know, there isn't an hour when it isn't with me. Whether I'm with her, or with someone else, or by myself, there isn't an hour when it isn't there in the background, like this voice that just doesn't ever go away, saying, "Why do you do this? How the hell can you do this? What sort of shithead fuckin' despicable thing are you that would do this?" And I've never told this to anyone else before. But it's always been true.'

She could not comment. Who was Joanna that she deserved better treatment from marriage than Sarah, Mrs Felix Grahame? And what sort of despicable thing was Susan herself that when she heard this terrible thing, she could only feel such joy that she was the one Mike had chosen out of all the world to hear it?

'This movie,' said Mike. 'This movie I've been talking about, the new one? Well, there's this woman. Celia. I've been screwing her.'

'Thank you,' said Susan. 'I can do without a roll of honour.'

'Listen,' he said. 'I've been screwing her. And I saw her yesterday, and she wanted to screw me, and I wanted, quite badly, to screw her. And I didn't. For the first time in my life. I really wanted to, and didn't.'

I knew it, sang Susan's rebel heart. I knew he wouldn't do it to me.

'If you ever cheated on me,' she said. Then, quickly, 'That is, if you ever were in a position to cheat on me, and you cheated . . . I'd kill you.'

'I know,' he said.

And yet she herself cheated, regularly, and with few pangs of guilt, on Sarah Grahame.

'We're a selfish pair, you and I,' he said. 'Joanna deserves better than both of us.'

And he held out his hand, and she went to him.

To pull away was an amputation, an amputation without anaesthetics, with just a slug of whiskey and a hard bullet to bite on. She pulled away.

'Joanna,' she said. 'Joanna. Joanna. Joanna.'

'Susan,' he said. 'Susan. Susan.' He reached for the Cola can, and again drew his hand back. 'Can I bum a cigarette?'

'Sure.' She lit one each for both of them, and he pulled gratefully on his.

'Haven't had one for six years.'

'She made you give up.'

'Feel ten years younger since . . . Listen. You know, now, that it's not that good with Joanna. I mean, it's good, and it'll always be good, but it's not *that* good.'

But Joanna was still her cousin, still her oldest friend.

'She thinks it is.'

'Yeah, but she thinks wrong. It's all wrong, all based on a lie, you know?'

She said nothing.

'You know?' he repeated.

His dark eyes were on her, not as they had been earlier, but hard, questioning. Shame flooded her as she looked to the ground.

'I know,' she muttered, and it was the greatest betrayal of all.

'How's Felix?' he asked.

'Sorry?'

'Felix. How is he?'

She saw no reason to look up from the floor, from the scuffed stained carpet, with the cigarette stubs lying like fat, dead maggots under the shadows of the seats.

'I haven't thought much about him lately,' she said.

'I figured not.' He moved closer to her, and tenderly, but not like a lover, lifted her face towards him. 'Someone will always love Joanna,' he said. 'And probably someone will always love me. But who's going to love *you* the way I could?'

She looked at him, lips parted, and did not speak.

'I could,' he repeated.

'I know.'

Subtly, his touch changed. 'So?'

She stood up. 'I need to think about this,' she said. 'I really need a bit of time to think about it.'

'OK,' he said. 'Take time.'

'Thank you.'

'But Susan?' He looked up at her, and for the first time she saw vulnerability in his eyes. 'Not too long.'

She looked down at him. 'I need time,' she repeated.

'Oh, Susan.' He reached for her hand, and stopped himself. 'This is driving me crazy, you know. I mean, I think I'm in love here. I'm thirty-seven years old and I think I'm in love, really and truly in love for the first time, and I'm scared shitless, and I have to know where I stand. So — not too long, OK?'

No one had ever appealed to Susan's kindness before. She felt it now, rushing warm through her breast, felt herself soften, want to give love, protection, shelter; and felt, along with it, a wild, almost drunken elation. So she, too, could be sweet, could care for another more than she cared for herself. How lucky, lucky Joanna had been for all these years.

'Not too long,' she promised. She climbed over the seat backs and into a seat. 'Did you say something about a film?'

He sent his cigarette butt to join the others on the floor, picked up his Cola can, and returned to the projection booth.


Joanna was late. Rick propped his feet on his precarious coffee table, scowled into the frowsy gloom of the apartment, and wished he had thought to bring a bottle of Oliver's good wine, or at least a six pack of beer, as a housewarming present.

The apartment — scarcely that, two mean rooms in a weather-ravaged building that lacked even air conditioning — was thick with the smell of a place that was not lived in, of doors and windows and drawers that were never opened, of a telephone that never rang. It was hot, uncomfortably hot on this warm night in the airless hills above Hollywood, but even in its heat, a chill of unwelcome struck through to Rick's bones. He had lived there a bare month before he had met and moved in with Oliver, and although Oliver had encouraged him to keep it on since then, he had rarely visited it. He did not like the place, and the place, all too clearly, did not like him. Well, he need not stay there: rich as he was now about to be, he could well afford to move somewhere new. He might even buy somewhere. Somewhere in West Hollywood, he thought, somewhere modern, with a jacuzzi as well as a swimming pool. Somewhere, he added vindictively to himself, considerably nicer than Oliver's.

How cold Oliver had been as he had left, not even trying to stop him, but standing, inscrutable, at the door of his bedroom, watching as he had packed clothes and toiletries and the week's *Van Der Meers* script.

'If you want to go,' was all he had said, 'then of course you must go.' And had added with that little sneer Rick always found so unkind, 'At least you'll be able to invite your friends home.'

And of course, he had already invited a friend home, his very best friend, Joanna. Rick's scowl turned to a smile as he remembered the sweetness of her voice over the telephone, the way it softened when she called him Ricky — and had he imagined it, or had it held just the merest hint of pleasure at the news that he and Oliver were finished? At any rate, there was no mistaking the alacrity with which she had agreed to come and visit him now that he was free, the studied casualness with which she had not suggested bringing Mike or even Susan. He wondered whether he would kiss her tonight, or wait until the next time: he had never been the one to make the first move before.

And there was a step on the rickety stair, and there she was, flushed under her new haircut, balancing a large casserole, a jug of wine, and a bunch of flowers.

'Sorry I took so long,' she said. 'The traffic's murder. Hello, Rick, how are you? Sorry.'

'I wondered where you were.' He kissed her, and took the wine. 'It's nice to see you. What lovely flowers.'

'They're for you, I thought the place could probably use some brightening up.' She looked around, and he saw the look which she politely concealed in her eyes. 'Can I have a glass of wine?'

'It's not a very nice place,' he said. 'Is it?'

'Oh, shove some plants round, buy a couple of cushions, and it'll be OK. Look, I bet you haven't eaten, so I brought you a shepherd's pie. Shall I put it in the oven, do you have a vase, and may I *please* have a glass of wine, because I'm *thirsty*?'

He watched, smiling, as she coaxed a flame from the stained oven in the corner of the living room, and found and filled an old coffee jar with water.

'I won't be here long, anyway,' he said.

'Oh?' She turned quickly from the flowers. 'You might go back?'

'No! I mean, I'm thinking of buying a place. Of my own.'

'Oh.' She bent her head — to hide a blush? 'Well, I suppose if you think it's time, you think it's time. Is the wine open yet?'

He handed her a glass. 'I am quite hungry, really. When will the shepherd's pudding be ready?'

'Shepherd's pie. It's an old English dish, and it's just the ticket when you're feeling rough. It won't be too long. Come and sit down, Ricky, and tell me how you're really feeling.'


Between talking, Joanna noted with an inward smile, Rick had managed to put away a more than fair portion of the shepherd's pie. But he was so young; and he had made the effort to move out, which could not have been easy. She must respect him for that.

'That was nice,' he said finally, scraping his plate for the second time. 'Thank you, Joanna, you are good to me.'

'Well.' She poured him more wine: he was on the verge of having had too much, but this evening, she felt, he deserved it. 'We have to keep your strength up, haven't we?'

'Well, I can cook for myself, you know.'

'Yes, that's one blessing, isn't it?' But they had talked enough, and more, about Rick: he should not forget that she was fond of Oliver, too. 'What did Oliver do before you were around?'

He shrugged, his face becoming a cold mask.

But she persisted. 'I know you won't mind me saying this. But . . . I hope Oliver's OK. I know he's as unhappy about all of this as you are.'

'Oliver.' He drank a hefty gulp of wine, and fixed on her a slightly too bright eye. 'You're always thinking of Oliver.'

'Well, I did meet him first, you know. And I do know he's unhappy, and that's . . . not nice.'

'Unhappy! Him! Joanna, only you would try to find human feelings for Oliver.' He paused, and suddenly, his face collapsed, became sloppily sentimental. 'And that's why I love you.'

'Well, thank you, Ricky.' She laughed: it was as well that he was not driving tonight. 'I love you, too.'

'Of course you do,' he said. 'And you carry on thinking about Oliver, and worrying about Oliver, and never so much as a thought for yourself.'

'Myself?' Maybe she should not, after all, have poured him that last glass. 'I think about myself a lot.'

'No, you don't.' He moved his plate, and leaned over the table towards her. 'I'm free now, Joanna.'

'Well, yes,' she said.

'I mean, free. We can . . . ' He stopped.

Maybe, she thought, she should suggest some coffee. If he had some.

'We can what?' she asked, moving to take his plate.

But instead, he grasped at her wrist. 'Oh, Joanna! We could be so happy together! Couldn't we?'

'We!' She stared at him, and tried in vain to loose her wrist. 'Rick!'

'Joanna,' he said. 'You know I'm in love with you, and I know you love me too, whether you realise it or not.'

'Rick!' She managed at last to free herself, and sat back, rubbing her wrist, and blinking her eyes in amazement. 'Don't be so silly, Rick, you know perfectly well you're gay.'

He sat back himself, and looked at her under dark brows. 'It seems I'm not,' he said.

Stay calm, she told herself, approach this sensibly. But what have I started, she thought, dear God, poor Rick, what have I started? 'Rick,' she began. 'Ricky. You're having a bad time, I know that. And you're a bit confused. And . . .'

'May I kiss you?' he asked.

'No! Rick, please listen to me.'

'Please?'

'No! Rick . . .'

'It's Oliver, isn't it?' he said. 'You don't want to kiss me because you're Oliver's friend. That's it, isn't it?'

'No! Well, yes! Listen.' Poor Rick, she thought, poor Rick. And how wonderful, how unimaginably wonderful it would be if this all turned out to be no more than a crazy, jumbled dream, from which she would wake next to Mike, with Rick several miles away and still with Oliver. But there was no such luck. Stay calm. Be sensible. 'I don't want to kiss you because I don't want to kiss you. Rick, you and Oliver . . .'

'You see!' he cried. 'It is Oliver! I told you so. Joanna, Oliver and I are over. History. Don't you believe me?'

'Will you stop this!' She rose, and began to clear dishes from the table. Calm. Sensible. 'And since you mention it, no, I don't actually believe that after an hour and a half of living apart, you and Oliver qualify as history. And . . .'

'You don't believe me! It's true, Joanna. Look, I'll prove it to you.' He gulped at the last of his wine, rose himself, and went to the telephone. 'I'll call him.'

'Oh, let's not bother him,' said Joanna. The last thing that Oliver probably was in need of now was a tipsily abusive phone call. 'OK, Rick, I believe you. Let's have some coffee, h'mm?'

'You think I'm drunk, don't you? I'm not. Look at me. I'm not.'

She looked at him; and looked again. No, despite his bright eyes and the wine he had consumed, he was not drunk. Looking steadily at her, he dialled a number. 'Oliver?' he said, after a moment. 'It's me, Rick. I'm at home. My home. Guess what, Oliver? Joanna's here with me, and guess what again, we're in love. That's right, her and me. Know what we're going to do now? We're going to go to bed. Her and me. *Her* and me. See you around, faggot.' He replaced the receiver. 'We're history now,' he said.

She walked to him, and before she knew what she was about to do, had slapped him across the face.

He sat down, hard, on the broken springed sofa.

'I'm sorry,' he said. 'I just thought you loved me, that's all.'

She stared at him, appalled: she had never slapped anyone before.

'Oh, Ricky,' she said. 'Of course I love you. But . . . '

'No you don't,' he said. 'I was dumb; you don't. Why should you? And Oliver doesn't, and my Dad doesn't, and my Mom's dead. And she was the only one dumb enough to.'

What had hardened in her softened; she took a step towards him.

'Go away,' he said.

'Ricky . . . '

'It's OK, Joanna.' He bit his lip, hard. 'Just go away, huh? Please?'

'Really?'

He nodded.

She left, quietly shutting the door behind her, and picked her way down the dark steps. On the bottom step, she sat down, cupped her face in her hands, and stared into the night, trying to decide what she had done that she should not, what she had not done that she should, praying, as she had not since a little girl, that what harm she had inflicted might not be devastating.

She had been there for maybe five minutes, or maybe fifteen, when, although she had not heard the telephone ring, Rick's voice floated into the sweet, stuffy air to mingle with the chirrup of crickets, and the scuffle of the night-time coyotes that scavenged the neighbourhood.

'Alan?' it said. 'Hi, it's Rick. How are you? Me? Oh. Oh, I'm not very happy at all.'

She stood up, laughed, shook her head, and tiptoed to her car.


'So this morning,' said Joanna, 'I found myself calling Oliver to apologise — for what, I don't quite know, but there you are. And he was very nice about it, although we didn't talk much, well he *doesn't* talk much about Rick, and said could he bring a, quote, unquote, friend, on Friday. And Rick called this afternoon, to say he'd forgiven me — *he'd* forgiven *me*, mind — and could *he* bring a, quote, unquote, friend, on Friday. So I suppose he means this Alan. Lord knows who Oliver means. Anyway, Friday should be fun.'

Susan, eyes glazed over her wine glass, gave a grunt which might have signified anything. Joanna glanced at her in annoyance. She had been looking forward to telling the story to Susan. Mike was never a satisfactory audience for anecdotes involving Rick; Nancy had spent the day taking Barbara to a nutritionist; and Kathy was still mysteriously unavailable. And it was such a good story, too. It was really too bad that Susan could not at least pretend to enjoy it. Then her look changed to concern. Susan had gone to bed so early last night, but looked the reverse of rested today. Joanna hoped she was not coming down with something.

'Are you feeling all right?' she asked.

Susan looked up at her then, and her eyes were cold. 'Fine,' she replied. 'Thank you.'

Joanna, mimicking her, stared pop-eyed back at her, and returned to her own iced tea. Susan was not sickening, obviously, but simply in a bad mood, and Joanna's sympathy with bad moods was scant.

'I worked hard today,' said Susan after a moment.

'Good,' said Joanna. 'Jolly well done you.'

Susan's cold eyes focused into hostility. 'When are you going to start painting again?' she asked.

'Oh, no.' Joanna stood up, selected onions from a basket, and brought them to the table to chop for supper. 'No, you don't do this to me, Susan. If you're in a bad mood, fine, go and be in a bad mood somewhere else. But don't start bullying me here, because I won't stand for it.'

A good thing about Susan was that you could say that sort of thing to her without her taking offence.

'Was I?' she said.

'Yes.'

'Sorry.'

The silence, as the sharp knife fell, and the onion fumes rose and stung Joanna's eyes and nostrils, was amiable enough.

'Joanna?' said Susan at last.

'Mm?'

'I'm not bullying now, but may I ask you something? I'm not bullying, I promise I'm not, but I'm just curious.'

'Curiosity,' said Joanna, pausing to wipe her eyes with a tissue, 'killed the cat. But it is allowed.'

'Well.' Although there was still wine in her glass, she poured herself more. 'I looked through your canvases again today. I didn't think you'd mind?'

'Feel free, my dear.'

'Well, anyway, I looked through them.'

'That must have been fun for you. They're not very good, are they?'

'No, they're not. And they used to be so . . . Joanna, what happened?'

'I told you. I got happy.'

'As simple as that?'

'As simple as that.'

'But doesn't it . . . *bother* you?'

There was that in her tone that demanded a serious answer. Joanna pushed the onions aside, sat down at the table, and rested her chin on a pungent hand.

'I suppose it should, really, shouldn't it?' she said.

'Well, I'd have thought so.'

'But you know, the funny thing is, it doesn't.' She paused, and searched herself for a moment for a deep regret that simply was not there. 'No, it honestly doesn't. I'm *so* happy, you know. I wake up every morning, and . . . there it is. Happiness. And I'd rather be this way than any other.' She paused again. 'I suppose that means I have no character whatsoever?'

'Probably,' said Susan. She rose, took her glass, and wandered into the garden, pausing unusually as she did so to kiss the top of her cousin's head. Under the jacaranda tree, she dropped to the sunlounger, and sat nursing her glass, while inside, Joanna hummed quietly as she chopped and stirred and fried.

Joanna was happy. Joanna's happiness was delusory, like the safety of an animated cartoon character who walks over the edge of a cliff, and keeps walking until he realises that what he is treading is not solid ground, but air. But Joanna, treading air, was happy.

She herself, if she chose to take Mike, would almost certainly not be happy. He would not be unfaithful, it was true; but there were other ways of inflicting unhappiness. He would resent her for forcing him to fidelity, would become ill-tempered, demanding, his selfishness constantly battering itself in conflict with hers. A selfish pair, he himself had called them, and what a thorny, embattled life they would give each other. And dear God, how she craved that life.

And Joanna, what would she do? Presumably one of two things. Either she would find another happiness, with another man — marriages seemed to break up so easily here, and there would be no shortage of men to fall in love with her, good lord, even gay men fell in love with her, and their partners bore her no resentment for it. Or — or what? Or she would not find another happiness, would simply suffer, simply hurt. And why, asked the cold voice in Susan's soul, should not Joanna suffer? She who had never suffered in her life, even her father's death being peacefully prepared for by a mercifully short illness; she who had a mother, a brother, a thousand loving, caring, loyal friends, who had had seven fat years of marriage to Mike, why should she not for once bear a little of the world's burden of loneliness, of pain?

She stood up, went into the garage, and once again pulled out the canvases of Joanna's paintings. She stood for some time looking at them, watching the flatness of the movement, the tameness of the colour, and as she did so, a phrase her cousin had used to describe herself returned to her ears.

'Smug fat married cow,' she muttered. And repeated it. 'Smug fat married cow.'

As she crossed the garden to the kitchen, she saw Mike, striding in from the street. Their eyes met in a look that was older than love, that was deeper than their souls.

Mike looked away first and sniffed the air. 'My God,' he said. 'How many onions is Joanna cooking?'

Because she did not want to work on her birthday, Joanna spent the whole of Thursday preparing for the party. In the morning, she cleaned, polished floors and wooden tables and chair arms, and scrubbed the kitchen to a gleaming shine that would last possibly an hour before cigarette ash, spilled wine, and large, laughing people tramping dust from the garden wreaked their delightful havoc. In the afternoon, she shopped like a rich woman, lavishing dollar cheque after dollar cheque; on drink, champagne for the first arrivals, jug wine and beer for those who came later, tequila, lime juice and Cointreau for Mike to blend into his famously lethal margaritas after the party had taken off; on food, bags fecund with groceries, pasta and vegetables for salads, eggs, cream, seafood, cheese for quiches, plastic glasses, paper plates, to be used and thrown away when their use was done; on, finally, and just for herself, a stop at the exclusive deli for lox and dark, extravagant coffee for the morning's breakfast. At last, legs and back aching, arms strained, she flung herself into the sunlounger with a glass of iced tea and a slice of the deli's apple pie for a rest.

It felt good to be resting and fully to have earned it: she had almost forgotten the sensation. But even Mike could not criticise her for laziness today. No more could Susan, who had yesterday appeared to be taking on, almost, the same tone as Mike. Perhaps they had been talking together about her. Well, they'd have a different cause for complaint this evening, because between cooking quiches and preparing salads, she would not have a minute to cook supper for them, and serve them jolly well right. Serve them jolly well right. She yawned, and knew the luxury of drooping eyelids.

A car stopped, there were footsteps, and Eileen was standing over her looking down at her quizzically.

'Well, Miss,' she said. '*You're* working hard.'

'I deserve this.' Joanna scrambled to her feet. 'Would you like a drink?'

'I came to see if you needed help with your preparations, but it looks to me like you aren't preparing.'

'Well, it looks wrong, because I'm all prepared, so there.' Triumphantly, she led her through the living room, and into the kitchen. 'You may admire the house. And all I have to do tonight is cook about a dozen different quiches, so Mike and Susan can bloody well put up with pizza.' She handed her mother-in-law a large whiskey. 'How have you been?'

'Thanks, honey, I'm fine.' Eileen took the drink. 'I was at the convent last night, and the nuns couldn't say enough about how charming you were. Sister Guadalupe said you were the most beautiful young girl she'd ever seen in her life, so what d'you think of that?'

'Young girl!' Joanna consulted her watch. 'Eileen, if we're going by English time, I've been thirty-four for almost two hours. Thirty-four.'

'Ah, you're just a kid. How's our cousin?'

'Oh, Susan's OK. Except I think she might be working a bit hard, she's been like a bear with a sore head all week.'

'Oh, too bad. I thought how pretty she looked on Saturday.'

'Did she? Must have done her good to get away from those blasted books. Isn't it a shame that James didn't work out?'

'Oh, that man is so cute, he asked after her today. He likes her, you know.'

'Yes, I thought he did. Did he really ask after her?' But then she remembered that other conversation. 'But you know, Eileen, you know this man I told you about she's been seeing?'

The line of disapproval appeared between Eileen's brows. 'The married man.'

'Yes, him. Well, we had a funny kind of a talk about him lately, and . . . I think she might be more fond of him than I thought she was.'

The line deepened. 'But he's married.'

'Yes, I know, but . . . Oh, you know.' Over Eileen's shoulder, she saw Susan emerging from the garage. 'Yes, cheese for the vegetarians, and fish for the fishetarians, and if anyone's allergic to both, they can just damn well go off to McDonald's. Hello, Susan, would you like some whiskey?'

'Fishetarians?' queried Susan. 'Yes, please, I'd love some. Hello, Eileen, have you been helping Joanna with the party?'

The glance she gave Eileen was positively warm, Joanna noticed. Along with overwork and unhappy love, there must be something good happening to her.

'Yes, fishetarians,' she said. 'You see, after all these weeks, we still have the power to shock and appal you. And no, Eileen hasn't been helping. She very nicely stopped by to offer to help, and I climbed straight on to my high horse, looked very hard indeed down my nose, and informed her from a great height that I'd done it all already, *thank* you.'

'Oh, you,' said Eileen. 'Well, I stopped off from work early, but if you're all done, then there's an end to it. Sure I can't chop some mushrooms?'

'Actually,' said Susan, 'if you have half an hour to spare, could I ask a favour, please?'

'Sure, honey.' Surprised and pleased, Eileen turned to her. 'What is it?'

'Well, would you mind awfully giving me a lift to do some shopping? I was going to wait till Mike came home, but . . . And *you*,' she added, swinging to Joanna, 'are absolutely not allowed to ask what shopping.'

'Wouldn't dream of it,' said Joanna. She clapped her hands like a little girl. 'Goodie! A surprise.'

She followed them down the drive to Eileen's shiny, compact car, and stood watching expectantly.

'Go away,' said Eileen. 'Go on. This is private between our cousin and me.' She waved goodbye, and watched Joanna return to the house. 'Now,' she said. 'Where to?'

'The nearest bookshop, please.'

'Bookshop.' Eileen paused, a little doubtfully. There had, Susan remembered, been few books around her apartment, and those that there had been were not well thumbed. 'Well, let's see. There are a couple in Westwood.'

'But isn't that rather a long way? There's a perfectly nice one on the beach.'

'Is there? Well, you direct me, then. You see, you know the place better than I do.'

The crowds at the beach were barely beginning to thin into the early evening, but inside the bookshop was monastically tranquil. Susan browsed for a while before choosing a book of photographs of California, not gaudy, but stark, black against grey against white.

'Do you think she'll like this?' she asked: it seemed only polite since Eileen had driven her there.

'Honey,' said Eileen, 'if you gave that cousin of yours a stick of candy, she'd be delighted.'

'I think she'll like it,' said Susan. She paid, exchanged pleasantries with the woman behind the desk, and they emerged into the already cooler air.

'This was really very kind of you,' said Susan. 'Thank you very much.' At the café next door, tables were beginning to empty rather invitingly: and an hour here would be an hour not spent with Mike and Joanna. 'May I buy you a drink?'

'Why, that would be just fine,' said Eileen. 'Thank you, dear.'

As they entered, a couple left a table by the railing, and they took the vacant place. They ordered whiskeys and waited, watching the swallow-graceful swoops of the young black men dancing on their roller skates.

'This was a stroke of luck for me,' said Susan. 'Your driving me. Mike always seems so tired when he comes back from work, and you can hardly ask Joanna to drive you to buy her own birthday present, can you?'

Eileen chuckled as the drinks arrived. 'Your cousin,' she said, 'is such a sweetheart. Such a sweetheart. I look at some other women, what they have to put up with, and every day I thank God for giving me the daughter-in-law he did. How she manages to put up with that great son of mine, God alone knows.'

No longer could Susan condemn the honey in her voice when she spoke of Mike.

'You must be proud of your children,' she said.

'Yes,' said Eileen. 'Yes, I am. They're good kids. Don't see enough of Colleen, but that's better than having her tied to my apron strings. For her. Would you like to see my grandsons?'

'Oh, yes, please.' Would she like to see Mike's nephews, what a question.

'Just happen to have them with me,' said the older woman with a rare, faint touch of sarcasm. She reached for her narrow strapped bag of good navy leather, and produced a small fan of photographs. 'David and Paul. Oh, and look.' Next to the shiny modern photographs were two others, dull black and white, on the thick paper of three decades ago. 'Colleen and Mike as kids.'

Restraining herself, just, from snatching, Susan took the pictures. The modern children, politely scrutinised first, were a disappointment, two anonymously brown-haired youngsters with nothing that she could see of their uncle in them, standing beside a barbecue with a woman who was a generation younger mirror image of Eileen. But Mike as a little boy . . . Carefully, Susan made herself look no longer than would seem natural, imprinting on her brain every line and curve of the image, to feast on later, alone in her garage.

'What sweet children,' she said. 'And isn't your daughter like you?'

'The spit, so they say. And in character, too.' She winked. 'That's why we get along better a few miles apart. Mike, now.' She took the photographs from Susan and smiled at her son, her love worn, luxuriously, out for all to see. 'He's all his father. And he gets more like him as he gets older. I look at him sometimes now, and I see Pat so clearly . . . We were very deeply in love, you know.'

'Well, of course,' said Susan, slightly surprised. But then Eileen had had that drink at Joanna's; and she was past middle age.

'Of course nothing,' she snapped. 'We were. Now, he wasn't an easy man to live with. Oh, waiter.' She caught the waiter's eye, and signalled for more drinks. Then she turned back to Susan, and winked again. 'He had an eye for the ladies, if you know what I mean. And sometimes more than an eye, too, and that took some living with, I can tell you. But.' Her small, gingery head lifted. 'He was my husband, and that was the way it was. And I'm talking too much, because I'm too old to sit outdoors and drink. Have you ever been close to marriage, dear?'

'Sorry?' Absorbed as she had been — so Mike's father, too, had cheated — Susan started. Then, almost before she realised it, she found herself answering the too personal question, and answering it, too, with an openness that a month ago she would never have believed possible. 'No. No, I haven't. That is, I obviously haven't been close enough to do it.'

'So, you're all alone in the world?'

'Well, except for Joanna. And Aunt Betty and Tom, of course.'

'And now Mike and me.' The new drinks arrived, and she raised hers to Susan.

'Yes.' Somehow, Susan was raising hers back: she, too, must be feeling the effects of the alcohol. 'And now Mike and you.'

'You know, dear,' said Eileen, 'we're all very well, but you need a family of your own. Lord, listen to the drink talking. But you do.'

How on earth had Susan got herself into this conversation, with Eileen of all people? But she was answering, not withdrawing into herself as she so easily could. 'People do manage to lead perfectly productive lives without being married, you know.'

'But somehow, my dear, I don't think you're one of them.'

'Well.' Was it annoyance, or was it a more straightforward curiosity, that prompted her to continue? 'But it can't have been easy for you, surely? Having a husband who had a . . . an eye for the ladies?'

'It killed me.' The greeny-blue eyes met Susan's with a lifetime of pain in them. 'All his life it killed me. Time after time, night after night, he'd be working late, and maybe he'd be at the office, and maybe he'd be in a hotel somewhere, and maybe he'd be God knows where he'd be. And I always thought he'd come back to me in the end, and he always did come back, thank God, but meanwhile, he'd be with someone else. My Pat. Seventeen I was when we married. He'd never smell of her, I'll give him that, he was always very careful to wash himself before he came home. But he'd have been with someone else.'

How could she have stood it, Susan thought, how could she have lived like that?

'But he always came home,' she said.

'He always did, thank God. You never quite knew, mind. You never knew who he was with, whether she was prettier than you — not that that would have been difficult, not when my two were small — or smarter, or have read more books, you never quite knew if he . . . Night after night, I'd pray. The children were in bed and asleep — nothing to do, there wasn't much on television in those days, or at any rate, we didn't watch as much of it — and I'd say my prayers in front of Our Blessed Lady in the bedroom, and ask her to send him home to me, and I'd cry and cry. Dear God, the tears I'd cry.'

For what? thought Susan. For the return of a husband who was an even worse rogue than Mike: at least he and Joanna had no children.

'I'm surprised,' she said, and stopped.

'Surprised what, honey?'

'Nothing.'

'Surprised I wanted him to come home at all?'

'You must have loved him very much.'

'I was his wife. I did love him, yes, and so did he me, in spite of it all, but that was by the way. We were married.' She looked up and at Susan, her old eyes shrewd above her drink. 'You young people today, you think you can live without the structures, but you can't, the world just doesn't work that way, and one by one you're finding that out. Well, look at Mike and Joanna.'

Susan's heart leaped uncomfortably: Eileen's eyes of a mother were so sharp, what could she have seen that no one else had?

'What about Mike and Joanna?' she asked.

'They lived together,' said Eileen. 'In London, before they were married, don't tell me they didn't, I could tell. But as soon as they became important enough to each other, you see, they did get married. And that's how they stay together. Mike picked me up from the airport for the wedding, and he couldn't look me in the eye, my son, he knew. He knew. But after the wedding — after God had joined them — he could look straight at me. Coming out of the church, I tell you, he looked straight at me. The first time for two days. And he's looked straight at me ever since.'

'Yes,' said Susan, since what was the point of taking issue?

'But it sounds as if you took your marriage vows a lot more seriously than . . . than your husband ever did.'

'Honey,' said Eileen, 'I'll tell you something because I'm an old woman and I've had too much to drink, but I'll tell you anyway, and it's God's own truth. When Pat stayed out all those nights till God knows what hour, I felt sorry for myself, I won't pretend I didn't. But I felt sorrier for him. And I felt sorrier still for his lady friends. Because while I was suffering, I wasn't harming anyone. And they were harming me, and if you harm others you harm yourself. And I don't care if you call that good Catholic conscience, or Buddhist karma, or whatever it is they talk about these days, that's the way human beings work.'

Susan was silent. Suddenly, in a way she had not for years, she wanted her mother.

'I've talked your ear off,' said Eileen. 'I'd better get you home before that daughter-in-law of mine starts wondering what I've done with you.'

They had a brief squabble over the bill, which Eileen won on the grounds that Susan was a foreigner, and were quiet on the drive home, Eileen concentrating rather harder than before on the driving, and Susan filing the conversation in her head for further dissection as soon as she had the time. Extraordinary, the picture it painted of Eileen's world. A woman gabbling prayers before a plaster Virgin for the return of a husband she would be more at peace without, and simply because he was her husband. A grown man cowering before his mother for performing a natural function, only to look her in the eye once more after the priest had, with whatever theatrical aplomb, slipped a ring on a finger and muttered some magic words. And all of that leading to Catholic conscience and Buddhist karma. Interesting, really. But extraordinary, quite extraordinary.


'I really like this bit the best,' said Joanna. 'Sitting around the living room, all poshed up and ready, having a drink, and waiting for people to come.'

She looked pretty tonight, the earrings sparkling above the dress that still matched her eyes so well, one round arm graced by the solid silver bracelet that had been Mike's unexpectedly extravagant birthday present. Mike, spruced for the occasion in clean jeans and fresh plaid shirt, lifted to her his plastic glass of champagne.

'Sure you remembered to invite people?' he asked.

'Oh, very witty. I'm surprised Kathy isn't here yet actually, it's gone quarter past eight. She never called me back, you know, I hope she's OK. Oh, and Mike, don't tease Candy and Dan this time, OK? They don't like it.'

'Now, would I tease Candy and Dan?' asked Mike.

'Teacher friends,' Joanna explained to Susan. 'They're very nice, but they're rather earnest, and Mike gives them the most awful time.'

'I very occasionally,' said Mike, 'crack a very small joke. It completely freaks them out.'

'Occasionally! You persecute them.'

'Now, Susan, would I persecute anyone?'

'I can't for the life of me imagine it,' said Susan. She was looking well, too, tonight, in the skirt and shirt she had worn for dinner with James.

'You two,' said Joanna. 'I don't know what you'd do if you didn't have each other to gang up against me. Kathy! We were just talking about you.'

'That's nice,' said Kathy, arriving. 'Hi, Joanna, happy birthday, don't you look gorgeous. I love your hair.'

'It's ancient history by now,' said Joanna. 'Where've you been all week? I wanted to make your dip.'

'Oh, I've been around. Hi, Susan. Hi, Mike. Oh, champagne.'

'For the first arrivals.' Mike handed her a plastic glass. 'How's it going, Kaz?'

She shrugged as she drank, and sat down on the sofa next to Susan.

'Be workin' again by the New Year,' said Mike, 'I guarantee. Celia said she might stop by tonight, you guys can meet her properly.'

'Great.' Kathy managed a smile. 'Maybe I can do my audition piece.'

'Are we the first?' A dumpy woman wearing heavy spectacles pushed her head around the door. 'I told Dan I didn't want to be the first. We're not the first, are we?'

'Sure are,' said Mike promptly. 'These guys aren't guests, they're from Central Casting.'

'Mike, do shut up.' Joanna got to her feet to greet the woman and the man who followed her. 'Candy, Dan, how lovely to see you. Have some champagne, and you know Kathy, don't you? And this is my cousin, Susan.'

'How do you do,' said Susan.

'Oh,' said Candy. 'I love your accent.'

It felt like a long time since anyone had said that to Susan, as if she had lived in Los Angeles for many years.

'It's great, isn't it?' agreed Kathy. 'Even when she's just saying hello, she sounds so intelligent.'

'Who's intelligent?' said Bill, arriving with Nancy.

'Don't tell him,' said Mike. 'He'll get an inferiority complex.'

'I know what intelligent means,' said Bill. 'I looked it up in a book.'

'Happy birthday, Joanna.' Nancy thrust at her a pile of gaily wrapped parcels. 'Alex made his himself, and Barbara wouldn't say what hers was, but she tells me it's definitely neat. And Bill and I couldn't decide between two things, so we got you both, we hope you don't mind.'

'Nancy!' Joanna took the gifts and put them on a table. 'You silly people!'

'Joanna, my dear! Happy birthday!'

The room, which had begun to buzz with talk, fell silent for Eileen's entrance.

'Eileen!' Joanna swooped on her with a cry of delight. 'Don't you look beautiful!' The older woman was wearing a dress of sea green that skimmed discreetly over her figure and softly framed her well kept, blurring face. 'Doesn't she look beautiful, everyone?'

'Oh, beautiful, I don't want to hear that word, standing next to you. Thank you, Mike.' She took the whiskey in the glass tumbler which he handed to her. 'Joanna, dear, you got him to wash his face.'

'And his neck,' said Joanna. 'And even behind his ears.'

Susan rose quietly, and went into the kitchen to pour herself more champagne.

'Talk to me tonight, Susan.' Mike, under the pretext of refilling his own glass, had followed her.

'Shut up,' she snapped. They had not spoken alone since the Tuesday evening.

'Tonight, Susan.'

'Shut *up*.' Importunate, unreasonable man, how could he expect her to make the decision tonight, on Joanna's birthday? But if it mattered that it was Joanna's birthday, then perhaps the decision was already made. She allowed herself a glance into his dark eyes. 'Maybe.'

'Maybe?'

She had not looked away quickly enough to miss the gleam that had come into those eyes.

'I don't know.'

'Is there more champagne?' Kathy joined them, her own alert gaze moving from one to the other.

'You can always tell the hard-core drunks,' said Mike, filling her cup. 'They're the ones first into the kitchen.'

The gathering was becoming a party now. More teachers arrived, Ted and Lauren, and a couple of uncharacteristically early film people. Mac made his beaming entrance, followed by Joanna's hairdresser, and then by the actor who had played the lead in *Marina*. The pile of presents on the table grew; groups drifted off into the kitchen and the garden; and the sound that arose was not that of several small talks, but of one humming, happy mass of conversation.

'Where's James?' asked Joanna, standing with Eileen under the fairy-light spangled jacaranda tree. 'I thought you two might come together.'

'He said he had some errands,' said Eileen. 'I think he just didn't want to arrive with me.' She winked. 'He might still have hopes for our cousin.'

'Well, I hope they're not too high, because I really think he'll be disappointed. Oh, look, there's Rick. Hello, Rick.'

'Joanna.' Rick, dark, pale, and unearthly beautiful in the magical light, was accompanied by a shortish middle-aged man. 'Happy birthday.' His kiss was as freely warm as if their previous meeting had simply not happened. 'This is Alan. Alan Horowitz.'

'Oh, of *The Van Der Meers*, right?' Joanna extended a hand. 'I'm so pleased to meet you, I've heard a lot about you.'

'Have you? That's good.' Alan and Rick exchanged smiling glances. 'And I've heard about you, too. Rick tells me you've been good to him.'

'Well, we're old buddies, aren't we, Ricky? Look.' She gently touched her earrings. 'Have you seen what he gave me for my birthday?'

'Pardon me.' Candy, Dan reluctantly following, had joined the group, and was looking hard at Rick. 'I'm sorry to butt in here, but I was just saying to my husband that I could swear I've seen you on the television.'

'Oh.' Rick smiled, and blushed fetchingly. 'Well, maybe you have. On the trailers for next week's *The Van Der Meers*?'

'I knew it!' she whooped in triumph. 'You see, Dan, it *is* him. He's the son. He's . . . '

'Ashley,' said Rick.

'Ashley, that's it! Why, *The Van Der Meers* is my favourite show! And Dan's, too, isn't it, Dan? You must tell us all about it! What's Jack Wordsworth really like?'

Alan watched fondly as Rick was drawn off with Candy and Dan.

'That doesn't seem quite fair,' said Susan, who had watched the episode. 'You're the director — you are the director, aren't you? — and he's been an actor for five minutes, and here he is soaking up all the glory.'

'That's the way it works here,' said Alan. 'Illusion. The famous guys aren't the powerful guys, and the powerful guys aren't famous. All illusion. If I'd been born pretty, like Rick, who knows? I might have been famous, too. As it is, I'm five feet six, with a face like a muffin. But,' with a stubby finger, he tapped his forehead, 'I have it up here. And I wouldn't change.'

'What'll happen to Rick, then?' she asked. 'When he isn't pretty any more?'

'Ah, don't worry about Rick. He stops being pretty, he'll start being handsome. That's how it works for guys. Different for women.' He looked at her, and shrugged, insultingly unconscious of the insult. 'Pretty women, I mean. Must be rough to be a pretty woman.'

Yet Susan, if she so chose, and by crooking a finger, could steal from her pretty cousin the most handsome man at the party.

'Must be,' she agreed.

'Uh-oh.' Joanna, passing, breathed down her ear. 'Here come Oliver and his friend.'

Oliver's friend looked a couple of years younger even than Rick; he was small, fair, and his bright-blue eyes were watchful.

'Happy birthday, darling Joanna.' Oliver embraced her, then held her at arm's length. 'You look quite, quite beautiful. I love your hair. This is my friend, Eugene.'

'Hello, Oliver.' Rick had disengaged himself from Candy and Dan, and slid a possessive arm through Alan's. 'You know Alan, don't you?'

'Yes, indeed I do.' The two men nodded, but did not shake hands. Then Oliver put an arm around Eugene. 'But I don't believe you know my friend Eugene? In fact, you two will have something in common, because he's another actor. He's just done Romeo off Broadway. Eugene, Rick's on a television show, called . . . ' Politely, he turned to Rick. 'What is it called, again?'

As unobserved as if she did not exist, Susan slid from the group. And walked directly into Mike.

'You're following me again,' she said.

'You're driving me crazy,' he said. 'Talk to me.'

She looked down — she would not look at his face — and watched his strong hand gripping the plastic cup of champagne. She was not to know how rough life was for a pretty woman. But it was Joanna's birthday. But Joanna was a smug, fat, married cow, and Mike's hand was holding the flimsy cup so tightly that it was cracking, and the skin around his thumbnail was bitten red and raw.

'Talk?' she said. 'Here? Now?'

'We could go down the street, and no one would notice. Please, Susan.'

'Hi, Susan, Mike.'

It was James Biggin, dressed in jeans, carrying a bottle of wine.

'Oh, hello,' said Susan. 'Have you just arrived?'

'This second. It's good to see you.'

'You, too. Come on, I'll take you to find Joanna.'

Leaving Mike, they went indoors, and found Joanna standing by the quiches and talking to Kathy.

'Birthday congratulations,' said James after the introductions had been made. 'Is that crab in the quiche?'

'I can personally recommend it,' Kathy told him.

'An expert, huh?' He turned to her with interest. 'And not one of the British contingent, either?'

'Part British.' Instinctively, she switched herself on, became vivacious. 'Part German, part French, part Swedish: a good mid-Western girl. You're from further East, aren't you?'

He moved closer. 'Now, how the hell could you tell that?'

Casually, Joanna drew Susan to the porch, leaving the two alone.

'It seems to be going OK, doesn't it?' she said.

'Seems to be. How are Oliver and Rick?'

'God knows. I left them to it. Who on earth's that?'

A tall, dark woman, pale skinned in a pale-grey dress, was walking down the path, a bunch of red roses dark against her light breasts.

'Hello,' said Joanna. 'I'm Joanna O'Connor. You're . . . ?'

'Hello.' Gracefully, the woman transferred the flowers from her own hands to Joanna's. 'Your husband tells me it's your birthday. Many happy returns, I'm Celia Fletcher.'

Indoors, Susan saw Kathy stiffen for a split second, and then resume, with renewed animation, her conversation with James Biggin.

'Oh, yes,' said Joanna. 'He's told me about you, you're going to be working together, aren't you? But what lovely roses, thank you so much, you shouldn't have. Come and have a drink, and let's see if we can find Mike.'

'Found.' Mike appeared out of the darkness. He laid a hand on Celia's elbow, kissed her on the translucent cheek. 'I see you've met Joanna. And this is Joanna's cousin, Susan.'

The woman's eyes, resting appraisingly on Joanna, brushed once, and with no pretence of interest, over Susan.

'Come get a drink,' said Mike. 'I hid some proper wine away from the riff-raff.'

Susan's cup was empty: she followed them in for the proper wine.

'What a lot of food,' said Celia.

'Joanna made it,' said Mike. 'She's psychologically incapable of feeding less than five thousand.'

'You made all that food?' said Celia to Joanna. 'How clever.' She returned to Mike: Joanna could not see, but Susan could, that under the table her foot had slipped out of its delicate sandal and was brushing his ankle. 'I'm hopeless in the kitchen

243

myself. But good wine I can appreciate.' She sipped, raised her eyebrows. 'This is *very* good.'

'I thought you'd like it,' said Mike. He was making no movement to draw his leg away.

Susan looked once at him, then left the kitchen and walked through the house and into the garden, through the garden and down the path into the street. She waited, leaning against a palm tree, for perhaps a minute, until he joined her.

'You didn't like that,' he said. 'Did you?'

'No,' she said. 'I didn't.'

'You don't have to worry,' he said. 'Not about her. Not about anyone.'

'I'd better not have to,' she said.

She walked, tall in the delicious power, she who had had so few men follow her, of knowing her love followed her, to the top of the hill, and stared out across the ink-black, lace-edged, moon-reflecting, moving Ocean. He stood next to her, his shoulder level with her head, smelling of clean flannel and masculinity.

'We have to do it,' he said. 'Tonight.'

'Of course we have,' she said. 'Lovely little birthday present for Joanna.'

'But don't you see?' he said. 'That's why we have to do it. It's the clean break, the only way. There'd be no going back afterwards.'

'Oh, don't be absurd.' Clean break, no going back. He sounded like a character from a bad melodrama. 'Anyway, the last thing it would be would be clean.'

'Oh, for Christ's sake, Susan!' She had angered him, she realised with a half shameful little thrill: his eyes were sparkling, his jaw tightening over a light mole on the neck she had never noticed before. 'For Christ's fuckin' sake! You want to do it, I want to do it, let's just do it! Why the fuck not?'

Thrilled or not, Susan was not to be sworn at.

'Be-fuckin'-cause . . . ' she began deliberately, but he tore through her.

244

'Don't give me that, Susan, that Joanna stuff, because I remember some things from school, at least. And one thing I remember is that if you want to do something to someone — if you're doing it to them in your heart — then it's as good as doing it to them really. As bad as. And you and I, Susan, we're doing it, in our hearts, to Joanna. And you know it. Every time we look at each other — every time, and don't look away, because you're looking at me in your heart — every single goddamned time we look at each other, we betray her. And because we're not . . . physically . . . performing the act, we're betraying ourselves, too.' He paused, and a sneer crept into his voice. 'Or are you too much of a hypocrite to see that?'

'I am not a hypocrite!' she snapped, her own anger flaring. But it was all so hopeless, hopeless. 'So what an excellently practical idea, Mike. Where do you suggest we do it? Here on the street? Or perhaps back in the kitchen under the table? If we can squeeze past Celia?'

'There's a place,' he said quickly. Susan felt a new thrill no less shameful; so he had thought of it, planned it all along. He jerked his head at the house on the corner, behind them. 'Guy who lives there's out of town. We could go in back of the house. No one would see.' The sneer returned to his voice. 'So what d'you say, kissin' cousin?'

The night was sweet with the sounds of cicadas in the trees and strains of music floating from the party; and suddenly Susan was tired, dog-tired, worn out with the effort of denying herself the only thing on earth or in the universe she truly desired. Susan was selfish, everyone knew it: she had made for herself a selfish life in London, and here she was, almost a month as a guest in Los Angeles without cooking a meal or washing a dish, without even being pleasant at times when her nature did not incline her so to be. Joanna was the unselfish one, had always been, it was Joanna who would put herself out for you, would want you to be happy, and comfortable, while Susan, on the whole, really did not care.

But it had never been asked of Joanna that she tear her heart bleeding from her body and fling it down the steep hill to the Ocean; it had never been asked that she add to it the only heart that had ever been more dear to her than her own. That had never been asked of Joanna, sweet Joanna, Joanna the smug, fat, married cow.

Almost unknowing, she put out her hand. And when he took it, a joy as wide as the Ocean flooded her heart.

'So,' said James to Kathy, 'would you like to go to dinner sometime? Or a movie?'

'Yeah,' said Kathy. 'Sure.'

He frowned. 'You don't sound that enthusiastic.'

'Don't I? Sorry.' She adopted a cheerleader smile, and waved her arms in the air. 'I mean, *yeah. Sure.*'

He laughed. 'Well, we could give it a try.'

'Yeah.' This time, her smile was genuine. 'We could give it a try. K J Schneider, I'm in the book. Would you excuse me for a moment? I have to find someone.'

The person she found was Joanna.

'Well?' she said. 'What did you think of James?'

'He's a nice guy.'

'Only a nice guy?'

'Nice guy isn't good enough? . . . Poor Joanna. Matchmaker, matchmaker, make me a match . . . Who are those two guys with Rick and Oliver?'

'Their dates.'

'Their what?'

'Oh, my God, you don't know, do you? My dear, the goings on! And serve you damn well right for disappearing for a week. You see, Rick's moved out, and . . . oh, it's such a long story, but anyway, the older guy is Rick's director, and the younger guy is some mysterious friend of Oliver's, and . . . they don't look as if they're having a very good time, do they? Should we go and break it up?'

Unobtrusively, they moved over, and hovered within earshot.

'But I suppose,' Rick was saying to Eugene, 'you have the opposite problem, don't you? Being so short.'

'It never really entered my head,' said Eugene. 'I always think height's such a boring subject that only pretty boring people talk about it.'

'Personally,' said Oliver, 'I find that some quite surprising things come in small packages.'

'Which reminds me,' said Rick, 'aren't those new pants?'

'Oh, God,' said Joanna.

'Leave them,' said Kathy. 'Let them fight it out.'

'No, I can't. Come on.' Skilfully, she inserted herself into the group. 'Is everyone OK here? You know there's food inside, don't you? Kathy, I'd like you to meet Alan, who's Rick's director, and Eugene, who's just played — is it Romeo? — off Broadway.'

'I read about it,' said Kathy. 'Great reviews.'

'And I've seen you,' he replied. 'In *Sheba*, at the Inge festival.'

'Really?' She pinkened with pleasure. 'Jesus, that was a difficult part.'

'You made it look easy.'

'Says the guy who played Romeo.'

'So how are you, Oliver?' asked Joanna, as the two drifted into their own conversation. 'We haven't really had a chance to talk.'

'I'm fine, thank you,' said Oliver.

'Of course he's fine,' said Rick. 'Can't you see how well he looks?'

'Actually, Rick,' said Joanna — she felt she had a right to expect at least civility from her guests, and besides, she was realising that she had not quite forgiven Tuesday evening after all — 'I was asking Oliver. But you are OK, Oliver. Good.'

'As a matter of fact,' said Oliver, 'I'm rather enjoying the peace and quiet.'

'He likes peace and quiet,' said Rick to Alan. 'It's his age. Although he's really not as old as he looks.'

'Rick, do shut up,' said Joanna. 'How's work, Oliver?'

'Nicely, thank you. I finished an article last week, so this week, I'm enjoying a well deserved respite.'

'You finished. Oh, well done.'

'And you, I hope, are still enjoying your vacation?'

'Oh, yes, I'm so lazy, I just love having nothing to do.'

'Oliver's pretty lazy himself,' said Rick.

'Rick!' Fully angry by now, Joanna turned on him. 'Would you please just either shut up, or go and talk to somebody else? I've had enough of you.'

'Actually, Joanna,' said Oliver, 'I really don't feel you need to come down quite so hard on Rick here. He was being nice enough to you.'

He looked at Rick. Rick looked at him, and tears rose to his eyes. 'Thank you, Oliver,' he said softly.

Oliver sighed. 'Come on, kid,' he said. 'Let's you and me go for a walk.'

Joanna watched in stupefaction as, shoulders touching, the two moved off down the garden path.

Alan dealt her a friendly clap on the back. 'I wouldn't worry about it,' he said. 'Blondie and me have been waiting for this for half an hour.' Winking at Eugene as he passed, he went into the kitchen in search of more drink.


The corner house, unlike most houses on the street, was surrounded by a fence, but it was low, and easily surmounted. Mike strode over in one long-legged bound, and then as Susan prepared to follow, lifted her, feather light in her flowing skirt, bodily after him.

'Too skinny,' he said, as he had said one afternoon two endless weeks ago, but his tone was different, as was the feel of his hands on her waist. Inside her, butterflies, ladybirds, and all manner of prickly grasses danced and tickled the length of her body. In the garden, just beside the house, was a fig tree, plump fruited, and underneath it, she turned to give herself to him.

Suddenly, he raised his head. 'Shit,' he said. 'Someone's coming.'

Two people, in fact: two sets of footsteps ascending the hill, two voices talking quietly, sometimes separately, sometimes together. Two other lovers had left the party. Stifling nervous laughter, like two school children about to be caught in a prank, Mike and Susan ran to the shelter of the house and pressed themselves against it, arm to arm, leg to leg, backs against the hard stucco wall, standing so close that they could feel the rise and fall of each other's chest, smell the wine and laughter and desire on each other's breath. The footsteps drew closer, closer still and stopped outside the house.

'Christ,' breathed Mike.

'Oh, no,' said Susan. If two others should have the same idea, should see the shut up house, the seductive fig tree . . . What would they do, what on earth would they do? Hand in hand, not laughing now, nor wanting to, they pressed further back into the shadows. The voices remained constant for a moment, and then the footsteps started again, went around the other side of the house, and at last, at long last, faded into the distance.

'Christ,' said Mike again, aloud. He freed himself from the wall, laughed again, once, then stopped, and looked at her, into her. 'My love,' he said.

But Susan, frowning, remained where she was. Something had changed; something was not the same.

'There's something strange,' she said.

'Did they frighten you? People will know soon enough, anyway. Come and sit under the tree, it's our tree now. My love.'

'No,' she said. 'There's something strange about this house.' Where she was standing, the top of her head touched the bottom of the windowsill. Her love was waiting, and she would go to him; but first there was something else, something about that house that simply could not be ignored. 'There's something very strange here,' she said.

'Susan.' Laughing, he reached to her. 'My darling Susan, strange is you standing like a sentry by that wall, while I . . .'

'No, wait a minute.' She warded him away. 'I know what it is.' She moved her head, moved sideways along the wall. 'The window isn't straight. Look. I'm touching the sill here, but if I move, you can see it's on a slant. Isn't that strange?'

'No, it's not. The house is slipping down the hill, is all. Susan . . .' And he reached for her again.

But again, she warded him away. Houses did not slip down hills, that was ridiculous, it was not the way the world worked. 'What do you mean?' she asked.

'What I say.' He sighed, beginning to be exasperated. 'A lot of these houses are. Ours probably is. Now, can we please . . .'

'No,' she said. 'No, we can't.' And again, to make absolutely sure she had not misunderstood, 'You're living in a house that's slipping down a hill?'

'My love, the entire city is built on the San Andreas Fault. What do you want?' His fingers traced her features, turned her face to him. 'My love?'

'Just a minute.' She slid down the wall to crouch on the ground, staring absently up at the dark leaves of the fig tree. Houses in Los Angeles slipped down hills. You have to have structures, Eileen had said, Eileen who prayed to a plaster Virgin, and thought that Kathy should have stayed with the husband who shot her; but Los Angeles was a city built on faulty ground, its houses slid with the inclination of the earth, not even the roof over your head, it seemed, was immovable here. Susan's heart collapsed and plunged, plunged. A vision of England assailed her, of stone Admiralty buildings in London, of graceful Georgian houses, of foursquare stately homes, of timbered, rough cottages that in seven centuries had never slid down a hill; and she saw then, as clearly as in bright, cruel, summer daylight, that she could not take Mike's love. It was not to be; was never to be; not for her. Her life would go on, of course: what else could it do? She would go home, soon, to her newly plastered flat, and she would live there, and stay there, alone, and people would come and people would go, but the house under the low grey sky would never move an inch. You have to have structures, Eileen had said. Susan did not care much for Buddhist karma or Catholic conscience, she would have cut Joanna and watched her bleed. But because she had seen a house slipping down a hill, it was herself she would have to cut, she who would bleed all the long years of her life.

But first, and worst, of all, she must cut Mike.

'I'm sorry,' she said. 'I can't tell you how sorry. But . . . I can't.'

He looked at her: he knew her so well, damn him.

'You mean that, don't you?' he said.

'Yes,' she said. 'I mean it.'

'You bitch,' he said.


Joanna, talking to Eileen, became aware of a figure walking up the path. Not Rick, she prayed, or Oliver, they had barely left, and this person was alone. But no, it was a woman, a latecomer, possibly, or . . . The figure came into view. It was Susan.

'Hello,' said Joanna. 'Where've you been?'

Susan shrugged. 'To London, to look at the Queen,' she replied.

'Oh, very funny. Well, you've missed all sorts of excitement. James has been pursuing Kathy like a mad thing, and that woman Celia is holding one of Mike's troglodyte movie people spellbound, and, oh yes, Rick and Oliver seem to be back together, at least they just went out for a walk together looking cosy, so that's nice, isn't it?'

'Lovely,' said Susan.

'Isn't this a marvellous party, dear?' said Eileen. 'I've been telling Joanna she won't want to cook tomorrow, so you must absolutely come to supper, the three of you. Won't that be fun?'

Susan smiled, her old, acid, London smile. 'If you're so desperate for company,' she asked, 'why don't you buy a guinea pig?'

There was an icy, eternal moment of silence.

'I'm sorry,' said Susan then. 'I'm afraid I've got a bit of a headache. Would you think me awfully rude, Joanna, if I went to bed?'

'Not at all,' said Joanna. 'You probably won't get much sleep with this noise, though.' She was damned if she was going to pretend sympathy, and tomorrow would have a few words to say on what was, and what was not, appropriate guestly behaviour.

'Well, I'll do what I can. I'll see you tomorrow.'

Damned, too, she thought, watching Susan's thin body wend through the crowd, if she were going to let her cousin's bad humour spoil her party. She turned to Eileen, to comfort her, but the older woman had already moved off, and was chatting, apparently quite happily to James. Then she looked around for Mike, and spotted him whispering something to Kathy, something that at last coaxed a smile from her. She went over to him.

'Want to dance?' she said.

He bowed, tall and familiar. 'My honour,' he said, and the two led their friends to dance on the moonlit grass.


But as it happened, she had no words with Susan the following day, because in the morning, a surprise telephone call came from a London colleague — curious that Joanna had not heard the telephone, but then, when she was in the shower, she sometimes did not — offering a spare room, and the day was taken up with packing, with buying tickets and presents for Joanna's mother, Tom, and various friends. Mike, too, although he did not usually work at weekends, had discovered a crisis at the studio, so it was Joanna alone who drove Susan to the airport in the gilded hour between the afternoon and evening. The airport was as full as it always was of meetings, of friends hugging, kissing, exchanging joyously babbled news; and Joanna was not surprised, when the seat had been reserved and the bags checked in, to find herself near to tears.

'I'm going to miss you,' she said.

'Yes,' said Susan. 'I'll miss you, too.' But her eyes were dry.

'You're quite looking forward to it, really, though, aren't you?' said Joanna. 'Going home.'

Susan shrugged, but did not deny it. 'I suppose I am English rather than Californian.'

'And you've been missing Felix,' said Joanna. 'Haven't you?'

'Felix?' Susan stared at her for a moment and then laughed. 'Yes. Yes, I've been missing Felix.'

'Well.' There was nothing, after all, that Joanna could say to this. 'Give my love to Ma, and to Tom, and keep me posted about the girlfriend.'

'Yes . . . yes . . . and you'll be coming over yourselves soon.'

'Oh, yes.'

'And do give my love to Mike, I'm sorry I didn't have the chance to say goodbye properly. I do hope he won't think me too rude.'

'No, of course he won't. And I'm sure he'd send you his.'

'Good.' She stood still, rummaged in her bag to check passport and ticket. 'He's a nice man, Joanna, you're lucky.'

'Yes.' Joanna knew all, or almost all, about Mike, she could not but know, and had shed for him fully as many tears as had Eileen for his father. But for all that, she was lucky. 'Yes, I am.'

'And who knows?' said Susan. 'One day, perhaps you'll start painting again.'

'Perhaps I will,' said Joanna. 'And then again, perhaps I won't.' They passed the news stand, and she stopped to buy a large bar of chocolate, which she handed to her cousin.

'You've got a long way to go,' she said.

'Yes.' Susan looked out through the window at the spare lines of the airport, and the feathery palm trees against the whitening sky. 'Yes, it's a long way to go.'

# FOR THE BEST IN PAPERBACKS, LOOK FOR THE 🐧

In every corner of the world, on every subject under the sun, Penguin represents quality and variety – the very best in publishing today.

For complete information about books available from Penguin – including Puffins, Penguin Classics and Arkana – and how to order them, write to us at the appropriate address below. Please note that for copyright reasons the selection of books varies from country to country.

**In the United Kingdom:** Please write to *Dept E.P., Penguin Books Ltd, Harmondsworth, Middlesex, UB7 0DA.*

If you have any difficulty in obtaining a title, please send your order with the correct money, plus ten per cent for postage and packaging, to *PO Box No 11, West Drayton, Middlesex*

**In the United States:** Please write to *Dept BA, Penguin, 299 Murray Hill Parkway, East Rutherford, New Jersey 07073*

**In Canada:** Please write to *Penguin Books Canada Ltd, 2801 John Street, Markham, Ontario L3R 1B4*

**In Australia:** Please write to the *Marketing Department, Penguin Books Australia Ltd, P.O. Box 257, Ringwood, Victoria 3134*

**In New Zealand:** Please write to the *Marketing Department, Penguin Books (NZ) Ltd, Private Bag, Takapuna, Auckland 9*

**In India:** Please write to *Penguin Overseas Ltd, 706 Eros Apartments, 56 Nehru Place, New Delhi, 110019*

**In the Netherlands:** Please write to *Penguin Books Nederland B.V., Postbus 195, NL–1380AD Weesp*

**In West Germany:** Please write to *Penguin Books Ltd, Friedrichstrasse 10–12, D–6000 Frankfurt/Main 1*

**In Spain:** Please write to *Longman Penguin España, Calle San Nicolas 15, E–28013 Madrid*

**In Italy:** Please write to *Penguin Italia s.r.l., Via Como 4, I-20096 Pioltello (Milano)*

**In France:** Please write to *Penguin Books Ltd, 39 Rue de Montmorency, F-75003 Paris*

**In Japan:** Please write to *Longman Penguin Japan Co Ltd, Yamaguchi Building, 2–12–9 Kanda Jimbocho, Chiyoda-Ku, Tokyo 101*